THANKS FOR READING!

Ruth Burton

THE
BENEFIT
of grace

A Novel of Pikeville, Tennessee

by Ruth Sapp Burton

Dedication

...to the people of my hometown, who are all the good between these pages, for allowing me to tell the story of our community through my eyes;

...to my husband—the best man I know; and

...to Jesus Christ, my Savior, who is even more than "tongue or pen can ever tell."

Thank You

Special thanks to:
John Hargis, *perfectlightgallery.com*
Anthony Ladd, *kneelindesign.com*
and
Carolyn Culver, my dear sister, fellow author,
and first cheerleader for this book

AUTHOR'S NOTE: While the Blue Hole in this novel is a product of the author's imagination, thousands of abandoned mines across the country await reclamation.

❧ CHAPTER 1 ❧

Before I was eighteen years old, I never spent a night outside my childhood home of Pikeville, Tennessee. Oh, sure, my family took some day trips to visit cousins down in north Georgia and even traveled to the Opryland theme park in Nashville a time or two before they tore it down to make way for a big shopping complex.

But when my daddy was still alive, he always wanted to be back at home to lay his head down on his own pillow each and every night. So that's what we did. After all, Daddy's opinion trumped everything else in our tight little world.

The only nights I wasn't in my bed at our faded yellow home on the outskirts of Pikeville, I wasn't more than a couple of miles down the road at my mawmaw's house or on a sleepover with one of my many cousins or a friend from school.

One time we even ventured up to Cincinnati to visit my daddy's uncle Newell who had gotten work up there in some kind of factory. You would think the distance might have required an overnight stay, but no. Instead, the family got up at some crazy dark hour and headed out before the sun even thought about coming up. We were in Cincinnati well before the time Uncle Newell got off first shift, and after a short visit, Daddy turned his beat up truck around and drove south. I dreamed of an overnight stay in a motel where you didn't have to make your own bed, but my dream stayed merely a dream.

"Katie Anne," Daddy patiently explained to me in his most persuasive tone, "you know Beulah'll be looking for me back home this evening. Don't want her to start worrying and call the law, do you?"

Beulah was his name for whatever old cow he was raising at the time in the little pasture next to the house. He routinely bought a calf each spring and fattened up the animal for the freezer.

In an early sign I would not be delivering my class's valedictory address, I routinely agreed Beulah trying to get into the house to make a phone call would end in a mess. By the time I figured out Daddy's scam, the pattern was too ingrained to change—not that I had anything to say about it anyway.

Momma's word may have been law to me, but Daddy's word was law to Momma. The fact was never spoken out loud in our home, but always understood. It helped tremendously that Daddy was usually quiet and easygoing, exactly the opposite of Momma's chatty energy. Daddy must have thought the Lord allotted him only a couple dozen words a day, and some days he didn't seem to use even that many. Sleeping at home every night was about the only hard and fast rule he ever enforced. Momma never questioned his decisions, at least not in my presence.

But since eighteen, when I left home, I'd never spent a full night in my parents' house again—or anywhere else in Pikeville, Tennessee. My new home of Nashville was as close as I wanted to be. Maybe closer than I wanted to be, but any farther away and I wouldn't be able to breeze in and out of my hometown the same day. When finally able to make my own decisions, I became as adamant as Daddy about returning to my own bed at night. Our reasons may have been different, but the result was the same.

The irony didn't escape me.

Now I was headed back home, even though I knew deep down inside I was making a huge mistake.

I knew it was a mistake as certainly as I knew I could stand to lose ten pounds, but I kept driving southeast anyway. My older model Mustang pointed in the direction of my childhood home as if the car knew the route on its own, so I allowed my mind to wander a bit as the miles sped by. The drive from my apartment in metropolitan Nashville to the little town of Pikeville, nestled in a gorgeous valley in the East Tennessee mountains, usually lasted only a couple of hours. This trip was different.

Whether subconsciously or not, I eased off on the accelerator and allowed other drivers on the road to pull around my car and travel on ahead. That was certainly uncharacteristic, going against my usual habit of driving in the left lane all the way, just as fast as I thought I could get away with. But this time I was in no hurry to get where I was going. The thought of the weekend looming ahead actually caused me to feel sick to my stomach, as if I were on the wrong side of the flu.

The emotional impact of the weekend was a topic I had successfully avoided thinking about, although a lot of

3

effort had gone into the preparations.

Even after a dozen years, a special reason was required to drag me back within Pikeville's city limits for an entire weekend. I had tried and tried to wriggle out of making the trip this time, promising to do my usual early morning drive down and then head back to my apartment the same night. The plan had always worked before, and I figured it could again.

Momma was having none of my protests.

"Katie Anne," she pleaded again during a phone call last week, "we need you here at least the day before the benefit and the day after. There's simply too much to do. It's a weekend mostly, and you can take a couple days off work if you need to. Tell them your family needs you. Everybody's got a family, so they'll understand. Give them a chance. You can plan on coming in on Friday and going back on Monday."

A benefit, the name we call a community fundraiser, was planned for my aunt Lora Anne, my mother's sister. She was diagnosed with a severe heart ailment some time back. She still kept health insurance through the plant where she worked before having to take a leave of absence, one of the few industries remaining in Pikeville after most of the other plants locked their doors and moved off to Mexico or elsewhere several years ago. Even though maintaining group health insurance put her a step ahead of many of her neighbors, her extended illness meant the bills were piling up and more were inevitable.

Aunt Lora Anne was the string Momma used to tug at my heart, and she seemed to pull it with cold calculation and no shame.

"After all your aunt Lora Anne's done for you, you know you want to be here to do what you can for her," Momma gently urged.

"But, Momma." I patiently tried to reason with her one more time. "I can actually do more right here. I can collect donations from some of the bigger stores for the auction. I can e-mail announcements to the newspaper and radio…"

She cut in before I finished.

"That sounds good. You do all that. There's still no reason you can't be here when I said."

"But Momma…" I repeated.

Her voice softened with understanding. "I know, I know. There will be a lot of people at the benefit you haven't seen since you left here, Katie Anne, but it's time you did. You can't hide forever."

&

As I reached the top of the mountain, ready to make my descent into the beautiful Sequatchie (pronounced "See-quat-chee") Valley, my nerves were on edge. The valley stretched out before me as far as I could see, a checkered landscape of farmland beginning to bud with the promise of a green spring awakening after a long winter.

Early spring was my favorite season of the year. Seeing the green bursting out to surround me filled some hidden spot in my soul I hadn't allowed myself to notice was empty. Each time the miracle of spring repeated, it was like a completely new, mysterious event. In years past, the process was a confirmation there were things I could count on, things I could hold tightly to in faith. Now I was no longer sure, so I did my best not to think about it at all.

I pulled across the oncoming lane of traffic on the two-lane highway and eased my Mustang onto the overlook, nothing more than a wide spot at the edge of the road. As I pushed my sunglasses up from in front of my eyes and perched them on top of my shoulder-length, newly highlighted blonde hair, I had to admit after all the time that had passed, this valley was still the only place to completely feel like home to me. Merely the sight calmed me. I shifted the gearshift into park and climbed out onto the tar and chip surface.

The sky was preparing to begin its nightly light show, about to fade from clear blue to a soft pink. Soon, a darker pink or even a light purple would emerge. Then the sun would continue its subtle journey over the top of the mountain until the blazing sphere dropped out of sight.

My ancestors were some of the original settlers who pushed the Cherokee Indians out of the valley long ago. Many last names of Bledsoe County's original settlers remained familiar, carried by their descendants: Standefer, Tollett, McReynolds, Worthington, Roberson, Swafford, Hankins, Rainey, Anderson, Thurman, Billingsley, and others. My momma was a McReynolds, and on her side I was kin to a good half the residents of the county.

Me? I was born Katie Anne Henderson.

The roar of an eighteen-wheeler gearing down for its entrance into the valley abruptly snapped me out of my musing. I spared one last look at the horses in the distance, flipping their manes and snorting as they enjoyed the beautiful spring day in their pasture. Settling into my car, I shifted to drive and pulled back onto the highway toward home.

When I was younger, I always imagined the valley as a place of safety. Surely if trouble came, I would be protected on either side by a formidable mountain. Nothing could touch me as long as I stayed in the valley between. I kept the delusion firmly in place until one night when my world shattered into a million pieces.

~

In denial about my weekend trip home, I put off telling my closest friend, Lainey Jenner, about my plans until the same Friday I was scheduled to leave. When I finally broke the news that the community of Pikeville was organizing a benefit for my aunt Lora Anne, all I got back in response was a blank stare.

We were grabbing a quick lunch at an outdoor café near the law office where we both worked. In a busy area of the city, many restaurants geared their service to the short breaks of office workers in the neighborhood. Neither of us needed to study the limited menu since this was one of our favorite lunch spots.

"Want to order a small salad each and then split a turkey sandwich?" I asked.

Considering we'd made a pact last week to encourage each other in healthier eating habits, her agreement came as no surprise. So far we were on track to fit into stylish summer fashions. Then again, we were still in our first week of the plan. We knew anything could happen from here. But a pact was easier to keep with a friend looking over your shoulder.

Lainey, an attorney at the firm where I work, encouraged me in many ways during the last few years since she moved to Nashville following an ex-boyfriend, wanna-be musician. Or, as she came to refer to him, "The dumbest mistake of my life."

Our friendship began one day when I walked into the

office's copy room while she suffered a semi-meltdown over the doomed relationship. I did little more than listen to her ravings and fetch some tissue for her, but my commiseration seemed to be enough at the time. We quickly formed a friendship expanding beyond the workplace, and she kept gently nudging me until I enrolled in paralegal training.

"You need to stretch a little, Kate," she suggested. "Get a plan for your life. Don't keep drifting."

Once I finally completed my degree as a paralegal, working by day and attending classes at night, Lainey began requesting me to work on her cases. She never made me feel she was talking down to me or believed she was smarter, which helped continue to cement our friendship.

I rarely need to explain anything to her—except when talking about small town living.

"What's a benefit?" she asked, the lines of her forehead scrunching together in question below short auburn hair cut in a trendy style.

Lainey was the original accessorizer, the kind with the earrings, necklace, ring, and scarf all matching a power suit, all matching stylish shoes. And not only for work, either. Even in jeans, she was never completely dressed without her accessories. Exactly the opposite of me. If I coordinated slacks to blouse, I was fairly satisfied. And my jewelry was of the all-occasion variety. Normally, women with Lainey's fashion sense drove me crazy, but I made an exception in her case, in light of her other fine qualities.

Although I couldn't imagine a better friend, I never knew when one of those subjects was going to rear its head and point out in stark clarity the huge differences in our backgrounds. Lainey was a Los Angeles transplant to Nashville, and as much as I may have tried to deny the obvious, I was a small town Tennessee girl.

Our cultures collided on a semi-regular basis. For instance, the time one of her more rural clients invited her to go snipe hunting and she told him she didn't like guns. Between bouts of laughter, I explained his invitation didn't involve anything to do with hunting. Instead, the term was country code for making out in the moonlight. Since then she hadn't missed an opportunity to tease me about "country code."

When something felt as familiar to me as holding a benefit for a person in need, explaining the whole concept from the ground up could be a struggle.

"You know, a benefit to help people," I replied.

"I repeat, what is a benefit?"

"Well, people pick a night, usually a Saturday, to get together to help somebody who needs help. It's usually when they have a medical problem, like Aunt Lora Anne, or if their house burns down, or something like that."

"You mean a fundraiser," she clarified.

"Sure, I guess so. But we call the whole thing a benefit."

As the waiter took our order, I glanced around the small room at the other customers seated at metal tables. Most were like us, nearby office workers hurrying to eat so they could return to their workplaces. A man in the corner had the morning's newspaper open, covering most of his face from view while he read. A group of six apparent coworkers pushed two tables together so all of them could sit together. Two women chatted across from us as they also waited for their food to arrive. Everyone in the restaurant appeared healthy and without a care in the world. I wondered if, beneath their polished exteriors, any of them needed a benefit of their own.

Lainey's voice drew my attention back to our table.

"How much money do you get at a benefit?" she asked. "Is the resulting amount enough to go to the trouble?"

"Oh, a few thousand dollars anyway, and sometimes the total is a lot more, depending on the urgency of the need and the turnout. How do people where you're from help somebody who needs it? Don't they have any benefits there?"

"Not really," my friend replied, obviously surprised by the suggestion. "I guess people could give money directly to the person if they wanted to. I never really heard of any kind of organized event to accomplish it. I admit, I've never even thought about it."

Although I'd tried to distance myself from my hometown, now and then I felt a spark of pride well up that wouldn't easily be tamped down. This was one of those occasions. In spite of all the times I bashed small town living, some things not even I could put a negative spin on. Small town people truly did come to the aid of their neighbors. At least, that's the way it was in Pikeville.

When I spouted all the negatives of rural life, I couldn't admit I was trying to convince myself more than anyone else. I had lost my faith in everything I was taught to believe while growing up. Everything had failed me. The knowledge tore at my very core, and I wasn't about to set myself up for the same thing to happen again. Fool me twice, shame on me.

Lainey's next question arrived at the same moment the waiter approached our table from behind her, carrying our food.

"So how does this benefit thing actually work?" She reached up to take her salad from the waiter's tray, one of her rings sparkling with the movement.

"People donate all kinds of different stuff for an auction

and a food sale. People play music and sing. Sometimes they have cake walks, anything to raise money."

"And what in the world is a cake walk?"

One more thing to explain. How could a supposedly educated woman like Lainey be so clueless? But I managed to keep the thought to myself.

"Kind of like musical chairs. They put circles on the floor, one less than the number of people walking, and whoever doesn't land on a circle when the music stops playing is eliminated. They take away a circle each round, and finally, when there's only one circle left, the person standing on the circle wins the cake."

"How does that raise money?"

I sighed. "People pay a few dollars apiece to walk for a chance on winning the cake. Try to keep up here."

"Excuse me. I know our friendship should have gotten me up-to-date on these hick traditions by now, but I must be a slow learner." She tried to soften the sting of her words with the hint of a smile.

I chose to ignore her peacemaking effort.

"Well, excuse me, it sounds like these 'hick traditions' help a lot more people than your whole method of doing nothing."

In spite of her pleasant expression, I felt the hackles begin to rise up on the back of my neck. I looked across the table and thought, *Sure, I can take her. I can probably slap her from here without even standing up.*

It was probably good Lainey couldn't hear the last part, because the first part was enough to cause her eyes to widen in surprise.

"Take a breath, Kate. What on earth is going on here? Are you actually advocating the small town way of life?"

"Of course not." I gazed out the window without seeing the people passing on the sidewalk. "But benefits have helped a lot of people. Besides, I never said all things about small towns are bad."

"For whatever reason you're going, I'm just glad you're going."

Lainey was the one person I'd allowed myself to open up with, at least partially. Without me spelling out the details, she realized how painful and emotional the weekend promised to be. My friend already had a long history of encouraging me to own my mistakes and grab hold of the blessings right in front of me. At times, I detected a longing in her eyes for the kind of family I routinely pushed away.

Who knew my closest friend would end up siding with my mother against me?

"Put this behind you so you can move on," she advised. "Maybe once you get this door closed, you can allow yourself to develop a deeper relationship with Jason."

"Ha ha. If—a big if—I ever go long-term, it won't be with a man whose idea of a good time is me watching him play football in the park with his buddies."

After taking a sip of her tea, Lainey urged, "Come on, he's not a bad guy. He's got a job, decent looks, his own place. More than you can say for some of the losers we've dated. He could be nice to cuddle up to on a Saturday night."

"Great. I'll see if I can set you two up."

"Fine. If he can go for a redhead dragging a ton of baggage, he's all mine," she teased, flashing a wide smile.

By unspoken agreement, we moved on to other topics. We quickly finished our lunches and split the bill. I was headed back to the office, and Lainey was due in court.

As we parted on the sidewalk outside the restaurant,

she gave me a final instruction. "Give me a call when you get in tonight, and let me know how things are going. You can do this, Kate."

⌒

Traffic was light on the two-lane state highway, and almost before I realized, I was beginning to navigate the new bypass around town that allowed travelers to completely avoid the small downtown area. On the spur of the moment, I decided not to be one of those travelers and instead made a left turn, taking me down Pikeville's Main Street.

Although the bypass opened only a few years ago, the new route had already drawn some businesses out of downtown, which was small enough to begin with. Still, many things hadn't changed. As I navigated the mile-long drag, I passed a few restaurants, a grocery store, and the town's two banks, with a building supply and lawyers' offices on the right.

In the middle of downtown stood the county courthouse, an impressive red brick building with a new farmers' market and veterans' park on the grounds. Throw in a few real estate offices, retail shops, and drug stores, and that comprised much of downtown. Except for the churches, anyway. There was no direction to head that didn't lead to a church within a couple of blocks.

Pikeville, the only incorporated town in Bledsoe County, began as a small frontier village that grew up around a large spring. Currently, a couple thousand people lived within the incorporated limits. With much of the traffic rerouted to the bypass, city leaders removed the three signal lights on Main Street, including the one in front of the clinic that drivers sometimes ignored when they thought no one was watching. It was official: Pikeville was a no-red light town. But I'd put its beauty up against any town anywhere. The downtown area remained as charming and tranquil as in my memories.

A transition from the business section of Pikeville marked the beginning of the South Main Street Historic District. Several graceful homes built around the early nineteen hundreds, some ornately trimmed, were lovingly cared for by their owners. While I was growing up, we knew to watch out for out-of-town cars in front of you, because drivers frequently slammed on the brakes without warning. In seconds, we'd see a tourist toting a camera appear, and the photography would begin.

But the house I grew up in was still a little farther down the road. I took a left at the stop sign, then a quick right. The same route I had traveled so many times before. The way home.

In another minute, I arrived. Already in the doorway, with the screen door propped open and a dishrag in her hand, stood Momma.

I was home.

The Blue Hole

~ CHAPTER 2 ~

One night a million years ago began with a bunch of us high school kids, mostly seniors with a few younger ones and a few older ones mixed in, hanging around in the parking lot in front of the old high school.

A "new" Bledsoe County High School was built more than thirty years ago just south of town. The old high school, deemed at the time to be outdated and unusable, now housed public offices and a day care. Solidly constructed, the brick building would probably stand forever, but was too expensive to update to meet all the new building codes for a school's use. No matter what other fancy name they gave it, everyone in town continued to call it the old high school.

In front of the imposing structure was a small parking lot we used mostly as a gathering place for teens and as a turn-around spot for cruisers. With not a lot of entertainment options in town—no movie theater, skating rink, or bowling alley—teenagers had the option of either cruising up and down Main Street, about a mile in total, or pulling in with the throng of other vehicles in the parking lot. Weekend nights allowed teens plenty of time for both activities.

Only a month separated the majority of the group, including me, from receiving our diplomas. Some of us were headed on to college, while others were set on learning trades or going into their parents' small businesses. We were full of ourselves and confident of our bright futures. At least on the outside.

I was all set to begin classes at Chattanooga State, a nearby community college. The school offered a satellite campus at the vocational school shared by Bledsoe and Sequatchie counties a few miles south of Pikeville. I would get in all my basic courses there and then make the hour-long commute to Chattanooga later on for other studies. My major was undeclared, and I was completely unconcerned about my lack of direction. There was plenty of time to decide later.

"Hey, Katie Anne, how 'bout coming over here to me?"

I glanced around to see a big, floppy-haired boy leaning up against a beat-up Ford pickup truck. His name was Wayne Deweese.

Wayne and I started school in kindergarten together and traded flower rings in the second grade. Then our parents explained we were third cousins, too close kin for rings to be involved. But if he couldn't be my boyfriend, Wayne apparently decided to be my protector and occasional antagonizer. In other words, he acted like my big brother. Sometimes the situation worked out great, and at other times it was a pain.

In a somewhat unusual response for me, I granted his request immediately and strolled the short length of the lot in his direction. Accompanying me were my best friend,

Trisha, and a few other girls in our group with nothing better to do than see what Wayne wanted of me.

I didn't have a steady boyfriend during my senior year of high school. My friends usually went out as a group, and I didn't want to tie myself down before college. Waiting there for me to arrive, I imagined, was a wide array of eligible men longing to make my acquaintance, prepared to open every door before me and hang on my every witty word. So I purposefully remained unattached, and Wayne continued to be my go-to guy when I needed a date for an event. The arrangement worked out well for both of us.

"Too much man here for only one woman" was the way Wayne explained his single status.

Standing around him were several other boys from our class. Brad and Dennis both lived on the mountain on the Walden Ridge side to the east, and probably put in a hard Saturday working on their families' farms before changing into clean Carhartt jeans and shirts and heading into town. Zeb, Deacon, and Hayden rounded out the circle. Our graduating class contained about a hundred kids, with only about four hundred in the whole school, so I knew them all at least by name.

"Let's do something," Wayne suggested, his meaty hand curled around a can I recognized as beer.

We were not a group of big drinkers, but beer and cigarettes appeared at our weekend get-togethers about the time we turned sixteen. Most of the time no one got drunk, although it happened occasionally. I usually stuck to Cokes and kept my mouth shut about other kids' beverage preferences. After all, what they did was none of my business, and I didn't see any harm in their actions anyway. My mother's stern and often repeated warnings fell strictly unheeded.

"Yeah, like what?" I asked. We repeated this same conversation at least once a week, along with the rest of the teenagers in town.

"How 'bout mudding? We can go by Jake's shop and get the old truck." Jake was Wayne's older brother and frequent mudding companion.

"That would be ideal—if there was any mud. You know we hadn't got any rain in forever. Where we gonna find any mud? Besides, even if we could, your old truck always stalls out before we even get in the middle of the deepest mud."

"Hey, don't be talking bad about my truck," Wayne warned.

I had crossed the line by insulting his truck. A big no-no. The fiercest debate among the boys at Bledsoe County High School was Ford or Chevy. No other trucks needed to apply. Fully aware of the rivalry, the females in their lives knew the easiest way to get a rise out of them.

We all hoped the three-year drought ended soon. In a farming community, everybody was affected by the weather. No rain meant lower crop yields, less pasture for animals, and farm ponds drying up. No rain meant less money flowing into the community.

For my friends and me, no rain also meant no mud. One of our favorite and most frequent escapades was getting off-road in old four-wheel drive trucks and maneuvering up and down through creeks and streams and huge mud holes. Mudding provided the most entertaining roller coaster in the country. No amusement park ride could ever measure up.

Under the best of conditions, the mud oozed up past the tops of the tires and almost into the truck windows. Of course, getting stuck was part of the fun. When it happened, as passengers we tried to jump across to another truck while the guys pulled out the stuck vehicle with chains. A strong winch was a boy's best friend. Out in the middle of nowhere, we could rev the engines and holler to our hearts' content.

But, again, no rain meant no mud.

Zeb broke in with a new thought. "I know where we can at least find some water. Let's go up to the Blue Hole for a swim."

❧ CHAPTER 3 ❧

In preparation for every big event in her life, Momma got a new permanent put in her hair. It didn't matter how many times the styles changed, if Momma needed to be dressed up, she marched up town to the drug store and bought a home permanent for one of the other women in the family to put in her hair. She used to try to convince me to apply the goop, but I'm sure it was best for both of us that I steadfastly refused.

I finally figured out a permanent was a sign of respect in Momma's eyes, an acknowledgment the upcoming occasion deserved some special preparation. But merely looking at her brought back memories of how bad the house smelled while the procedure was underway. Worse than two skunks tied together. Nevertheless, the benefit was surely a good enough reason for a home perm to be involved. I should have been expecting it. I only hoped the house had time to be aired out.

As I opened my car door, I noticed the light, springy curls atop Momma's head bouncing in time with the gentle breeze of the late afternoon. For a few seconds, we stood still and sized each other up.

My mother always looked like just Momma to me. The only difference was these days she appeared even younger than she did when I was a little girl. I still didn't understand how she could have looked like a plain old lady to me when I was a kid on the playground and now be an attractive middle-aged woman. Some kind of reverse aging process. Or perhaps all little children think their mothers look horribly old, and only when they grow up do they begin to see the real person underneath.

Momma began chattering before I had a chance to say a word.

"I was wondering when you'd get here. Was the traffic bad? Did you have any trouble getting off work early? I put on a pot of beans this morning, and I hope the cornbread isn't too cold. I left it in the oven to keep warm. If you'd a been here sooner, it would have been hot. Aunt Lora Anne called a little while ago and said for you to run by and see her as soon as you got in. But I told her, I said, 'Now, Lora Anne, you give the girl a chance to get a bite of supper and then we'll be going on to the school to set up for the benefit.' You can visit your aunt later."

By the time she paused for a breath, I had crossed the small patch of manicured grass and reached her embrace.

The word aunt came out of Momma's mouth as "ain't," the same way I grew up pronouncing it. I clearly remember my mother disparaging some city cousins for saying aunt the way the rest of the country did. "Now, why would you want to go and call kinfolk an ant? It's downright disrespectful. It's not right. I don't want to be called a bug," she declared. "I don't care what other people do, my nieces and nephews better keep on calling me 'ain't.'"

Momma and I hugged warmly and traded cheek kisses.

As usual, I answered none of her questions. My delay in communication was a throwback to my teenage days, plus the realization that much of what Momma said was her style of greeting and not necessarily an expectation of information.

"Here, let me help you get your things. No need to make two trips," she advised, as if the distance from the driveway to the house stretched for miles instead of merely a few short yards.

I retrieved my weekender bag from the car, and we walked inside the small house together. Momma kept up a running commentary on everything from what flowers she expected to bloom first to the latest message on the sign outside the church.

"When I passed by on my way to the drugstore day before yesterday, Minnie Lee had put up about the benefit on the church sign like she promised to. The notice has been there all week. She changes the sign on Monday, so everybody who goes that way—which is nearly everybody—has got a reminder about it. That Minnie Lee is so good about putting announcements on the sign, and when nothing much is going on, she still comes up with something to really make you think. Why, only last week the sign said, 'What if God is waiting for a sign from you?' What a question! It sure did make me think. People all the time saying they're waiting on a sign from God, and maybe He's waiting on a sign from them. I wonder how Minnie Lee thinks of all those things. She always did good in school. You know, she was in my class."

Taking in my surroundings while listening to Momma with only half an ear, I was surprised by the few changes in my childhood home. Stepping from the back porch into a utility room, I recognized the same old washer and dryer that occupied the same space all my life, and the same sink where Daddy washed his hands when he came in from work or rinsed off the garden vegetables.

I drew in a deep breath, and the familiar smells of home brought with them unexpected emotions. The food, of course, reminded me of all the meals we ate together as a family while I was growing up. The hint of laundry detergent made me long for the soft, worn linens against my cheek as I drifted to sleep listening to the muffled sounds of Momma and Daddy getting ready to enter their bedroom across the hall. And lilacs. Momma always smelled like lilacs. A sense of belonging swept over me like the rushing creek out back, although I struggled not to show it.

The utility room led directly into a kitchen/living room combination. At one time, a wall divided the two rooms, but Daddy knocked it down years ago in favor of one larger room. The living room contained a door to the outside, but the entrance could have been nailed shut for all the use it got. We were a back-door-only kind of family. The linoleum on the kitchen floor was worn but clean, and continued down the hall to three bedrooms and a bath. A modest house by most people's standards, but as far as I knew, Momma and Daddy were happy within these walls and never wanted more.

Anytime I opened the back screen door and stepped into the house, I never failed to think about Daddy. This time was no exception. The house never felt right without him. He'd been gone since my second year in high school, killed in a logging accident. Until then, the extreme danger of logging as an occupation never registered with me. Daddy worked as a logger all his adult life, his body toughened for the grueling task. If possible danger ever crossed my mind, I would have dismissed it immediately. Daddy knew what he was doing.

One morning he headed out at daybreak, the same as always, dressed in his work clothes, carrying his lunch in a dented black bucket and a tall thermos of black coffee. My uncle Cooper came to the high school and got me from third-period economics. Miss Frady stood at the board, writing out the homework assignment for students to copy. When Uncle Cooper entered the room, I looked up and saw him, and then put my head down and continued writing the assignment in my notebook. Tears stung my eyes and overflowed onto the paper. I knew something was terribly wrong, and I didn't want to face the bad news, whatever it was.

It took Uncle Cooper saying my name three times, louder each time, before I was forced to look up. He guided me out of the school and into his pickup. I don't remember the ride or much of anything else, except a lot of crying and people hugging me and talking about God's will. The devastating blow put the first chink in my holy armor. I could never quite reconcile God's will with Daddy being gone.

Momma was always the talker in the family, her words serving as the music that provided the background to our daily lives. In contrast, Daddy guarded his words as carefully as a miser counted his pennies. So it was all the more shocking how quiet our house became after his death.

༄

Momma snapped me out of my mental wanderings with some questions she did expect to be answered.

"What were you able to gather up for the benefit?"

While beginning her interrogation, she adjusted the oven temperature with one hand and opened the refrigerator with the other. Momma was the original multitasker.

I had promised from the beginning of the benefit planning to contact some Nashville businesses, asking them to donate items for the auction. I thought I'd done quite well.

"I've got a trunk load of all different kinds of stuff. A lot of different businesses gave me things." I leaned one hip against the scarred but immaculately clean kitchen counter and began naming off a long list of widely varied goods. "A set of wrenches from this auto parts place around the corner from work, and several new music CDs from a radio station that's a client of our firm, and a poster of the Country Music Hall of Fame signed by some of the stars."

"Anything else?"

"Yep. I saved the best for last. A weekend in Nashville for two with tickets to the Grand Ole Opry."

"Land sakes! That aught to bring in some good money. Another big moneymaker will be the football. Tommy Joe got his coach up at Knoxville to sign one to auction off. They always go real good."

My cousin Tommy Joe was in his first year playing football for the University of Tennessee Volunteers on the Knoxville campus. So far he'd experienced little playing time, but he did get to dress out and sit on the bench with the rest of the team. Huge news for our family. In fact, huge for all of Pikeville, since most residents enthusiastically followed the Vol teams during both basketball and football seasons.

"Sounds great, Momma."

"And several ladies from the church are baking pies and cakes. I put in a special request for Miss Rachael to make one of her coconut cakes with the good kind of icing. They bring top dollar. Somebody paid a hundred dollars for one at the last benefit."

Hearing a woman's name preceded by "miss" prompted a smile from me. In Pikeville, as in many small southern towns, the title was commonly used before the first name of every adult woman, whether the lady was married or not. The title "mr." went before every older man's given name. Last names were most often used only to identify which family the person belongs to.

I reported one final donation.

"Lainey gave me a hefty check as a donation from her."

"That shouldn't surprise me. I knew from the first time I saw that girl she had a good heart, I don't care where she was raised."

Coming from my mother, the words were high praise indeed.

"I told her I'd give her a call when I got here to let her know I arrived safely. She worries about me nearly as much as you do, Momma."

"It shows she's got her head on straight, Katie Anne. There's a lot could happen to a woman on the road alone. You go ahead and call her. I'll finish getting supper ready for the table, and then we've got work to do. We need to go on over to the high school and get things set up for the auction. It'll take all day tomorrow to get the food ready."

Momma continued with her supper preparations as I carried my overnight bag down the hall to my bedroom, the second door on the left. It was funny how after so many years of living somewhere else, I still considered the room to be my bedroom. Apparently Momma must have agreed, because everything looked the same as I left it when in haste

I abandoned my family and my hometown years earlier.

"I swear, if you don't at least clear a path to the bed, I'll wear you out," was Momma's constant refrain during my teenage years. Of course, I knew she didn't mean a word of what she said, so the violent threat didn't have any real impact. When Momma got tired enough of having the mess in her house, she regularly broke down and cleaned the room herself. After about two years of living on my own, I realized my mother/my maid was no longer on the job. Even though I hated to clean, I preferred to live in a fairly clean house. Once I figured out the solution, I became an adept, if unenthusiastic, housekeeper.

In the center of my bed rested the same old teddy bear I slept with throughout my childhood. Even during high school, although I would deny it. On the walls was the same light yellow color painted in three coats to cover up the dark paneling underneath. Against the far corner sat a painted wooden dresser with photographs lined up atop a crocheted doily. I picked up the frame on the far left and looked directly into the eyes of my past.

Staring back at me from the photograph were young versions of Momma and Daddy in the front yard, standing as stiff and upright as fence posts and all dressed up for church. Daddy clutched a baby version of me out from himself, as if he were offering me up to some unknown person behind the camera.

Perhaps my parents were afraid of losing me the same way they lost a little baby boy born two years before me. My brother, Earl Samuel Henderson, Jr., lived only twelve days.

They say he was born with a hole in his heart and the life leaked right out of him. Both my daddy and momma longed for a houseful of children, but there weren't any more after me. Both my burden and my blessing. I was all of their children, all of their hopes and dreams, all of their love, wrapped up in one package.

Momma was named for her parents, Ray and Ettalene McReynolds, my pawpaw and mawmaw, in a combination producing the name Rayetta.

"By the time we got to your Momma, we run out of names, so MawMaw thought and thought, and it was the best she could do," PawPaw explained to me. He loved to tease, and I was an appreciative audience—and quite easily duped. "We was just glad it wasn't a boy. Wouldn't a been right to hang Rayetta on a little feller."

PawPaw and I spent a lot of time together while I was growing up, and some jealous comments from a couple of my many cousins pointed to me as his favorite. Their opinions didn't bother me a bit. All I ever did to earn the title was follow him around the farm. They could have done the same thing.

"Katie Anne, Katie Anne, come on, girl, and give me a hand!" The little made-up song ran through my head in PawPaw's low-pitched voice. He usually sang to me as soon as I jumped out of the car at the homeplace. Momma headed into the house in search of MawMaw, but my destination was PawPaw.

My young girl's heart nearly broke into pieces when PawPaw died. PawPaw and Daddy, both of them abandoned me. Only later did I learn of the obstacles PawPaw faced every day in his battle against alcohol, but to my young eyes he was perfect in every way. His great love, after MawMaw and his family, was the land. Since I loved it too, I rated tops in his book.

In the same way, I suspect MawMaw loved me a little bit extra because I loved PawPaw. Even so, she'd deny it with every breath. Instead, she was known to claim, "I don't favor none of my grandchildren, but some of them favor me." I didn't know which group she now counted me in, but I would find out shortly. She would never utter the words out loud, but I would know where I stood with her in short order.

There were no photographs on my dresser of Daddy's family, the Hendersons. We saw them occasionally during my childhood, but not often. They lived up this side of the Kentucky line. His mother died when he was only a toddler, and then the rest of the family kind of drifted apart. We heard from a couple of them at Christmas and possibly another time during the year. For the last several years, I'd seen my Henderson relatives only at a funeral home when there was a death on Daddy's side of the family. A few people with the last name of Henderson lived around Pikeville, but we weren't any kin to them, at least not that we knew of.

The next frame was one of those collages with a place for pictures from each of my school grades. Right there in those little rectangles, I could trace my childhood. The little girl in kindergarten sported a grin wide enough to hide a mind full of mischief with room to spare. Beginning in the first grade, Momma decided I needed bangs. She cut them herself, about as high as they could go. Remembering how she was forced to wrestle me down to cut them, no wonder she whacked them off within a half-inch of my scalp. That way she wouldn't have to put us both through the ordeal nearly as often. But I couldn't claim the look flattered me any.

By fifth grade, it appeared I had finally grown into

my two huge front teeth. Finally, I didn't resemble the Easter Bunny nearly as much. When I headed to middle school, my miniature bangs were merely a nightmare from the past, and early signs of my big hair days were already on the horizon. If all of my friends weren't haunted by similar pictures of hairdos better described as lapses in judgment, I would have burned the photos. I consoled myself with the fact I looked no worse than anyone else in my class at the time. And actually, our styles were already calmed down from those of some of my older cousins who went through the really big hair days.

The photo from eleventh grade made me think of J. T. Simmons. The same morning the photographer appeared at the high school, J. T. pulled me aside in the hall, and without a word, lavished on me the longest liplock of my life. When he thrust his tongue into my mouth, I thought I'd surely die of shock. Realizing my kissing experience peaked in the eleventh grade was a little disturbing to me. Our romance, however, lasted the average length of any of my recent romances, only a couple of months.

When my eyes drifted to the photograph of my graduation, I couldn't help but stare. I had never seen this one before. Within three days of the ceremony, I shook the dust of Pikeville off my shoes and swapped them for Nashville business heels. Now I wondered how I could have been so naïve to think I could roll into the big city and expect the doors to open wide and welcome me in. The fact they opened enough the first week to get me a cheap apartment and a temporary job was something I put down to good luck. I suspected Momma credited God's grace.

How young I appeared in the photograph, I thought, propping my left elbow on top of the dresser as I stared at the scene before me. Peering closely, I decided no graduate ever looked more unhappy than I did in my cap and gown. As I remembered how I felt facing the camera's flash, my bleak expression contained no mystery. Graduation, a milestone I'd dreamed of since kindergarten, became merely another occasion to suffer through. When the photo was snapped, I was already counting the hours until I could get into my cousin Drew's pickup for him to sweep me out of town. Anywhere but here. Another passage of my life was merely a blur.

The next photo proved even worse. Trisha and me, seven or eight years old, arms wound around each others' shoulders, giggles ready to erupt from our round, dirty faces.

I gripped the cheap wooden frame with the same intensity I reached out to steady myself on the dresser.

"Oh, no," I moaned. A sudden and sharp slice of pain cut through me, the first of many wounds I expected to suffer this weekend.

❧ CHAPTER 4 ❧

If there was ever a time in my life I didn't know Trisha, I don't remember it. But my first vivid memory of her was a little high-pitched scream, more like the yelp of a puppy when you barely stepped on its tail.

We lived on different roads, but our families' acreage backed up to one another, with a little spring creek in between that ran high during warm weather but nearly dried up about the time the leaves began falling in autumn. The creek fed out of a small lake about two fields over and eventually emptied into the Sequatchie River on its way to the Tennessee River.

Following the sound of the yelp to the creek bank, I spotted Trisha and her brother. His name was James, but she usually called him Brother. Sometimes I did, too.

"Hold it still," James demanded. He clutched a little bluegill fish in one hand as he tried to steady a small, white bucket with the other. More than a year older than Trisha and I, he was probably five or six at the time. We were still young enough none of us were supposed to be at the creek alone.

Of course, in our minds we weren't alone, we were with each other.

Trisha danced around with the bucket, excited at their first catch.

"We got one, Brother! We got one!" she exclaimed.

"I told you we would. Now let me get it in the bucket 'fore it wiggles loose."

Both of them stood in the middle of the creek, which spanned only a few feet across from one side to the other.

One big flop later, the terrified fish escaped and landed on the bank. Before any of us could reach it, the fish reclaimed its freedom by flipping over and over, one somersault after another, landing back in the water with a relieved splash.

"Look what you done!" A disgusted James faced his sister, eyes glaring. "We had one. You shoulda kept the bucket still."

Trisha, ever ready to accept blame, paused with her eyes cast downward. She was a sad sight, bottom lip pooched out and the weight of the world on her shoulders. She had disappointed her hero older brother.

Beginning a pattern to play itself out many times over many years, I jumped between Trisha and her antagonizer.

"You're the one dropped it, James. Don't go hollering at her."

"Girls!" he snarled. "Can't even hold a bucket."

James advanced toward me, balling up his fists. My quick temper lit up to boiling in seconds. Our eyes locked in steely glares. No two gunfighters ever squared off with more righteous indignation.

Ever the peacemaker, Trisha tried a quick diversion. She climbed back down into the creek.

"Come on, Brother. We'll get us another one."

James heaved a sad sigh, letting us both know he was relenting only because he had nothing better to do, and turned toward his sister. He trudged back into the water after her, and I followed.

We ended up catching some minnows and a turtle, but no more fish that day. The turtle might be the only reason I remembered the incident so vividly. The little thing was about the size of a small plum, with a head not as big as my little fingertip. With a forest green color on the top of its shell, the turtle's bottom was a soft buttercup yellow with a half-dozen kelly green diamonds stamped on for decoration.

Unfortunately for the turtle, I decided on the spot to adopt it and become its new mother. After all, if its original mother had been doing a good job, we wouldn't have caught it in the first place. With great thought and creative input from both Trisha and James, the turtle was named Mr. Tuttle. As soon as I got back home, I snuck a good plastic bowl from Momma's upper cabinet, ran some water in the bottom, and added the handful of rocks and grass I stuffed in my shorts pocket. An instant turtle mansion.

Mr. Tuttle tarried with us a few short weeks before the Lord called him on to turtle heaven. Of course, James officiated at a lovely creekside service with Trisha and me serving double duty as both pallbearers and choir members. Trisha's other brothers, Sam and Eddie Jr., joined us at the ceremony. A few sincere tears were shed at Mr. Tuttle's passing, and the mourners greatly enjoyed digging a hole for the grave. Throwing the dirt back down on top of the cardboard coffin provided even more fun, and by the time the shallow hole was refilled, our grief over Mr. Tuttle's passing was greatly eased.

For several weeks afterward, in honor of Mr. Tuttle, we gave up catching wildlife and switched to playing pirate. The goal of whoever played the pirate was to catch one of the others acting as a ship crossing the creek. The game proved a big hit with us but a rough one. After James suffered a particularly nasty scratch from a tree root jutting through the side of the bank, we switched to exploring for a while.

Our imaginations ran wild as we gathered bones we believed were relics of dinosaurs and bits of cloth from long-ago wagon trains. Those questionable artifacts mingled with authentic arrowheads that turned up whenever new ground was plowed, left by Indians who used to inhabit the area or others who marched through on the Trail of Tears to a reservation in Oklahoma. The trail they took cut right through Bledsoe County. Any new discovery thrilled us to no end and ignited several new days of drama.

We had the run of a good bit of the county, nearly as far as we wanted to roam, but the creek was supposed to be strictly off-limits to me.

"Don't you dare go down by that creek, Katie Anne," Momma hollered out the screen door each time I left the house during the summer.

She was cursed by a deathly fear of water. Her youngest brother, Wallace, had wandered off and drowned in a pond as a toddler, and that was it for her and water. The sorrow broke her heart. All water was bad; she didn't care if I could stand up straight and touch the bottom.

"The most water I want anything to do with is in the bathtub," she frequently declared.

Poor Momma, to have only the one child and that child be me. I figured out early that forgiveness was easier than permission almost every time. And I could usually persuade Trisha to fall in right beside me.

&

"Are you sure your mommas know where y'all are at?"

Trisha's grandpa, Pa Turner, peered down at us with big green eyes shaded by bushy grey eyebrows. The sparkle in those eyes let me know he was suspicious of our escapade from the very beginning.

In Trisha I found a perfect partner for adventure. She merely needed to be coaxed occasionally. The opposite of me. I was always ready to jump, and I could usually talk Trisha into jumping with me, however reluctantly. The trail ride episode was one of those times.

We finished the fifth grade and would be entering middle school in the coming fall. Classes had already been out for a few weeks. We were bored silly, but couldn't complain to our parents without being handed a long list of chores to fill up our time. Approaching them was a no-win situation. The responsible thing to do was to find our own amusement.

We decided to go on a trail ride.

Trail rides came around a few times a year. The local horse club organized overnight rides on some of the old, rural roads in the county. Sometimes they were in conjunction with a horse show or parade or other event, sometimes not. At least a couple dozen or so people usually showed up for a ride. Most traveled on horseback, but some drove buggies and others rode in wagons. Fine horses mixed with nags, ponies, and mules. The rides gave animal lovers a chance to experience a reenactment of what travel entailed when horses actually provided horsepower.

Pa Turner waited patiently for an answer, hairy arms folded across his barrel chest.

"Yes, sir," I replied for both of us.

Lying as bold as brass while maintaining eye contact was one of my finest talents.

He undoubtedly recognized my answer for the big load of nonsense it was, but far be it from Pa Turner to spoil the day. He was the one adult who never interfered with our fun. In fact, he shared in our mischief any time he could, if only by watching from the sidelines with a wide grin on his face. His granddaughter and I provided some of his best entertainment.

"Leave them girls alone," he frequently instructed his wife, the nervous Miss Adabelle, whenever she looked ready to scold us. "They're not bothering a thing."

I justified bending the truth by telling myself it could be the truth. After all, I left a note on top of my unmade bed telling Momma of my whereabouts. She would find the paper later the same morning when she went in to make my bed, and would have plenty of time to calm down before I got back home around this time tomorrow. Trisha left her own note only after much encouragement from me.

"You're gonna get us both a whipping," she warned even as she finished writing.

I ignored the often-repeated phrase. After all, Trisha chanted the same words over and over each time before agreeing to join me in whatever new shenanigans I dreamed up. Not that Trisha couldn't stand up for herself when she needed to. She had stood up to me many times. In fact, when she set her mind on something, it was set.

But this time, my mind was set. We were going on the trail ride.

Earlier that morning, we had snuck out of our houses and slipped off to meet at the school bus stop in between. The little shelter was covered, and since I arrived there first, I pressed up against the front corner so no one passing by would spot me and stop our plan before it got started.

"Katie Anne! Katie Anne!" I could hear Trisha calling loudly before I heard her footsteps.

"Hush. I'm right here."

"I brought everything on my list. Did you get yours?"

"Sure did," I replied. "Momma and Daddy went over to MawMaw's house to see Uncle Cooper's new truck. I told them I'd seen enough trucks, I'd stay home. It gave me all the time I needed."

I showed Trisha a small plastic bucket filled with what I thought we would use: a couple of peanut butter sandwiches wrapped in aluminum foil, four bottles of water, and a clean shirt. I traveled light.

In turn, Trisha held out her bucket for my inspection. It contained much the same items as mine, except she had brought fruit, too. She sprang from a family of committed fruit eaters, and Trisha never ventured far from home without a banana or apple.

"Let's go," I urged. "We've got to time this just right."

Trisha fell in beside me as we made the long trek to her grandparents' house. The Turners owned a little place with a few acres on the outskirts of the other side of town. We hiked slightly out of the way to circle around town and away from the prying eyes of anyone who might be tempted to question us. We soon spotted the Turners' unassuming house, the sun's rays bouncing off the light blue vinyl siding.

"Looks like Pa's already gone," Trisha whispered.

"Good. We're right on schedule."

A weathered barn and a little holding pen set to the left of the house. Behind them was a pasture where Smoky made his home.

"Here Smoky, here boy. Got something for you." Trisha pulled an apple out of her bucket and offered the fruit to the big pony as I grabbed a bridle from inside the barn.

By the time I got back outside, Smoky, who was nothing but a big pet Pa Turner kept for his grandchildren, was still slowly ambling toward the apple. When he strolled close enough to begin eating out of Trisha's hand, I flipped open the gate and slipped on the bridle. Smoky understood the tradeoff for his life of ease was to occasionally haul around some kids, and he usually fulfilled his duty willingly.

Since there were two of us, we decided to forgo the saddle. We often doubled bareback.

We managed to sneak away without Miss Adabelle spotting us. Trisha thought she was away at a women's circle meeting at church that morning but wasn't sure. We trekked the long way around the back of the barn in case she was at home.

In short order, we arrived behind the old high school, the beginning point for the trail ride. Pa Turner, driving a wagon pulled by two mules, spotted us right away.

As soon as I reassured him we had permission from our parents to ride, he nodded and guided his team to the middle of the procession. Trisha, perched in front, coaxed Smoky in behind him. Within minutes, the group set off down the valley to travel an old road that wound its way up the side of the mountain.

Our mommas didn't catch up with us until about two o'clock in the afternoon. Neither of us even saw them coming. They snuck up from the back, Trisha's momma jerking her off Smoky only seconds before my momma grabbed my arm and administered a quick but fierce tug. When I tumbled to the ground, she quickly reached down and snatched me back up to meet her wrath.

I knew Pa Turner couldn't help us now.

Momma kept me busy the rest of the summer. I didn't get back on Smoky again until September.

࿔

Trisha loved jelly on her mashed potatoes, turtles but not frogs, adding up numbers in her head, newborn piglets, and romantic poetry. I knew her better than any other soul on earth. Even though she was unquestionably different from me, I completely understood her.

She was shy and soft-spoken, whereas I never met a stranger and possessed no internal editing system. I didn't mind sharing with the world anything entering my brain.

I admired Trisha greatly, yet I often teased her about the long, lovey-dovey poems she could recite from memory. A faraway look stole over her face each time she quoted the work of a famous romantic poet.

"Who are you saying those words about?" I asked. Then I named all the boys in our class I could think of and dared her to confess her crush's identity.

Usually, Trisha merely blushed and turned her head away. Occasionally, however, I did pry an answer from her.

Once she replied, "I'm saying them to the man I'm going to marry."

"And who is he?"

"I don't know yet."

"Who do you think he is?" I pressed.

40

"Somebody we don't even know now. I can't think about marrying one of these boys around here, can you, Katie Anne?"

"Lands, no. There's no telling where our husbands will be from. Momma wants me to marry a Pikeville boy so she knows I'll stay close by. If I move away, she says she'll move right after me. I told her she might as well pack her bags, 'cause I'm not staying here in this town the rest of my life."

Trisha then launched into a lengthy description of the man she imagined she would eventually marry.

"He'll have wavy dark hair to curl around his collar when it gets long, and he'll have clean hands and work at some kind of inside job, maybe a lawyer or a store clerk or one of the men who go around inspecting at restaurants. He'll bring me flowers once a week, even if he has to pick them at the side of the clinic where all those pretty ones grow. I'll have his supper ready when he comes in from work, and of an evening we'll dance close together in the living room to the songs on the radio."

No marriage I'd ever seen resembled her romantic description one bit. However, if anybody could accomplish it, Trisha could.

Her wedding plans were even more detailed.

"I can see it all. The ceremony will be so beautiful." Trisha's delicate features nearly glowed as she described her perfect future. "I'll be in the most gorgeous white gown you've ever seen, with miles and miles of lace and a long, flowing train. And my hair will be up in the back with a little curl hanging down each side of my face. And the church will be in soft candlelight, with big columns where the choir pews usually are. But we'll have to move all the pews into a classroom for the day. My brothers can do it after the Wednesday night service. It won't take long. And you'll be my maid of honor, of course."

"Don't you dare put me in an ugly yellow dress, even if it is your favorite color. You know I don't like to wear anything yellow," I warned.

"Don't worry, you're going to be in an extremely flattering peach or maybe a soft, sky blue. My brothers will be the groomsmen, and I want them to wear a black suit with a tie to match your dress color. Maybe my fiancé will have enough sisters to be the bridesmaids. Or maybe my brothers will be married by then and I can ask their wives to stand up with me, too. Or else I'll have to pick some of my cousins, and the rest will get mad when they don't get to be bridesmaids. But I'll have the most gorgeous wedding you've ever been to. Wait and see."

Even the honeymoon was covered in Trisha's plans.

"We'll go on our honeymoon to the beach in Destin. Teresa and her husband went there when they got married."

Teresa worked as a bank teller and attended church with us. A few years older, she was the person we looked up to as our role model in many areas. We were more than willing to follow in her footsteps to the perfect life.

"She said the sand is nearly white in that part of Florida, and they've got a lot of good seafood places to eat. She brought back seashells they picked up on the beach so they didn't have to spend their money on souvenirs."

All the wedding talk bored me to death.

"When the time comes, I'm going to the courthouse and get the legal part over with quick. Or maybe Pigeon Forge. As far as I know, those kind last as long as the church ones and they don't cost nearly as much."

"Oh, no, you can't do it, Katie Anne, you just can't. You've got to have a romantic wedding like mine. I can see absolutely the whole wedding…except the groom's face."

She giggled. "Don't worry, I'm in no hurry to fill that part in."

⮑

Once we finally entered high school, Trisha all of a sudden decided to change her first name to Michelle. Instead of the more accepted practice of filling out court papers and filing them at the courthouse for a judge's approval, she decided it was enough to make the announcement to our homeroom class. Our fellow students showed decidedly little reaction to the news, although Mr. Boynton, who also served as the baseball coach, for some unknown reason grinned as big as a cat licking cream.

However, Trisha's mother, Miss Justine, didn't find the whole thing funny.

Trisha and I barely walked in the door at her house after school that afternoon when Miss Justine started in on her. She had seen our keyboarding teacher, Miss Yolanda Freeman, with her long fingernails, big bosom, and flowing wavy hair, at the telephone office earlier in the day. Miss Freeman spilled the beans about the name change while making her monthly payment.

"I am flat-out not calling you Michelle," Miss Justine declared. "I named you Patricia, your Daddy shortened it to Trisha, and that's as far down the road as I'll travel. And nobody else is going to call you Michelle either, understand me?"

Miss Justine could work up a good head of steam

when she got rolling, which wasn't notably often. A short, slightly round lady with prematurely graying hair, she usually matched her daughter's quiet manner.

"Well, I think I should have some say in what people call me."

"If you didn't like your name, you should have spoken up when the decision was made. I'm not about to change it now."

Obviously, logic was not going to win the day. Retreat was clearly my best strategy, so I tiptoed out the back door and left Michelle to take her lumps alone.

The news had already spread to the Henderson household by the time I made the short walk home. Of course, I should have expected it. Momma and Miss Justine were close friends, and whatever one of them knew, the other one would find out in short order. I suspect my and Trisha's antics added to their need to share information with each other.

"Whose idea was all this Michelle business?" Momma demanded.

I tried to brush past her, but her reflexes were too quick for me. Her arm shot out, warning me not to take another step.

"I didn't know she was gonna do it today."

Momma picked up on my exact words, knowing I would try to wriggle out of trouble any way possible.

"But you did know she was going to do it sometime, didn't you?"

"Maybe. It is her name. I don't see why you all think it's such a big deal."

Momma let out a long-suffering sigh.

"It's a not such a big deal to me, but it is to Justine.

She named her daughter after her cousin on her daddy's side who moved up to McMinnville and married that I-talian man. They're both in real estate, doing real good. They even bought a little place close to them for her mother to live."

How we got into real estate, I didn't know and didn't care.

"Y'all are four-thirds crazy. Let it go."

"First off, you watch your mouth, girl. Second off, you don't need to be putting any ideas into Trisha's head."

Momma's voice suddenly softened. She reached out a hand to tuck a stray piece of my hair back over my shoulder before her arms reached out to draw me close. My head rested on her shoulder.

"Katie Anne, you're a sweet young woman with a good heart, but you're always ready to jump before you think about where you're going to land. Maybe you didn't have anything to do with this Michelle business. I'm not actually even talking about that now. I am talking about the big influence you have over Trisha. Every time you go off, she follows right after you. It's a big responsibility when you have so much influence over somebody else. Think about what you're doing before you do it."

The Blue Hole

❧ CHAPTER 5 ❦

What we called the Blue Hole was an abandoned mining area on the mountain. Thousands of communities all across the country were left with former mine sites still waiting to be reclaimed, although most of them didn't have water. The only thing left at our Blue Hole was exposed rock and a monstrously huge, deep pit filled with water a striking shade of blue that didn't seem natural but was. Something about the mineral content caused the water to appear a brilliant blue. I'd heard the reason explained countless times, but I continued to file away the fact under "useless information." Science was never my strong point.

None of us kids remembered a time when the area had been mined. We knew it only as a good place for swimming. The country kids' public pool. Although the night air felt warm, it was still too early in the season to swim.

"No way I'm swimming out there in the pitch dark tonight. My daddy said he doesn't mind me going out there during the day, but it's way too dangerous at night," answered

Debra, a petite brunette always picked first for sports teams. If she wouldn't swim, none of the other girls would either. "Besides, it'll be freezing."

"We don't mind if you didn't bring your swimsuit." Hayden leered and gave her a long look that made me think he might be sweet on her. "I promise not to look. Scout's honor."

His remark met Debra's frown.

Wayne was impatient with the debate and ready for action.

"Anything is better than standing around here doing nothing. Let's ride up to the other side of town and see if anybody's up there. Either they'll have a better idea or they'll prob'ly go with us."

❧ CHAPTER 6 ❦

Momma's familiar voice carrying through the thin walls from the kitchen into my bedroom finally broke into my reminiscing.

"Katie Anne, are you about settled in yet? Supper's nearly ready, and it's time to run and get MawMaw."

MawMaw had always been one of the most important people in my life—and one of the most complex, although she would probably be surprised by my description. In her own eyes, she was a simple country woman, unremarkable in every way.

In my opinion, nothing was further from the truth.

Ettalene Swafford McReynolds grew up in a different world but was exceptionally sharp about the new one. She may have finished only the ninth grade in formal education, but I'd put her common sense up against any college graduate I knew.

Not only did she seem to be able to see into my head, she could also see deep within my heart.

When I was a little girl, I thought she must be a mind reader. I had seen psychics only on television, but they completely captured my imagination. One time I told MawMaw she reminded me of one, and then I surely wished I hadn't. To say she didn't take my characterization well was an understatement.

"Hush your mouth, girl, and don't you never say it again," she ordered, tightening her mouth in disgust. She also assigned me to look up five Bible verses warning against the evils of witchery. To her, the world was filled with traps set by the devil, who gleefully awaited the opportunity to drag us down. She was determined neither she nor anyone else in her family would succumb on her watch.

MawMaw was my mother's mother. Tall and slender, she wore her long, gray hair wound up in a bun fastened to the back of her head. The only times I'd ever seen the long strands down were late at night when she braided her hair for sleep and early in the morning when she brushed and put it back up again.

She bore ten children in her own home and proudly stated she never spent a night in a hospital in her life. One of her favorite tirades was "these young girls running their babies to the doctor with every little cough. No use in it a-tall. Might as well keep your money in your pocketbook for all the good it does."

MawMaw was what some people might describe as a lady with a lot of opinions.

She was also a lady with the strongest faith in God I'd ever come across. No matter the trouble, she was ready with, "The Lord already knows how it's going to work out. We'll go on about our business and let Him take care of it."

And it wasn't as if she hadn't known trouble. PawPaw

didn't become a Christian until on his deathbed. He had just turned sixty-three years old when he died a few painful days after a tractor accident. In the previous years, he had relied on whiskey to take care of his problems. Thankfully, in the end, he turned to the Lord before his time ran out. That, MawMaw said, was the answer to her greatest prayer. For years, she'd been lifting up his name each Wednesday night at prayer meeting.

MawMaw's life was rough in some ways before PawPaw died and rough in different ways after he died. But no matter what occurred during the previous week, every Sunday morning found her sitting in her pew, fifth from the front on the left. And even though she knew all the words to every song, her hands gripped a hymnal anyway as her clear alto rang out in praise to her Lord.

But MawMaw's personality featured a humorous side, too. She loved to talk, and she loved a good joke. Maybe she would have a new one for me when I picked her up.

Gingerly, I set the photo of Trisha and me back onto the dresser and picked up my car keys.

"I'm on my way," I called to Momma as I passed through the kitchen. "Back in a jiff."

"Don't lollygag around. All I lack is pouring the tea."

With a promise to hurry, I grabbed my keys and headed for the door. I backed the Mustang out onto the road and headed south to MawMaw's house. After little more than a mile, I reached the familiar turn-in to her home.

&

Some people talked about their roots. I could actually see mine.

Broken timbers and scattered stones marked the original homeplace, a simple, four-room wood structure already lost to fire by the time I was born. About a dozen cattle usually grazed inside fenced acreage where my great-grandparents originally settled.

When PawPaw and MawMaw first married, they followed the common practice of the day by moving in with his parents until they could build their own home. The older house stood several hundred yards to the side in mere ruins. Beside it was the home in which my grandparents raised their family. Now MawMaw and one of her sons were the only inhabitants of the big white farmhouse, planned to accommodate a sprawling family, with fireplaces providing warmth in nearly every room.

The home was built in the style of many in the same time period. A wide hall split the middle from back to front, with a stairway off to the right leading to a second-story landing. Entering from the front, you could see right out the back door. To the left of the hall were the front parlor and then MawMaw and PawPaw's bedroom. On the right were the dining room and a large kitchen.

Four upstairs bedrooms sheltered the couple's nine surviving children until they grew, married and established homes of their own. In one of the bedrooms, you could still see the bullet hole where one of my uncles "accidentally" shot through the ceiling. The reason why and who was to blame varied according to who was retelling their version of the story.

Bathrooms and electricity were added a short time after the home's construction, when the luxuries became commonplace in the area.

A short path out the back door led to PawPaw's barn,

the wood aged to a faded gray yet the construction still sturdy. A small fenced area allowed the animals freedom to go in or out of the barn at will. A cattle chute for loading animals into a truck did double duty to administer treatments and vaccinations.

My uncles were trying to convince MawMaw to sell the old homeplace and move into something smaller and more modern, but they may as well be trying to convince a preacher to drink whiskey in front of the whole town. MawMaw wasn't budging.

Before I had time to pull off the hardtop and onto her gravel driveway, MawMaw hurried out of the house and over to the car. I intended to get out and open the door for her, but she moved too fast for me.

"I do hate to put you out like this, Katie Anne. I used to walk farther than this every day just in trips to tote water from the spring. It's hard for you young people to believe. Now you think anybody who grows up without a microwave is plumb backward, although I do love mine."

"Hey, MawMaw. You know I wanted to come get you myself."

I leaned over the narrow console to grab her for a warm hug, breathing in the familiar scents of firm hold hairspray and baby powder.

"Yep, you're a good one, Katie Anne, and always have been. Tell the truth, ain't you glad to be out of the big city?"

Well, she didn't wait long to start in on me. We weren't even out of her driveway yet. I was bracing for an inquisition over supper, but apparently MawMaw decided not to wait for backup from Momma. She thought she'd set things rolling at the first opportunity. At least you knew where you stood with her, and I knew she disapproved of me moving away from

Pikeville. It didn't even matter where I had gone, only that I had gone.

"Now, MawMaw, there's nothing wrong with living in Nashville. I've got friends there and a good job and a nice place to live. You ought to get Momma to bring you up there sometime."

"You could have all them same things right here, plus your family, and I don't need to go nowhere. I didn't lose nothing up there, so I don't need to go after it," she stated with conviction, placing her plain brown pocketbook on the floorboard at her feet. She was dressed in her normal uniform of cotton housedress and tan lace-up shoes with white anklet socks.

"There just aren't the jobs in Pikeville." I responded almost absently, throwing out one of a number of excuses ready in my arsenal.

"We've got lawyers here, too, and they've got secretaries."

"They don't pay anywhere near what I make. Pikeville salaries won't compete with a big law firm in a city like Nashville. And besides, I'm not a secretary, I'm a paralegal now. I told you when I finally earned my degree. Remember?"

"Call it whatever big, fancy name you want to, but you don't need to make as much money to live in Pikeville as you need in the city, do you? You could move in with me. I got all them bedrooms upstairs going empty ever night, nary a bed slept in except for your uncle Cooper. Or you could stay with your momma. You could save up money and buy your own piece of ground. You got plenty of kinfolks to help build a place on it for you."

I couldn't argue with her logic, but my stubbornness demanded I try to anyway.

"From what I hear, with all these Florida people moving in from the south and all the Michigan people coming down from the north, land prices here are getting as high as anywhere else."

"That's true," MawMaw conceded. "But I guess their money spends as good as anybody else's. I'm hoping they'll come and spend some at the benefit tomorrow night."

What a lucky break! While I racked my brain trying to devise some way to turn the uncomfortable conversation away from my personal living situation, MawMaw turned the topic herself. I took full advantage of my unexpected good fortune and kept up a steady stream of details about the benefit during the rest of the short ride back to my mother's home.

෨

When we arrived, hugs all around were once again in order. Then we sat down to a veritable feast that guaranteed I would not be losing those extra ten pounds as long as I remained under Momma's roof. She had prepared all of my favorite foods: country-fried steak with mashed potatoes and white gravy, green beans, slaw, corn, and biscuits. I knew the vegetables came straight from last summer's garden out back and into the house, where they were canned and stored, ready for use. And the biscuits were from scratch, the only way Momma fixed them.

Pinto beans and cornbread were on the table, too. They were probably the only foods not necessarily cooked with me specifically in mind. I don't believe there was ever a time while I was growing up when we didn't have pinto beans and cornbread on the table for supper and a lot of times for lunch, too.

I knew better than to pick up my fork before the blessing was said. The move would get a person hurt in a hurry. Even so, I tried not to catch anyone else's eye, lest they be able to read how much time had passed since God and I had been on speaking terms.

In the same way she did before any meal she sat down to, Momma bowed her head and began her familiar greeting to the Lord: "Our gracious heavenly Father, bless this food we are about to partake and let it give us strength to do Thy will. Thank You for granting safe traveling mercies to Katie Anne and bringing her back home to us. We ask Your blessing also on Lora Anne, for You to heal her body if it be Thy will. Bless the benefit for her and all those who give as You have given them. In the name of our precious Savior, Jesus Christ. Amen."

As soon as we filled our plates with the tempting food, the phone rang.

"Don't it happen every time," exclaimed MawMaw. In spite of her rail-thin figure, she was a woman who enjoyed her food and didn't want to be bothered by any interruptions while doing so.

Listening to her words, I marveled at how easily I slipped back into the rhythm of the unique dialect that was the language of the rural South. The words flowed with a gentle cadence which brought to mind the perfume of line-dried clothes, the breeze blowing over a newly mown hay field, and my daddy's gentle hug after a day's work.

With a growing influx of new residents with their own speech patterns and the influence of television, I wondered how long before this particular dialect was lost forever. Not more than another generation.

"Hello," Momma answered, picking up the phone and moving on into the living room to talk to the caller. After a couple of minutes of muffled conversation, she said goodbye and replaced the cordless phone on its base.

"That was Farrah," she informed us. Farrah was the daughter of my mother's brother Garner which, of course, made her my first cousin. Only two years older than I was, she could have hailed from another galaxy for all we connected. In fact, perhaps she did. At least it would be a good explanation for our differences.

At the face I made, my mother reached toward me and rapped the table top with her knuckles the way she used to rap whichever part of my body she could reach.

"She's done a lot toward the benefit, young lady, and I expect you to be nice to her. You're not the same person you were when you were little, and Farrah's not either."

"I guess not, since she's even got a new name." I sniggered.

What was with the pattern of people around me suddenly deciding to change their names?

My remark prompted a snorting laugh from MawMaw, too.

"She's got you there, Rayetta. I swan, that girl of Luther's takes after her mother's people. I don't know what got into her to make her run around telling ever'body to call her Farrah. What's wrong with the name Clara Jean? It's a good, strong name, and it's the name give to her. This trying to change your name business is foolishness, that's all."

"She said it goes better with her business name," Momma defended her. "Farrah's Flowers looks better on the sign. Besides, she's bringing all her big ferns and the stands to go with them to put around the auctioneer's spot tomorrow night. She'll make the front of the gym real pretty."

"I know she will, Momma, and I'll try to be good," I promised. With a grin, I looked over and couldn't resist adding, "but I can't make any promises for MawMaw."

"I wouldn't be casting any stones, *Kate*," Momma emphasized.

Ouch, got me there.

&

My first bite of gravy nearly set me swooning. Nothing I'd ever eaten tasted better than gravy mixed up in an iron skillet with meat drippings. And nobody made gravy better than Momma—unless it was MawMaw.

After making the mistake of ordering restaurant gravy a few times, I quickly learned to strictly avoid the menu offering. Not even places specializing in breakfast came close to Momma's perfection. Of course, making gravy and homemade biscuits for breakfast every day of her married life earned her quite a bit of experience.

I was so caught up in savoring the magnificent flavors bursting wildly on my tongue that I nearly didn't catch the significance of MawMaw's comment.

"Who's Edgar?" I questioned.

A nervous glance backed up by a frown of warning darted from Momma across the table to MawMaw. But MawMaw merely sat there silently, acting as innocent as could be.

An awkward silence settled over the table. Silence at a table with Momma and MawMaw was unusual enough to let me know I wanted details. The reason was bound to be interesting.

"Well, who's Edgar?"

"Tell the girl, Rayetta," MawMaw prodded.

Momma pursed her lips tightly for a moment and then reluctantly obeyed. "He's a brother to your aunt Dora." Aunt Dora was married to another one of Momma's brothers, Alvin. "You may have met him before. He lived over in Spring City a while after his wife died, and now he's got a little place down the road. You turn at the Four-Way Store and go back in there. He's retired, but sometimes he helps out at the farmer's co-op during busy season."

A nice little description, but none of her narrative warranted the unease Momma was displaying. I knew there must be more.

"And?" I prodded.

"And what?"

"And she's keeping company with him, that's what," blurted out MawMaw, unable to keep silent any longer.

I couldn't have been more surprised if the corn started dancing.

A deep red blush swept over Momma's face, reached her hairline, and continued on up into the roots of her permanent as far as I could see.

"He's only a friend," she firmly protested. "We've shared supper a few times, and he comes over to see some television. That's all. There's nothing going on."

MawMaw cut in. "You better get him in church with you now, Rayetta. If you don't start it at the very first, you can't expect him to pick it up later."

Ha. MawMaw's advice for all ages. No matter how old her daughter got, her advice never stopped.

But neither did her words distract me from the real issue for more than a moment.

Momma dating? I was so shocked I didn't quite know how I felt. My first thought was, *What would Daddy think?* Of course, I reminded myself, if Daddy were here she wouldn't be dating someone else. I couldn't picture my mother with anybody but Daddy. *Why would Momma even want to date?* Nope, I didn't want to think about those reasons. Better to leave that sack of frogs alone lest any of them jump out unwanted and roam around free, loose in my brain forever.

My next thought was, *How did my mother end up with a better dating life than I have?* How depressing. The next thing I knew, MawMaw would have another man.

The subject was definitely making Momma nervous. She kept fiddling with her napkin and staring down at her lap. She was caught in an impossible situation, squeezed on both sides, between her mother and her daughter.

Although enjoying her discomfort just a bit, I decided to give her a break and changed the subject by asking for another biscuit. Shrugging off momentary guilt over the extra calories involved, I told myself Lainey was probably breaking our diet, too. The thought reminded me of my promise to call her, and I resolved to do so as soon as we finished eating.

Passing me the biscuit plate, Momma jumped on the diversion and quickly reached to grab a random thought out of the air.

"Harmon Suggs is working down at the tire store, did you know?" she asked MawMaw. "I saw him going into the post office yesterday when I was passing on my way to the grocery store. Looked right good."

"How much did they give him for killing that little girl? Two years?"

"He served two years, but I think he got five. Must be on some sort of probation. I sure hope he don't start drinking again."

I searched my memory and finally identified Harmon Suggs. From what little I knew, he suffered the same downfall as my pawpaw: alcohol. In a terrible accident while Harmon was drunk behind the wheel, he hit another vehicle head-on and a little three-year-old girl died. She hadn't been in a child safety seat. His son, Curtis, was in my graduating class, but I didn't know him well.

"I reckon he's had a hard time," sympathized Maw-Maw. "I pray he straightens hisself out. He can still have a good life if he's got a mind to. It's been so wonderful to see him in church. It's the best place to start over."

Where was the sympathy for the parents of the little girl who died? I wondered. But I wasn't in the mood to debate two against one so I kept my opinion to myself.

By the time we finished supper, I felt so tired I wanted to collapse on the comfortable but worn leather couch in the living room and pull the soft, multi-colored afghan over me. Selfishly, I felt like doing anything but going down to the high school and putting in two or three hours of work getting ready for the benefit.

But I'd barely placed my fork on my empty plate when Momma announced we were leaving the dishes for later. The statement in itself proclaimed loud and clear the importance of our task ahead. To my knowledge, my mother had never left the table without jumping up and doing the dishes right away. And heaven forbid a dishwasher ever cross the threshold of her home.

That was one more way in which Momma and I were vastly different. I had always believed in dishwashers. Not nearly on the scale with how I believed in the blood of the Lamb, despite our recent differences. But right up there with

Santa Claus and birth control, neither of which saved you but still made life more enjoyable.

Not Momma. Doing dishes was some sort of sickness with her, but evidently she was making progress in her recovery, because we left the dishes in the sink.

After being badgered into going back into my room to get a light jacket, I rejoined the two most important women in my life and proceeded to the high school.

The Blue Hole

~ CHAPTER 7 ~

On that night so long ago, we all piled into our vehicles, at least a dozen or more, and pulled out for the other end of Main Street, where another small parking lot served as the other turn-around spot for teenagers. Trisha and I were the only two riding in the car I borrowed from Momma for the evening.

Momma was already talking to Uncle Cooper about looking for some reliable, sensible transportation for me to drive back and forth to college classes. I was talking to Uncle Cooper about finding me something sharp and unsensible. As Wayne frequently pointed out, "Even if it breaks down, you'll look good sitting by the side of the road." So far, though, I remained stuck in Momma's boring sedan.

Our trail of cars and trucks looked like a late night parade descending on the town square as we made our way slowly but noisily to our destination. Tires squealed and engines revved, but we crept along, killing time.

When we arrived at the turn-around on the north side

62

of town, we found a few more friends settled in, lounging on the hoods of vehicles parked in a semi-circle around a utility pole. One of them was Jesse Myers, a boy who graduated last year and worked in his uncle's mechanic shop. Although Trisha hadn't yet admitted her crush to me, I suspected she was interested by the nervous way she acted around him. And Jesse seemed to be giving her extra attention lately, too.

"Hey, Trisha." Jesse spotted her as soon as she opened the car door, and his face lit up.

A smile immediately bloomed on my best friend's face. Her answer was to head in the direction leading straight to him. I thought I'd give her a few minutes for a private greeting, so I walked over to Debra and the other girls as they climbed out of their cars.

"Is something going on there?" Debra nodded toward Jesse and Trisha. She quickly reached her own conclusion without waiting for a reply. "Good for her."

Realizing nothing was happening at the other end of town either, Zeb jumped up in the bed of the nearest truck.

"Attention, students. I have an announcement." He did a good job mocking the school's morning intercom broadcast delivered daily by our uptight principal. "We are going on a field trip this evening to the Blue Hole. While we are gone, you will not be expected to act like the gentlemen and ladies we know you are not. Please line up in a disorderly fashion and proceed to the designated site."

Not to be outdone, Wayne hopped up in the truck's bed alongside Zeb and raised a fist in the air.

"Start your engines, boys, and let's head for the water."

His command sent most of the group to their vehicles. Since the road into the pit wasn't paved, I didn't want to drive my momma's car into the adjoining field and risk bottoming out and losing all my driving privileges, so I piled in with Wayne. Zeb had beaten us to the truck and was already in the cab with a boy we called Ralph, even though it wasn't his real name. When they saw me coming, they jumped out of the cab and moved to the bed. Their mommas were raising them to be gentlemen after all.

I called out to Trisha, who was still over talking with Jesse.

She ran toward me. I opened up the truck door, climbed in, and began to scoot over and let her in beside me. But she stopped short.

"Umm, Jesse asked if I'd ride up the mountain with him. He's all by himself. I said okay."

For once, I resisted the urge to tease.

"Do you want to come with us?" Trisha asked.

When I told her I would stay where I was and ride with Wayne, a brief smile of relief flickered across her face. I had sized up the situation correctly. Three was definitely a crowd.

"I guess I should call home and let them know where I'm at." Trisha tried to whisper to me, but Wayne, who was swinging his right leg into the driver's side of the truck, heard her too.

"Come on, girl, we'll be back before they even know we're gone. Why take a chance on riling them up for no reason?"

Trisha, ever trying to please, dropped the subject and turned back to Jesse's truck.

All at once, the squeal of tires filled the air as the trucks left the parking lot and headed up the mountain.

❧ CHAPTER 8 ❦

Aunt Lora Anne occupied her own special place in my heart. The best way I knew to describe her influence in my life was to say she was always there. I'd never known a world without Aunt Lora Anne in it. She was the youngest of MawMaw's three daughters. Aunt Patty Lynn was the oldest, and my mother, Rayetta, was in the middle, with less than two years' time between each of their births.

"The Lord give me three little boy babies, then three little girl babies, and then three more little boys," was the way MawMaw told it. "They say bad things come in threes. I don't know about that, but good things sure did come in threes for me. I wouldn't take nothing for my babies, no matter how old they are."

In reality, MawMaw's final set of threes was a set of four. But she rarely spoke about the little boy she and PawPaw lost or even acknowledged his birth. Not for a moment did I suspect the loss didn't wound her deeply, but she believed in keeping her pain private.

The three sisters—Aunt Patty Lynn, Momma, and Aunt Lora Anne—were each others' lifelong best friends and confidantes. Even that description doesn't capture the gentle nuances of their relationships. Sometimes they reminded me of one person in three similar bodies.

Looking back at old photographs quickly revealed how attractive all three were from the time they were small girls, through their teenage years, and then as women. Not that they still weren't, I guessed, but you sure didn't expect to find out somebody might have thought your mother looked hot, no matter how young her age at the time. Add in the recent attentions of a man named Edgar, and the creepy factor hit big time.

Within our family, the women were often called "the triplets." They earned the nickname honestly, over time developing a peculiar habit of dressing alike. Not all the time, but often enough so their unusual attire proved hugely embarrassing to me as a kid. If their identical outfits were limited to around the house or among family, the practice might not have bothered me overly much. But the identical triplet look came out big in public. If one of them found a flattering outfit, the purchase must be made in threes, one for them to wear and a matching set for each of their sisters. Occasionally MawMaw joined in, but not often.

Dressing alike tapered off somewhat over the years, but the three sisters still used the same hair coloring, an unusual shade of blonde no one could ever mistake as natural. Add in their comparable heights and weights, and the result was pretty close to triplets. Hard to argue with the evidence.

To the younger me, Aunt Lora Anne was my mother minus all the responsibility of seeing I grew up to be a decent person. Of course, the one difference made her way more fun. She let me get away with a little bit more than Momma, as long as my actions didn't involve anything dangerous.

I was Aunt Lora Anne's namesake. Not the Lora part, of course, but her middle name, Anne. She was Lora Anne and I was Katie Anne, at least to everyone in Pikeville.

"This girl's part mine, too," she frequently announced with pride. "She's got part of my name, and I reckon it's the closest thing to my own daughter I'll ever get."

She was probably right. She acquired a daughter-in-law with the marriage of her oldest son, Bryant, but at the pace their relationship was developing, Kayla probably wouldn't graduate to daughter status anytime soon.

Aunt Lora and Uncle Herbert had three sons but no daughters of their own. In spite of her wishes and prayers, she produced only boys. And she didn't mind publicly announcing she was greatly disappointed from the beginning. Bryant was the first to let her down. He was a year younger than me and a year behind me in school.

"I tell you, when the doctor said, 'It's a boy!' my heart dropped to my shoes. I was for certain I was carrying a girl. Why, everybody said so."

I'd heard her repeat the story countless times, accompanied by great dramatics and hand gestures, which highlighted my family's manner of storytelling. Any one of them could spin a thirty-minute story about a ten-minute trip to the grocery store that made you sorry you weren't along. I'd always believed their dubious shared talent was the result of growing up without a television. Instead, they learned to provide their own entertainment.

"When they asked me what his name was, why, all I could say was, 'Cathy.' My heart was set on my baby being named Cathy. I thought it was the most beautiful name in the world. Ever since my class studied Catherine the Great in school, I tucked her name away inside me, knowing I found the name of my firstborn. She was going to grow up to be somebody great, too.

"Of course, everybody in the room laughed, even the nurses, thinking I was cutting up. But I wasn't. I was straight serious."

I didn't know what Bryant thought about the story and, as far as I knew, nobody ever asked him. It was the truth, so why shouldn't it be told? My family probably told a lot of truths that should have been kept silent, and kept silent a lot of truths that should have been told. We mixed up the concept quite often.

Aunt Lora Anne's disappointment didn't end with Bryant. She had two more sons to go, each one bringing a letdown—if you believed the story the way she told it, which nobody did. We all saw right through her, fully aware the sun rose and set in her world with every little thing one of her boys did or said.

"Then, just twenty months later when I found out I was expecting J. Arthur, I prayed and prayed for a girl. I was certain the Lord wouldn't give me another boy. Back then my doctor didn't tell you ahead of time what kind of baby you were getting like they do now. All you could do was wait and see. Not that we ever decorated a nursery anyhow. We didn't have to have all the same color to match. We used what we already had.

"November seventeenth, right on the dot at two o'clock in the morning, the same doctor said the same words, 'It's a boy!' Herbert knew better than to laugh then, after the fit I throwed when Bryant was born. He told me, 'Hon, we'll keep on trying.' But I knew he was tickled about another little fishing buddy.

"Then when Levi was born, don't you know, I cried and cried my heart out. I knew by then he'd be the last one and I never would get my Cathy. But as the preacher told me, 'The Lord knows best.' And I tell you, now I wouldn't trade my boys for any Cathy in the world."

In fact, the only reason Aunt Lora Anne could repeat her Cathy story without appearing to be an ungrateful mother was everyone knew she adored her sons with the fierce devotion of the most loving mother. The only thing required to get her in a fighting mood was the slightest hint one of her boys was the least bit imperfect. In other words, she spoiled them rotten.

In the way of so many traditional southern mothers, Aunt Lora Anne picked up after them, fed them, pampered them, and tried her best to anticipate their every whim. Prospective wives found the situation difficult, if not impossible, to overcome.

⁊

There I was, stuck in the kitchen every Sunday afternoon at MawMaw's house, washing dishes while all the boys played ball out in the yard. Boys sure had life easy. Take out the trash and that was all, job done. Mow the yard every once in a while. Girls like me were expected to be shriveling our hands in dishwater every time a fork hit the sink. On top of that came making beds, sweeping floors, and whatever other torture Momma could dream up.

The words "it isn't fair" were uttered by me at least once each Sunday, followed by Momma's familiar refrain, "Sugar, life ain't fair, get used to it."

I wasn't the only girl with her hands in the sink. I had plenty of company. All of my girl cousins were right there alongside me. All except Clara—oops, Farrah—who "almost died when she was a baby." Apparently I was the only one who couldn't figure out why the detail still mattered when there were dishes to wash or some other chore to do. No wonder she stayed at the top of my hit list.

But if you kept your head down and your ears open, a lot of good information could come your way during Sunday dinner cleanup at MawMaw's. Sunday still remained the one time a week the whole family, or at least most of the family, gathered together. Doing the dishes gave the women time to talk without unwelcome comments from the men every time they crossed the line from facts into a little speculation.

My tendency to break a dish or two along the way if I handled them more than a few seconds made me the perfect choice to man the rinse sink. That way I didn't have far to reach the drainer, and usually somebody with a dishtowel plucked the dish right out of my hands before I made the transfer. So, basically, I stood in front of the sink for half an hour or so with my hands playing in the water. As long as I didn't splash too much, I was pretty well overlooked.

In fact, there in front of the kitchen sink, absent-mindedly swishing water round and round, I finally found out the real reason for PawPaw's frequent bouts of headaches, bloodshot eyes, and sluggishness. Aunt Patty Lynn let the forbidden information slip out after one of these Sunday dinners.

"Charles heard tell Daddy got in a bad way up to the club the other night." She delivered the news in a voice barely above a whisper.

My ears immediately perked up. All of the most

interesting information came in whispers. I instantly shot into high alert mode.

I had learned from past experience if I kept my head down, quietly continued moving my hands through the dishwater, and didn't make eye contact with anyone, the women were lulled into thinking I was daydreaming instead of listening to them. Nothing was further from the truth. It was all part of my sneaky plan to make them drop their defenses and drop something juicy right into my lap, or dishwater, as the case may be. Whenever one of them began to whisper, my ears perked up along with everyone else's.

The "club" was nothing more than a plain block building by the side of the road up the valley where drinking men could drink in peace without the disapproval of their wives hovering nearby.

"Charles saw Troy Lee over at the co-op when he was picking up a load of feed yesterday." Aunt Patty Lynn continued whispering. "Said Daddy must have got ahold of some bad liquor. Either that or he was having some kind of flashback. Said he started talking crazy about somebody trying to kill him. Said it took a while to get him calmed down."

"I swear, I'd like to choke him when he pulls one of these spells." MawMaw shook her head in disgust as she covered the rest of the greens with plastic wrap. "Why the man won't stay away from that place, I don't know."

I realized PawPaw having a "spell" meant nothing more than a long drinking binge and "that place" was the club.

Then MawMaw's daughter-in-law, Aunt Rachael, who was married to my uncle Vernon, cut in. She was principal of the middle school, and the rest of the women were a bit in awe of her doctorate degree in education. Since they looked up to her, they assumed she looked down on them, and their backs bristled any time they perceived a slight, which occurred on a regular basis.

"He needs to be taken to the Veterans Administration hospital in Murfreesboro and let a staff of professionals help him with his addiction," she helpfully suggested. "They could also work with him on any lingering Post-Traumatic Stress Syndrome from his war experiences or any other unresolved issues bothering him."

Mistake.

Huge mistake.

I nearly giggled out loud, realizing how deep Aunt Rachael had stepped in it, but I kept my head down to avoid drawing attention to myself, hoping the conversation on the forbidden topic would continue. If anyone realized I was listening, talk would shut down quicker than a rabbit could run.

If you hadn't grown up under it, our family's loyalty system could be hard to figure out exactly. But there were some clear cut rules. One: While in a group you could be critical of a family member only if you were a blood relative. In-laws better keep quiet or we closed ranks awfully fast and slammed you out in the cold before you even know we were reaching for the door. As poor Aunt Rachael should have known after all those years of being in the family. A formal education obviously didn't cover all the important topics in life after all.

An in-law could criticize only in a one-on-one conversation, but with the understanding the conversation would probably be repeated endlessly to anybody who wasn't around to hear the words the first time, so there was still great potential to get yourself in trouble.

Rule two: If you and your immediate family members were out of the room, you were completely fair game. Once again, though, only for blood relatives. In-laws were expected to keep their mouths shut unless asked to comment.

Of course, rule number two kept a lot of women out of the bathroom and in the conversation. They wouldn't talk about you if you were in the same room.

Rule three: PawPaw, MawMaw, and their three daughters were strictly off-limits at all times and in all places, unless one of them brought up one of the others. That was a very unlikely scenario. But even then, the rest of us could only listen, not participate.

Rule four: Nothing particularly good about you was ever said in your presence. Any least bit of flattery might cause you to get "the big head." In our family, contracting a case of "the big head" was one of the worst possible character flaws, and we stood firm guard against cultivating it.

If you knew how to play the game, you were all right. But if you didn't, they could eat you alive.

Since Aunt Patty Lynn was the one who brought up the subject of PawPaw, she obviously felt duty-bound to lead the fight for his honor. She wasted no time before whirling around from the long table to face Aunt Rachael, shaking a fist full of utensils she was in the midst of gathering.

"Daddy does not have an addiction." This time there was no whisper in her voice. Instead, she delivered a clear, firm statement that forcefully relayed another strong message at the same time: back off. "He drinks too much sometimes. Period. He's just letting off a little steam. Plenty of men do the same thing."

A silence descended over the kitchen.

After a long, tense moment, Aunt Rachael realized retreat was her best strategy and left the kitchen to "see if Vernon is ready to go."

The conversation continued, but the talk was all aimed at Aunt Rachael and who did she think she was to judge Daddy. Having a fancy degree didn't mean you knew it all. She would do well to remember her place.

Quickly bored with the sudden change of subject, I also cut out as soon as I could and joined my boy cousins outside where all the fun was taking place. If I wanted to hear Aunt Rachael chewed up and spit out, I knew I would have many other opportunities at many other get-togethers down the line.

"Hey, here's miss dishpan hands." J. Arthur's eyes were focused on the football he was tossing straight up into the air and attempting to catch when it fell down again.

Bryant, J. Arthur, and Levi knew teasing me about "girl chores" was guaranteed to get a rise out of my quick temper, and they never failed to zing me good.

&

Even years later, thinking about Aunt Lora Anne's fried egg sandwiches made my mouth begin watering for one. I didn't know why, but nobody had ever been able to cook one like her. Those sandwiches were a staple of my childhood, and the ingredients were always on hand in her kitchen. A couple of eggs fried in bacon grease, then layered between light bread smothered in mayonnaise.

In my family, a woman who didn't cook was automatically suspect. After all, everyone knew food equaled love, right? If you really loved me, you'd have seconds. Yes,

I fell victim to the Clean Plate Club. Over the years, I'd tried and tried to revoke my membership, but I still couldn't figure out how to resign. My lifetime membership stood firm. Unconditional love from the well-meaning women in my life taught me my worst habits.

Admitting not going to church was another serious infraction that got disapproving eyes cut over at you in stern criticism. Now, not everyone was required to attend, but at least the woman should. And she should take the kids so nobody could blame her if they didn't turn out right. At least she tried.

There was plenty of evidence my momma tried with me. All you had to do was inspect the Sunday school records. All those check marks, Sunday after Sunday, year after year. And Sunday nights and Wednesday nights, too. And every revival. And Vacation Bible School. And youth trips to Gatlinburg. Willingly or not, either way, I was there.

Not to say everyone in town went to church every time the doors were open. Don't get me wrong, there were plenty who did, I was certain. But even those who didn't attend knew the big three: Sunday morning, Sunday night, and Wednesday night. So even if they didn't go themselves, they still knew Wednesday night was church night. No sports practices and no community meetings on Wednesday night. We didn't even have homework. Nothing to keep people from going to prayer meeting except themselves.

Aunt Lora Anne was a major part of my church life as well as my family life. Determined to see her sons behaved in Sunday school, she usually ended up teaching whatever class they were in at the time. Their class was usually the same one I was in. Since Trisha's family attended the same church, she was with us, too. Aunt Lora Anne made it her personal mission to see we all behaved.

We must have memorized enough scripture to compile an entire Bible. The Ten Commandments, the Twenty-Third Psalm, the Beatitudes, the Lord's Prayer. Looking back, the list seemed a lot longer at the time. Of course, we were forced to quote a zillion individual verses, too. We covered a sampling from the Old Testament right through the New.

And Bible drills. Every so often, we lined up in front of the whole congregation on a Sunday morning with our Bibles clutched firmly in front of us. Aunt Lora Anne called out a verse, and the race began to see which student could find the reference first. I proved pretty good down in our basement classroom, but once in front of a crowd I sprouted all thumbs. Momma rarely had reason to be proud of my performance.

In spite of our general rowdiness, Aunt Lora Anne was patient and let us get away with a little bit sometimes. She also knew how to settle us down in a hurry.

She was always a great storyteller, completely mesmerizing us with elaborate recreations of Bible stories, painting detailed pictures in our minds of the exciting scene when Pharoah's army realized the Children of Israel were escaping their evil clutches, but the Red Sea was collapsing down on them in torrents of waves. She authentically conveyed the magical wonder of a precious little baby taking His first sweet breath in a stable, with sheep and donkeys as witnesses.

My favorite Bible story was when little Samuel awoke to hear a voice speaking to him, but he didn't know who it was. He thought it must have been the priest, Eli, and ran to him. But Eli said it wasn't him. This was repeated a couple of times, until finally Eli realized the voice must be from God.

The next time Samuel heard the voice, Eli told him to say, "Speak Lord, for Thy servant heareth."

I always thought Samuel was lucky to have an Eli, somebody to tell him the voice he heard actually was the Lord. Otherwise, those messages could be hard to figure out. Or maybe I never listened close enough to know.

Trisha's favorite story from the Bible was about the servant girl who told her master to go see Elisha who could cure his leprosy.

"Talking to him took a lot of courage," she said. "What if she was wrong? They could beat her or throw her out or sell her to somebody else or something."

I secretly liked to pretend I was the servant girl too, confident in my faith and ready to tell anybody where all of the answers could be found. Of course, back then I thought I owned all the answers. What a great surprise to me later on when I found out I didn't.

The boys liked the gorier stories, such as when the dogs licked the bones of Jezebel. Yuck.

When I was eight years old, the message began to sink in that those "unsaved" people everyone at church was talking about included me. I needed Jesus in my heart. For days, when Trisha and I were in private, we talked of little else.

"I sure don't want to go to hell." Her chin quivered up and down as she spoke. "But I don't want to go up in front of everybody either. And then you got to get baptized. What if the preacher can't pull me back up? I could drown down in there."

With Trisha's fear of water, she should have been my mother's child.

"No, you couldn't. It's not that deep. All you'd have to

do is stand up."

"But what if I hit my head on the side of the baptistry going down?"

"You can baby talk all you want to, but I'm going up."

And I did. The next week during revival, I nodded to Trisha, who stood next to me as the familiar strains of *Just As I Am* rang out from the piano. That's the song they always played for the invitation. I stepped out from the pew and headed up the aisle toward the altar.

Just as the preacher claimed, the first step was the hardest. I didn't even remember the rest of the journey. I thought I was making the walk alone, but when I got up front, Trisha was right behind me. There were smiles everywhere there weren't tears, and in some places there were both. Momma, MawMaw, and Aunt Lora Anne for sure.

"You'll remember this forever." Aunt Lora Anne whispered softly in my ear as she came through the line to give me "the right hand of fellowship" our church extended to every new Christian.

I gave my heart to Jesus that night. For a long time, I'd been trying to take it back, but no matter what I did, He wouldn't let me go.

The Blue Hole

ॐ CHAPTER 9 ॐ

Only ten to fifteen minutes elapsed before our little procession arrived at the Blue Hole—or as close to the pit as we could drive. The original roadbed was long overgrown and impassible, meaning the best way in was through an adjacent piece of property. The parking area we used was nothing more than a level field plenty large enough to hold all of our vehicles pulled in with no regard to a specific pattern. The first ones in opened the twelve-foot gate, and the last ones in were careful to shut it back. We all knew the quickest way to create trouble was to leave a farmer's gate open.

By the time Wayne, Zeb, Ralph, and I arrived, several of our friends were ahead of us and some were already climbing toward the top of the pit. None of us knew exactly how deep the pit plunged or where the deepest part was located. We did know to be careful of the jagged rocks in some places which could cut as sharp as a razor, and we also knew pockets of water were cold enough to cause deadly cramps to even the strongest swimmers.

Truth be told, we even knew we weren't technically supposed to be swimming at the Blue Hole, but everyone did. Abandoned mining sites with water pools all over the country not yet reclaimed according to law were still being used every day by swimmers. Some were even large enough to run boats on. We were merely making our own fun where we could.

Some of the guys—and girls, too—were already walking a little unsteadily by then. This was shaping up to be more of an alcohol night than usual. They had obviously dipped into the coolers occupying the back of nearly every truck on the property. Empty cans were tossed carelessly back into the truck beds. Beer was the drink of choice, but a couple of moonshine jars began making an appearance, too.

"Here, honey, carry a few of these cans for me." Zeb thrust a six-pack of beer toward me, along with one single can. "Go ahead, have one for yourself on the way."

My friends had witnessed me drink a few times before. I didn't notice any effect other than an occasional short-lived buzz. I sure didn't want Momma to catch me, but what could she do anyway, except holler at me and make me feel bad for a while? I thought I was a little too old to be forced to memorize scripture verses for punishment anymore.

I popped the top of the can and guzzled the first of the beer. Each time I tried it, the taste got a little better, until now I could do more than tolerate beer. I was actually beginning to like it.

Trisha and Jesse seemed to appear out of nowhere, strolling close together, holding hands. In a silent exchange between best friends, I semi-discreetly raised my eyebrows as I stared at their joined hands. In the dark I couldn't see her blush, but I knew her well enough to know red stained her cheeks.

Without Trisha asking, I handed her the beer in my hand and motioned for Zeb to toss me another single can.

Wayne grabbed an old raggedy quilt stashed behind his truck seat. With a flourish, he turned to me and waved an arm before us.

"Lead on, Katie Anne."

☙ CHAPTER 10 ❧

The combination of Momma and MawMaw kept up a steady stream of conversation on the way to the high school, flipping topics too often for me to keep up, although I didn't try very hard, I admit. By then, my nerves had completely taken over. Although we were merely setting up for the benefit, I would probably see people I hadn't faced in years. People who might not be glad to see me.

As if she could read my thoughts clearly, MawMaw reached over from her position in the front passenger seat and gently patted my arm. Just when I thought she wasn't paying any attention at all, without a word she let me know she was still on my side.

Her brief touch refocused my thoughts on the conversation underway in the car. The ladies' latest subject was gardening, something that didn't interest me in the slightest, but could keep the two of them rambling on and on for hours at a time. Remembering my manners, I fought the temptation to tune out their voices once again.

"My little tomato starts are coming up real pretty." Momma wasn't content with buying small plants like everyone else. No, she had to put an actual heirloom seed in the soil and raise the plant up all the way. Anything else was cheating. "By the time it gets planting weather, they'll be ready. The almanac recommends waiting till the sixth day of next month."

The almanac. The final authority on all issues farm-related. The best time to plow, when to plant, and harvest schedules. In my family, the almanac was given the proper respect it deserved, second only to the Bible.

MawMaw responded, "I'll likely be getting Cooper to plow my ground this year. Old Mr. Scott just ain't able to since his stroke last fall."

"You know Cooper won't care a bit to plow your garden spot. He would have done it all this time if Mr. Scott hadn't already been used to doing it regular for you."

My uncle Cooper was the only one of MawMaw's children who never married. He always had women chasing after him, but once they began getting too familiar with the rest of the family, he was finished with them.

After PawPaw died, Uncle Cooper moved out of the little house he built himself on a few acres down the valley and moved back in the family homeplace with MawMaw. The arrangement appeared to suit both of them. And the rest of the family felt easier knowing he stayed nearby for MawMaw in case she needed help.

"I hope you're remembering Mr. Scott in prayer, Rayetta. Lands, they's so many people in this world needs prayer."

Ever since I could remember, MawMaw kept a written prayer list, an extremely long list. Many times over the years,

I'd come across her on her knees in the middle of an easy conversation with her Savior. I knew my name appeared on her list, and I was lifted up in prayer every day. Fine with me, I'd take all the help I could get.

"I put Ashley and Ricardo on my list this morning. They need so much help, bless their hearts."

A couple of different young women named Ashley came to mind, but who in the world was Ricardo? The name certainly wasn't a common one in Pikeville. MawMaw's comment puzzled me, but Momma caught on right away, and a frown instantly shot from her mouth all the way up to the lines on her forehead. From her position in the back seat, she quickly scooted up between the car's bucket seats and poked her head forward. Too far forward for me.

"Momma, do you have your seat belt on?"

She completely ignored me to zero in on MawMaw.

"Do you mean Ashley and Ricardo from your stories?"

"Yes, honey. They've been having so much trouble lately. First they suffered through the terrible tornado and lost their house and everything in it, and now somebody stole their little baby yesterday."

"You can't put them on the prayer list. I keep telling you all that happens on your story ain't real. It's made up for the television." Momma's voice got higher and higher, her aggravation growing with every word.

But MawMaw was getting aggravated right back at her, meeting Momma's frustration head on.

"Don't you think I know, Rayetta? I'm not senile yet. Maybe their real names ain't Ashley and Ricardo, but I was just giving their television names to have somebody specific to pray for. It don't matter what their names are, somebody in there needs prayer. They don't make all them situations up. Somebody is going through it. Whoever writes it or somebody. And they need to get their baby back, the sooner the better!"

Momma could see she was getting nowhere fast but needed to try to get in the last word.

"Don't you dare mention them when Miss Frances asks for Sunday school prayer requests this week. If you absolutely have to say anything about it, give it as an unspoken request."

"I'll study on it and do what the Lord leads."

There, MawMaw restored my faith in her by beating Momma in The Last Word Game. While Momma sat back in her seat and MawMaw folded her hands demurely in her lap, I stifled a grin and did a little touchdown dance in my mind.

≈

Several cars were already lined up in the parking lot at the high school when we arrived. I pulled the Mustang up to the front curb to unload my passengers and all of the auction items I collected in Nashville. I shifted into park, shut off the ignition, and started around the car.

A man walking from the parking lot toward the school beat me to the other side and opened the car door for MawMaw.

"How are you tonight, Miss Ettalene?"

"I'm still above ground, thank the Lord. It's a blessing itself. Although getting out of this car might do me in. These low-slung vehicles are made for young folks, not for old women like me."

From her position inside the car, Momma chimed in

with her solution.

"Katie Anne can drive my car tomorrow. I don't know what she wants to hold onto this old thing for."

I shook my head in amazement. Momma didn't appreciate my taste in vehicles. My Mustang was the inevitable favorite of every teenage boy who crossed my path. When I bought the car several years ago, it was the cheapest transportation I could find. Then muscle cars came back in style in a big way, and I allowed myself to take undue credit for anticipating a popular trend. After deciding not to trade in the car for a newer model last fall, I spruced up the interior some and had the exterior repainted in a color the brochure described as "blazing saddle red" but looked like plain old bright red to me. Regardless, the car was definitely an eye-catcher.

While the man concentrated on helping MawMaw, I got a better look at him. He wasn't anybody I remembered specifically, yet his face seemed sort of familiar. Everything about him shouted average, including his height. A little on the slim side, he had flecks of gray sneaking into dark brown hair. A short-sleeve shirt and jeans put him in typical Pikeville uniform for a man of his age, which I guessed as mid-fifties.

"I know this with Miss Lora Anne is hard on you, ma'am."

MawMaw's gaze locked on his sympathetic face as she slowly straightened up.

"Yes, I purely hate to see any of my children suffer. We sure do appreciate you being here to help tonight. All our neighbors carrying the burden with us makes it lighter."

As soon as MawMaw moved up the one step to the sidewalk entrance, the man flipped up the front seat and offered his hand to help Momma get out of the car, too.

In true Momma form, she began telling me what to do before she set the first foot on the pavement.

"Leave those things in the trunk be until we get the tables and all set up like we want them."

"I'd be glad to help you carry in what you've got here," the man offered.

"Why, thank you, Harmon, but let's get inside first and see where we need to start. No sense in having to move it all twice."

I searched my memory. The only Harmon I could think of was Harmon Suggs, the man who killed the little three-year-old girl while driving drunk, the ex-con. And here MawMaw and Momma were treating him like a dear friend. The situation didn't compute with me. Surely this wasn't the same man. What would he be doing here?

While he and Momma talked, I sneaked another look at him. His nose appeared to have been broken at some point, and he had a faint scar beginning at one end of his mouth and extending down a couple of inches. I wondered if the wounds were the result of the car wreck or whether he got them in a rough prison environment. In spite of them, he wasn't a bad looking guy for his age. Certainly no one would ever guess by looking at him that he'd spent time in prison.

"Katie Anne, you can leave the car right here and we'll come back out later to get the things we brought. You're not blocking anybody in."

Glancing up, she noticed my curiosity about the man who was a stranger to me, and she realized we were not acquainted.

"Harmon, this here is my daughter, Katie Anne."

Our eyes me briefly, and then he dipped his head

at me in a nod but didn't speak. The unwelcome thought flashed across my mind that perhaps he had heard about me, too. After all, I didn't know how much of his family was still around Pikeville. There remained an outside chance his son and my former classmate, Heath, had said something to him about me at some point. Or maybe somebody else in town blurted out too much about me when the topic of Aunt Lora Anne's benefit came up. Anything was possible.

But if he recognized anything about me, he didn't let on.

"Well, let's roll up our sleeves and get on inside," Momma ordered.

While I turned back around to lock the Mustang, a habit I soon learned in Nashville, Momma took Harmon by the elbow and led him up to the school's large double doors, happily chattering away.

The way they were huddled together had me wondering if old Edgar faced any competition for Momma's affections from a younger man—and an ex-con, to boot. I was definitely going to have to jumpstart my dating life as soon as I returned to Nashville.

❧

Entering the doors of my former high school, I could almost feel the years fall away. I paused and took a moment to glance around. Not much had changed. The same worn tile led to the cafeteria directly ahead. Classrooms were off to the right, with both the auditorium and gym to the left. The shiny glass trophy case looked a little more crowded with plaques and awards than I remembered. Obviously, Bledsoe County was still turning out successful athletes. Go Big Blue.

Both MawMaw and Momma spent time working in the school's cafeteria over the years, putting their natural cooking talents to use by making institutional food palatable.

I could still hear myself begging Momma the summer before I entered high school.

"Can't you please find someplace else to work? Another school? Maybe the grammar school. Nobody wants their mother and grandmother looking over their shoulder all day long."

"Why? What are you trying to hide?" Momma knew the best defense was a good offense. "Are you planning on doing something you'd be ashamed of us seeing? Besides, we'll be busy working, we won't have time to interfere with you and your buddies."

In reality, the situation wasn't so bad. I saw the two of them only briefly during my lunch period. It wasn't as if they wouldn't have found out everything I did anyway. Somebody would have called them every time I more than sneezed. As things turned out, they merely cut out the middle man, or woman, and got the information firsthand about five seconds faster.

The old halls down the classroom corridor to the right were dark and shadowy, but to my mind's eye they were as bright and busy as the last time I walked them as a student. I could hear echoes of the bells ringing to signal class change and the stampede of adolescent feet eager to flee the confines of one class only to enter another.

When I was part of the group, I had my life all figured out. The future lay ahead of me as a clean slate, and I owned the only pen available to write on it.

"Well, well, would you look at the bad penny, showing up again."

I whirled around, ready to take offense and jump on whoever dared confront me here. Angry words died on my lips as I stared into the familiar green eyes of my old friend and sometimes high school stand-in date, Wayne Deweese. The big, gangly youth of my memory had developed into a big, muscular man, and the shaggy hair was now cut short off his forehead. But the piercing blue eyes were the same, and I could feel them boring holes into me.

On his face was a soft, sweet, welcoming smile.

"Where have you been so long, honey?" he asked.

"Oh, here and there," was all I managed to choke out before I grabbed him in a warm hug. I held on for several seconds, taking in the scent of soap and leather before releasing him and stepping back for another look.

"Time sure has been good to you, looks like."

"Not too awful bad yourself."

Our first minutes of conversation were stilted as we mentally circled one another. But Wayne's kind eyes soon resulted in me feeling as relaxed in his company as ever.

Then came the question I dreaded.

"Why'd you stay gone so long?"

While my brain scrambled to form a coherent answer, over Wayne's shoulder came another figure from outside, a man who looked familiar but I couldn't place immediately.

"Let's go, buddy. We gotta get the mic system set up."

He never stopped moving while he talked, and continued toward the gym. By the time Wayne turned around to look at him, his long strides had already taken him halfway down the hall.

Wayne threw me an apologetic grin and began to follow the man.

"Guess we'll have to catch up later after all. But we

will catch up," he promised, closing his fist and cocking his trigger finger at me like a gun. "Later, tater."

≈

With a couple dozen people hurrying in and out of the school's gym, benefit preparations were well underway by the time I noticed a flurry of activity out of the corner of my eye. Tables stretched out the length of the gym and were loaded down with merchandise donated for the auction. Some people I recognized mingled with others I didn't recognize as they carried in item after item. Lamps, a microwave, and homemade quilts shared space with pocket knives, wrench sets, and various assorted toys. A whole batch of certificates offered free car washes, tanning bed sessions, haircuts, and oil changes.

Momma put me in charge of arranging the auction items while she, MawMaw, and a few other ladies concentrated on getting the food area ready. They gave the whole place a good cleaning and then sent a couple of my cousins for the keys to my car to bring in the paper goods and other items. A good design put the school's concession stand directly outside the gym, so everyone could see the food both coming and going. Plenty of opportunity for impulse purchases.

Momma knew my talents were better put to use somewhere other than the refreshment category.

I was trying to find the perfect spot to display a gor-geous photograph of the "big falls" at Fall Creek Falls State Park when I heard my name called out. The waterfalls claimed the title as the highest east of the Mississippi River. Niagara Falls may have been the widest, but Fall Creek Falls was the tallest at 256 feet. The barnwood-framed picture should bring a good chunk of money on the auction block tomorrow night.

"Katie Anne, your aunt Lora Anne just come in." Momma hurried across the gym to me. "Come over and see her. She won't be able to stay long. We don't want her to get too tired out tonight so she don't feel like coming tomorrow."

Quickly abandoning my latest task, I met Momma and we headed toward the doorway together. A small group gathered around Aunt Lora Anne's wheelchair, with Uncle Herbert behind, but a couple of people stepped aside when they saw me approaching.

Since Aunt Lora Anne got so sick, she and Momma and Aunt Patty Lynn didn't look much like triplets anymore. Weight loss had stamped a gauntness on Aunt Lora Anne's face that was hard to reconcile with the round, smiling features I knew so well. She temporarily removed an oxygen mask from over her mouth and nose, stretching out her thin, frail arms for my embrace.

Drawing on a strength I didn't know I possessed, I willed my eyes not to fill with tears as I reached out to her. It took me a moment to be sure I could speak without my voice trembling.

"How's my darling aunt doing tonight?" I knelt down directly in front of her wheelchair.

"Honey, I'm just sitting around being lazy these days. Your uncle Herbert tries to get a little work out of me, but I just won't do it. I tell him, 'You and the boys can wait on me for a change.'"

Big talk, but I knew she was aggravated to no end to be the person waited on. In her world, the wife's duty and desire were to care for her husband and children, not the other way around. I wondered how many cups of coffee she'd served Uncle Herbert while he sat in his recliner and how many trips to the kitchen she'd made over the years. No telling.

Her whisper feathered my cheek.

"You know you're my favorite niece, but I can't let them other girls hear me tell you."

"And you know you're my favorite aunt, but we'll keep the news a secret between us."

We looked at each other, and a wink sealed the familiar deal.

After our initial exchange, I turned my attention to Uncle Herbert.

"Who's the handsome chauffeur you've got in charge of this chariot?"

"Why, he's some old man I can't seem to get rid of. He follows me around everywhere I go these days."

"Hold on, gal," Uncle Herbert cautioned with a mock sternness. "You might be rolling yourself all the way back home if you keep up that kind of talk."

The opposite of my daddy, Uncle Herbert sported pasty white cheeks, a large rosy nose, and a ready smile. His cap advertised a feed grain store, and I knew underneath were mere remnants of a bygone mop of unruly red hair. He wore his pants hitched low underneath his belly, allowing him to brag he still wore the same size he did on the day he got married. In their wedding photos, he looked like a different man entirely. When they exchanged vows he was quite handsome, and I suspected Aunt Lora Anne still saw him that way in her mind.

"Have you ever seen such an uproar? And it all over me." A note of wonder crept into Aunt Lora Anne's reedy voice. "I aught to be ashamed to be the cause of all this fuss."

"Come on in here and see what all we've got set up so far."

We slowly made our way across the cables being laid by Wayne and the man I'd seen in the hallway. Aunt Lora Anne replaced her oxygen mask, but I could see she was taking in every detail. It rubbed against her grain to be trapped in the wheelchair while others were working, but she could find no way around the situation. We strolled the entire length of the gym, Uncle Herbert and me cutting up back and forth to fill in with conversation so Aunt Lora Anne wouldn't waste energy by trying to talk.

Our little caravan exited the gym and circled around to the concession stand outside the gym doors. By then, Momma and MawMaw had shooed the other women out of the cramped space and were finishing up organizing the benefit food supplies.

"Now, Lora Anne, you need to get on home and see to yourself tonight," MawMaw ordered. "Herbert, you take her on to the house and see she gets right to bed. We've got things well in hand here."

"Yes, Miss Ettalene," replied Uncle Herbert. Years of dealing with MawMaw and her daughters taught him the lesson that anything less than complete agreement was futile.

With a flurry of hugs and goodbyes, the two disappeared down the hall toward the front doors.

When I turned around to reenter the gym, I came face to face with someone else I dreaded seeing.

The Blue Hole

❧ CHAPTER 11 ❦

In my memory, I could almost feel myself grasping Wayne's hand as he pulled me along behind him toward the Blue Hole. We followed a small, worn path through the brush for a few hundred yards. The night was pitch dark, with barely a partial moon providing the only faint light.

We stepped as carefully as we could through the emerging undergrowth. After all, we were in the beginning of snake season, and we knew the silent creatures became more active in the spring. If one of us got bitten out here, we probably wouldn't see which type of snake was to blame, and the knowledge was critical in treating the wound. A snake with a triangle-shaped head meant poison, and we would have to get to the hospital quickly. A bite from a non-poisonous snake might hurt like the dickens but should leave no lasting damage.

The boys, wearing their usual work boots and jeans, were adequately protected, but most of the girls were in shorts and tennis shoes. I wasn't even that prepared. Instead, I sported flimsy sandals. So although Wayne was merely a dark shape before me, I struggled to keep up with him. I hoped he was making enough racket to warn any nearby snakes of our presence in time for them to slither far away. Both in front of us and behind us, I overheard bits of conversation from the other kids, quieting the nervousness rising up within me.

All at once, the path ended in a huge clearing. At the center was the Blue Hole, a sprawling body of water in a basin of solid rock. A steep hill of rock and brush being taken over by kudzu formed the nearest side of the pit.

Kudzu, originally imported to the United States from Japan, was introduced as the perfect solution to soil erosion in the South, but the solution had long since turned into the problem. The plant grew wildly out of control and proved nearly impossible to kill. Multiplying as much as a foot per day, kudzu could nearly consume an old barn or an abandoned house in a single growing season.

The dim light from the moon shone down on the huge pool of midnight blue water in the pit, illuminating the calm surface and giving the appearance of an oversized vat of inky darkness.

The open space where we were standing covered an area about as massive as a football field. I knew spring flowers beginning to blossom were being trampled under our feet, but I couldn't see them well enough to determine their variety.

The side of the Blue Hole directly in front of us was probably the most dangerous area due to its steep cliff. From the clearing where we stood, you could walk almost level all the way to the side of the pit. If you weren't watching what you were doing, it would be easy to get too close to the edge and slip over. Even the most foolish of divers usually avoided this side. The water under the cliff was known to be the deepest and the coldest. Even worse, jagged rocks jutted out from the edge of the wall.

"Look at me, boys, I'm a high-wire walker." Dennis hollered from a spot near the water's edge. With arms flung out, he stretched on his tiptoes, pretending to balance atop an invisible wire.

"Get back from there, you idiot! You're not nearly good enough to join the circus as anything but a clown." Wayne's warning was only half joking, but Dennis finished his act with a flourish and leaped down toward us.

The best place to swim was on the direct opposite side of where we gathered. The ground sloped off enough around the hole for long-ago miners to drive trucks in and out when the pit was the site of an operating business. From that side, hiking down to the water's edge proved easy enough for any able-bodied person.

We started heading that way.

ॐ CHAPTER 12 ॐ

Not more than a dozen steps in front of me in the school's hallway stood my cousin Leah, the middle daughter of my uncle Leonard and aunt Lillian. Only two years separated us in age, but during our childhoods the two years stretched out like a vast gulf which could never be spanned.

Leah was always the older, smarter cousin, and I was always the younger, dumber one. Our individual roles were firmly established in the family pecking order. Her younger sister Lisa was my age, and Leah never wanted to play with the "babies," as she frequently sneered at us. Even though most of the bickering remained concentrated between the two sisters, I sometimes got caught in the middle. As a result, Leah and I were never particularly close growing up, and since we became adults we hadn't spent much time together.

But a welcoming smile lit up Leah's face, and either she was a perfectly good actress or she was genuinely glad to see me. I decided to cling to the latter explanation until proven wrong.

"Katie Anne!" As Leah greeted me, she closed the short gap between us and wrapped her arms around me in an enthusiastic hug.

Her short, stylish hair gleamed a beautiful shade of warm mahogany that made me glad I'd invested the time to add new highlights to mine last week. She wore black stretch pants and a checkered flannel shirt she probably pilfered from her husband's closet, apparently chosen mainly to cover her advanced pregnancy.

"I know I'm too wide for you to wrap your arms around me, girl, but do your best. I'm liable to drop this baby out on the ground any second now."

"You look pretty good to me."

I was telling the truth. Although Leah had a rough start out of high school, her life now looked picture perfect. Even the careless way she was dressed couldn't dampen the impression of a savvy, intelligent woman who exuded self-confidence.

"I hear you're in the legal business." She took hold of my arm and pulled me off to the side of the hallway and away from the steady stream of pedestrian traffic continuing to move in and out of the gym.

"Yep, you heard right. Who would have thought we'd both end up on the right side of the law after all?"

"That's for sure. I know Momma and Daddy sent up some powerful prayers on my behalf. If I have to pay for my raising with this little one, I'll be in bad trouble." Leah patted her tummy. "It took a big mop to clean up my mess."

Leah worked in social services, but she put her parents through plenty of sleepless nights while on the way there. A disastrous teenage marriage drove her parents to tears and prompted them to hit their knees night after night to plead for their erring daughter. Of course, she wasn't the first girl to fall for the smooth line of a long-haired, no-good boy whispering into her ear. Unfortunately, Leah married him.

For a smart person, Leah spent long enough figuring him out. By then her pride kept her hanging on in the marriage even longer. In fact, the deadbeat was the one who eventually left her. He found another woman to put up with his drinking, drugs, and running around.

Leah took it hard when he left her. The only way she could take it, I guess. I thought what bothered her the most was her own bad judgment in taking up with him in the first place. There certainly wasn't much love left by the end.

"I'm sure you'll have the perfect child," I reassured her. I had no basis in fact for my opinion, but it seemed the thing to say at the time. After all, I held plenty of other opinions based on nothing.

"Do I detect a note of sarcasm in there?"

"Certainly not. Let me go on record here as predicting this child will be as stunningly beautiful and intelligent and talented as her cousin Kate." I punctuated my teasing remark with an airy wave of my hand.

"Who could ask for more? I'll be perfectly happy for your prediction to come true. Look at you, the career woman taking the big city by storm. Every time I talk with Aunt Rayetta, she tells me how proud she is of you and how well you're doing. To hear her tell it, you're running the entire law firm single-handedly."

What?

Suddenly I felt myself entering a parallel universe. All I ever heard from Momma was how dangerous the city was for a woman alone, how I was wasting my life away from my family, how my life would be much better if only I moved back to Pikeville. And on and on in many variations of the same theme. Surely Leah misinterpreted my mother's remarks.

The only other explanation was that Leah gilded the lily because she wasn't mean enough to relay my mother's true attitude. Either way, I decided not to argue with her. I would take whatever good I could get and be happy. No need to look a gift horse in the mouth and all.

"Is Zach here with you?" I asked.

Fortunately, Leah's taste in men had undergone a definite U-turn. Employed by the state's social services agency, several of her cases involved the legal system, resulting in her working with Zach, a lawyer with the district attorney's office. Zach encountered a tough time overcoming her defenses, but love and hormones finally prevailed. A powerful combination, after all. They married a couple of years ago.

"No, not yet anyway. He was coming, but he got called out on some case over in Dayton. He said he'll stop by, depending on what time he gets through. These things crop up all the time for him, but I told him no excuses tomorrow night. Be here or else."

As Leah finished talking, I heard a commotion behind me and turned to see MawMaw with her arms half full of disposable aluminum pans. The other half were tumbling to the floor, generating a loud racket as they bounced off the hard tile.

"MawMaw, why didn't you get me to help you with those?"

"I didn't think I needed help. They don't weigh a thing, but they're awful hard to keep corralled."

As I stooped to pick up the pans from the floor, Wayne appeared around the corner of the gym. Following him was the man he was helping set up the mic system.

"Wouldn't you know who I'd find in the middle of a ruckus." Wayne feigned disgust as he bent over and handed me a couple of the pans.

"Don't just stand there being a smart aleck, help me up," I demanded.

"Whatever you say. I know better than to provoke a bully."

He reached his big hand down, and I grasped his wrist and pulled myself up. As I did so, Wayne tugged me close to him in a warm sideways hug. His embrace lasted merely a few seconds, but the action warmed my heart like a blazing fire.

"Now my mess is cleaned up, let's get on with things," MawMaw ordered. "Leah, you help me take these pans into the kitchen while Katie Anne finishes up for the auction. I think we're about to get it whipped for tonight."

In only a few words, MawMaw put us back on track.

"We're nearly finished with the sound system, too," Wayne informed us. "Once we've done a sound check, we'll be on our way."

"We sure do appreciate you fellas and all you're doing," MawMaw said over her shoulder as she headed down the hall. I transferred the pans I clutched to Leah's arms before turning back into the gym as instructed.

The framed photograph of Fall Creek Falls still waited for me to find the perfect spot to display the artwork. I carefully picked it up and tried a couple of different locations before settling on a prominent position in the center where it could be seen from many angles.

Afterward, only a few other items remained to be set out. I made short work of them, and then I gave myself a mental pat on the back for a job well done. A couple of tables were left empty for donation items brought in by people as they arrived at the benefit tomorrow evening.

As I finished up, the back of a recliner entered the gym. Sticking out from underneath was a set of jean-clad legs.

A muffled voice rang out from behind the chair, asking for directions.

"Where's this go?"

"Come straight ahead. Now turn right, go more to your left, a little farther...put it down right there."

The chair eased to the floor. Drew, one of my aunt Patty Lynn's sons, emerged from behind.

"Hey, Katie Anne. Good steering. That thing was getting heavy."

"Not everybody can be the brains, somebody's got to be the back," I replied, allowing a grin to spread across my face. "How you doing, Drew?"

"Getting handsomer every day."

"So I can see."

Tall and slim, Drew had a head full of short, dark bristles of sprouting hair and a beard to match. An avid hunter, he was clad head to toe in camouflage clothing.

Before we had time to delve deeper into conversation, my uncle Cooper came in pushing a small chest-type freezer on a cart ahead of him. As he greeted me, he wheeled the freezer to the side of the tables.

"We can leave this thing on the cart for now, but help me remember to make sure the auctioneer knows the cart doesn't go with the freezer. It belongs to the furniture store. I told them I'd have it back first thing Monday morning."

When Uncle Cooper finished speaking, he advanced the few steps to me and before I knew it, he picked me up right off the ground and swung me around.

"Katie Anne, it's about time you came to see me." The deep voice was the same reassuring sound I took comfort in as a child.

"You're a man who knows how to sweep a girl off her feet, for sure."

"Truer words were never spoken."

Oh, the men in my family. At least they didn't suffer from a lack of confidence.

As my feet touched the floor once again, Uncle Cooper told Drew to see if Harmon Suggs needed any help bringing in the television. Evidently he didn't, because he appeared in the doorway hefting a fairly large box.

Drew grabbed one end and helped Harmon set the box carefully on a nearby table.

"Go on and take the thing out of the box," Momma instructed from the doorway. "But be sure and save the box so whoever makes the winning bid can put it back in to take it home in."

Momma was cradling a box of large plastic garbage bags and held them out to me.

"Katie Anne, by the time you line the trash barrels in here, we should be about ready to go."

"What about all the stuff in the car?"

"Harmon and Cooper already brought it in."

I got busy on the trash barrels as instructed, and Momma stayed true to her word. She was waiting for me after I tossed the now empty bag box into one of the barrels and walked out into the hallway. Gathered with her were a dozen or so people, all of whom looked satisfied with their accomplishments. One by one, they said goodnight while Uncle Cooper flicked off the last of the lights and began pulling all the heavy metal doors tightly closed.

MawMaw didn't let any of the non-family members out the door without giving them a personal thank you and a hug for their help in setting up for the benefit. Relatives didn't get the same thanks and didn't expect to. We were merely doing what we were supposed to do for one of our own. However, we all did get the hug and an admonition to drive carefully on the way home.

As my luck would have it, I got special instructions.

MawMaw lingered behind when others headed to their vehicles, keeping a hand on my arm to delay me. With only the two of us and possibly Uncle Cooper still in earshot, she turned to look straight at me in concern, tilting her head slightly and drawing me close to her.

"Katie Anne, don't you be too hard on your momma this weekend."

"Now MawMaw, what makes you think I'd be hard on her?"

"Don't you go acting like I don't have the sense the good Lord gave me. You two have left this thing simmering on the stove long enough. Any fool can see it's in danger of fixing to boil over and burn both of you."

Leave it to MawMaw to put the world into perspective while relating it to food preparation. I wondered if Uncle Cooper overheard our exchange, but I knew he would never mention a word if he did. A couple of my relatives could actually be discreet on occasion, and he numbered among them.

Having had her say, MawMaw was satisfied. She

started down the sidewalk, her bony fingers continuing to grasp tightly to my arm.

Wayne intercepted us as we approached my car.

"Me and Donnie Ray are going up town to get us a bite to eat. We worked late and didn't have time for supper before getting here. How 'bout coming along?"

When he said the name Donnie Ray, my brain finally clicked and figured out the identity of the man with him. He was the older brother of our classmate Dennis. Come to think, I heard he and Wayne were partners in an auto body shop. They were obviously close friends, too.

MawMaw answered for me.

"You go on with the young people, Katie Anne. Cooper can take me and Rayetta home."

"That sounds good, Wayne. Do you mind if I ask Leah along? Zach is working late himself."

"Sure. We'll be at the pizza place. Come on when you can."

❧ CHAPTER 13 ❧

Wayne and Donnie Ray were sprawled on chairs around a rectangular table, sipping through straws in plastic cups when Leah and I entered the only pizza restaurant in town. The welcoming aroma of marinara sauce awakened a hunger I didn't know was in me. We placed our orders and filled our beverage cups at the counter before approaching our friends in the dining section.

Wayne greeted my cousin first.

"Leah, don't that man of yours know better than to let a good-looking woman like you out on the town alone on a Friday night?"

"What about me?" I demanded, acting angry.

"Don't take this the wrong way, honey, but I don't think of you as a good-looking woman."

I faked a slap to the top of his head as Donnie Ray spoke up in my defense.

"Wait till Amanda gets here. She'll straighten Wayne right out. She's kept him on a short leash ever since he said I do."

Now I was even more glad I had come. It would be interesting to see what kind of woman could put a ring on Wayne's finger and a muzzle on his mouth.

Leah and I settled into chairs of our own, me next to Wayne and Leah next to Donnie Ray.

I didn't expect an introduction to Donnie Ray, and I didn't get one. People of my age in Pikeville didn't learn much about making formal introductions, simply because we didn't have to. While we were growing up, we knew most everyone we saw, if not by name then at least enough to know what family they were from. I suspected the situation had changed in the last several years, what with retirees and other folks flocking to the area to escape traffic congestion, freezing winters, and high property taxes elsewhere.

Before our conversation progressed beyond the preliminaries, the restaurant door opened once again, admitting my cousin Drew, followed by Debra and Zeb, good friends from high school who ended up married to each other. Both of them were now teachers in the local school system, Debra in math and Zeb in agricultural education.

I wondered if they still considered me a good friend. After all, we shared a lot of history together, but both were with me to witness the worst night of my life.

"Looks like y'all got the same idea we did," Drew greeted us.

"Pull up to the table and we'll make it a party," Wayne invited.

Zeb spotted me first, and his eyes widened in surprise. Debra caught on a minute later with an identical expression. Part of me fought the urge to laugh at their off-guard reactions, and the other part wanted to crawl under the table and out the back door.

If there had been a way out of the situation, believe me, I would have taken it. But there wasn't, so my best course of action was to smile back at them as sincerely as I could fake it.

Unaware of any tension, Drew plopped down in the chair next to me. He was never the type of guy to pick up on any subtleties. Debra and Zeb settled into seats across from him, next to Leah.

By the time a server delivered steaming hot pizzas to the table, we had traded sincere smiles and any lingering awkwardness had vanished. All conversation halted for the next few minutes as we filled our plates and then our stomachs. From around us came noises from a few other tables of diners, along with background strains of country music videos playing on an overhead television.

Two couples in booths next to each other appeared to be on weekend dates.

"I'm so glad to see you, Katie Anne." Debra broke into my thoughts at the same time I took a sizable bite of pizza. I maneuvered the sliding cheese and hot crust back onto my plate and made quick work of chewing so I could respond.

"It's great to see you, too. All of you, in fact. Even you, Wayne."

I was startled to realize the truth of my words. These friends were among the small group of people on the face of the earth who knew me best. There was unexpected comfort in the knowledge. But Debra's next question woke me up to the reality that no matter how well they believed they knew the heart of me, they knew little about my adult life.

"Tell us what you've been up to."

On the surface, a simple enough inquiry.

I gave as brief an answer as I could possibly get away with. Mostly I wanted to sit back and listen to the conversation around me while trying to blend into the woodwork for a little while, enough to establish a comfort zone. However, before I could make my retreat, I was back in the hot seat. Zeb jumped in with what was probably the number one question every Nashville resident was asked at one time or another.

"Do you ever see any big country music stars up there?"

"A couple." I reeled off a few names I knew they recognized. "Sometimes you see them next to you in traffic and they seem out of place driving their own car. Or sometimes they're walking in the mall. People in Nashville are generally pretty good about letting them have their space and not bothering them."

For anybody interested in music of nearly any type, Nashville was a great city. Of course, country music and Nashville went together like biscuits and gravy, but many other genres of music also thrived in "Music City, USA." One bonus I greatly enjoyed about my adopted home was the excellent and abundant music.

I should have expected the interest from Zeb. He was the musician in our class. So many of my memories of him were accompanied by the soundtrack of an acoustic guitar he constantly strummed. We always believed he possessed real talent.

The bell over the restaurant door chimed again, signaling the entrance of another customer. In a reflex action, I glanced toward the front of the restaurant, and my heart skipped a beat. Striding up to the counter came a ghost from my past.

Jesse Warren, the last person on earth to touch Trisha's hand in this life, was in the process of pulling his wallet from his back pocket when he turned his head. His eyes skimmed over the people in the room before he returned his attention to the tired woman behind the counter.

If he saw me, he made no indication. He handed her a few bills and she handed him two pizzas. He turned on his heel and walked out, never looking back in my direction.

I wasn't sure he recognized me. After all, high school happened a long time ago. I hoped my style had improved, if nothing else.

Judging from the momentary silence to descend over the table, I knew I wasn't the only person who noticed Jesse's entrance and exit. Leah was the first to recover from the intrusion and jump back on our interrupted discussion.

"You're the one everybody thought would end up in Nashville, Zeb."

"Not Zeb. He's too ugly. You got to be able to sing and be pretty all at the same time," Wayne joked.

"How can I be pretty after all those times you slung me all over the mountain and back in that old rattle-trap truck of yours? My face bounced back and forth from the dashboard to the window, the dashboard to the window. Nearly ruined my good looks."

Drew couldn't stand not being a part of the teasing, and he jumped in with all he owned.

"Yep, it's a good thing Debra's standards are so low. She's the only one would have you."

"What about you? How come you always dress in all that camo?"

"Got to. Makes me invisible. Can't let the women know I'm coming."

The verbal sparring shot back and forth in a light-hearted manner. Donnie Ray couldn't get a word in edgewise and didn't make an effort. He proved as quiet as the other men were boisterous. Wayne, Zeb, and Drew continued to try to outdo each other telling tall tales. Choosing a winner would be impossible since any of the three could talk a tick off a dog.

We had long since finished eating and were relaxing around the table, simply enjoying each other's company. With great effort, I pushed the thought of seeing Jesse to the back of my mind. Instead, as I looked around, I realized an unfamiliar emotion was flooding over me. I hadn't felt the sensation in such a long time that identifying it took me a moment. It was a feeling of belonging, of being some place in the world I knew I fit. No pretense, no fear of being found out as a fake, no desire to be anything other than what I was. Amazing at any time, but especially so soon after seeing Jesse in the flesh, not only in my nightmares.

Wayne began his next story.

"You want to talk about scarring up somebody, do you, Zeb? How about the time you turned me into a flaming marshmallow?"

A roar of laughter erupted from the table, drawing curious stares from the other diners. Those few words were all Wayne needed for the rest of us to remember the incident. We had all heard the story repeated so many times it was securely stored in our collective memories.

"What's this about flaming marshmallows?"

We were so caught up in reminiscing that we failed to notice the arrival of Leah's husband, Zach, until he leaned over her shoulder and pecked her cheek with a kiss.

"Haven't you ever heard about our local stuntman,

darling? Have a seat and Wayne will tell you all about it." Leah patted the seat of the chair beside her and loaded her empty plate with a couple slices of leftover pizza before pushing the food over to him.

"No, I'll tell it," Zeb declared.

"No, you won't," Wayne insisted, waving his hands in front of him. "I'll tell the truth of it. If I leave the telling to you, you'll leave out the best parts. I mean, the true parts, the ones showing everything was all your fault."

"I said I'd tell it, and I will." A sly grin spread across Zeb's face. "This happened when we were eight or nine years old. You have to keep in mind what a runty little thing Wayne was at the time. He didn't hit a real growth spurt till the end of grammar school. See, at this time his momma and daddy were real worried he'd never amount to a thing. That's what it looked like was going to happen. And not only was he little, he was dumb as a stump. So little Wayne came to me for help. His best buddy. We were together all the time. I guess his parents hoped some of me would rub off on him.

"We loved to watch the old cowboy shows on television where they jumped down from the wagon onto the backs of the runaway horses and where they catch the bad guy by throwing a lasso around him. Strictly in black and white, of course. The real thing. We practiced with a rope, trying to toss a lasso around each other, switching out the bad guy role. I don't believe Wayne could ever do it, but I believe I lassoed him every throw. Least that's how I remember things. Then I'd reel him in slow, dragging him to me on the hard ground. As I recall, he was pretty much a baby about it. He'd cry at the least little sign of blood from a scratch."

Wayne kept up a steady stream of protest while Zeb continued his retelling.

"We kept trying different things, experimenting to see if we could come up with anything Wayne was good at. First one thing and then another. Nothing worked. The boy wasn't good at anything. Then on TV one day, they showed a little piece on stuntmen and how they could survive fires. Our ears perked up. We looked at each other and knew we'd found Wayne's destiny. He wanted to try. He always did love fire.

"I found this old bomber-type jacket with thick leather, especially on the sleeves, in my closet. This was still summer, so I knew I wouldn't have any use for a coat for a long, long time. We got this idea—I swear Wayne was the one who thought it up—to douse just a dab of lighter fluid on the sleeves, light it on fire, and I would take a picture of Wayne wearing the coat while it blazed. He needed the picture to prove he was a real live stuntman. He'd be a hero to all the third graders. Who could ask for more?

"Somewhere in the back of our minds, we must have known how dangerous the idea was, because we knew enough to wait to try it when Momma wasn't home. She could get real funny about blowing stuff up or setting stuff on fire."

Wayne protested. "Stuff like me, you mean."

Zeb continued as if he hadn't heard the interruption. "Everything went according to plan. We went outside into the back field. We got the jacket ready, Wayne put the thing on, I lit the match, and whoosh! The arms of the jacket exploded like flaming marshmallows, and Wayne took off running. Luckily, it wasn't more than a few steps till he hit the pond next to the barn. My poor jacket sizzled all afternoon."

"I'm just lucky you didn't kill me!" Wayne cut in. "A dab of lighter fluid, my eyeballs. You emptied the whole daggum can on my coat!"

"Never mind that now." Zeb nodded to the rest of us. "Class, what's the worst part of the story?"

"No picture!" we called out in unison, picking up his cue as we had done many times before when the story was told.

"Right answer, class. Instead of picking up the camera to get the picture, I got flustered and ran after Wayne. Jumped right into the pond with him. I heroically saved his life but didn't get the picture. What was I thinking! Besides, I was the only one ended up hurt. I got blisters on my hands pushing the coat underwater."

The story underwent minor variations each time I heard it, depending on which one was doing the retelling, Zeb or Wayne. After all this time, how much was fact and how much was fiction was impossible to figure out. Surely there was a grain of truth buried deep, but I hoped the actual fiasco wasn't nearly as terrifying as the retelling led us to believe.

Debra let out an audible shudder. "Sure, we laugh about it now, but it was such a dangerous thing to do, you big fools!"

"Little Wayne always did like fire," Zeb added. "But my momma definitely didn't. She got home about the time he took off toward the pond. If I hadn't already been in blisters, she'd have blistered me herself. I thought she'd never settle down."

"The whole thing was all your fault anyway," Wayne accused. "Now, since you told one on me, it's time for me to tell one on you."

"Better hush up, old buddy. The statute of limitations may not have run out on some of this stuff." Zeb nodded in Zach's direction. "Don't forget, we've got somebody from the district attorney's office among us tonight."

Leah answered for her husband. "If he were forced to prosecute every fool redneck stuntman in this county, he never would get to leave work. It scares me to death to have this baby, knowing you all are going to be influences on it." A pat on her protruding stomach punctuated her remarks.

"You're a fine one to talk," Wayne replied. "You're the first girl I ever knew to get arrested."

Leah's smile was genuine, but a faint blush slowly crept up her cheeks anyway.

"I believe that's a story to save for another night. Let's say my husband was fortunate to get me after the Lord had a little time to make some improvements on me first."

Wayne quickly agreed, uncertain whether his foot was stuck in his mouth from his latest comment.

"I guess I'll call it a night, too. Katie Anne, I reckon my Amanda got held up somewhere along the way. But we'll see you at the benefit tomorrow night. You ready to go Donnie Ray?"

"Anytime." Donnie Ray finally got a word in the conversation.

I was touched to the core when both Debra and Zeb circled the table to embrace me in farewell hugs.

"You really are looking good, Katie Anne," Debra softly whispered in my ear. "If you get a chance during the benefit, let's girl talk a few minutes. You don't know how good it is to see you again."

"It's great to see you both, too."

Debra began tugging Zeb to the door by one arm. "Let's go, buster. You've got a busy day of chores ahead of you before the benefit tomorrow."

"I sure am glad I don't have you for a wife, dragging

me around like that," Drew called from where he slouched near the door.

"Like I tell Zeb, the day may come when he doesn't want me for a wife either, but I guarantee he doesn't want me for an ex-wife!"

Drew eyed her, confused for a second until the meaning of her words sunk in. "Ho, now, don't even mention ex-wives. You could have went all night and never said that bad word."

Still sparring verbally, the three of them left the restaurant while the rest of us completed our goodbyes.

Back in my Mustang, I pulled out of the parking lot and headed for home with my burdens the lightest they had been in quite a long time.

❧ CHAPTER 14 ❧

During the short drive back toward Momma's house, I found myself grinning at the silly antics of my old friends. Our lighthearted time together struck me as somewhat of a mini high school reunion. I felt as if I'd passed some sort of unwritten test in my own mind. Not only passed, but sailed through with flying colors. Aced the exam. My friends may have welcomed me back into the fold with raised eyebrows but no spoken censure. Even catching a brief glimpse of Jesse couldn't spoil my mood. For tonight, it was enough.

In the midst of my self-congratulations, I glanced down at the dashboard and noted the time in glowing red numbers. Not too late, but late enough for Momma to be in bed, especially with a big day coming up tomorrow. If so, I expected her to leave the little light on the stove hood on like usual.

How many nights over the years did I tiptoe in late at night after she headed to bed? I still had the routine down pat. Softly squeeze the screen door handle enough to allow admittance, gently turn the doorknob and push open the door, tiptoe over to the stove, and press down the switch to extinguish the light. I was all right until I turned off the light. The click generated an unreasonably loud noise in the hushed darkness. In the still of the night, the sound was loud enough to wake the dead—or, at least, Momma.

It never failed. From her bedroom would come a quiet whisper, "Katie Anne, is that you?" On the occasions when I had nothing to hide, I might shoot back a sarcastic remark along the order of, "No, it's a serial killer come to murder you in your bed. Go back to sleep."

Then again, on nights when I didn't want to awaken her more than necessary lest she get up and venture close enough to smell the lingering cigarette smoke in my hair or beer on my breath, my automatic response was, "Yes, Momma. I love you. Goodnight." She would reply in a whisper, "Love you too, sugar," and doze back to sleep.

Without fail, the stove light blazed like a beacon in the darkness for me. No matter how far away from home I traveled, the bright rays welcomed me back. In fact, the light was never really for my benefit anyway. I made the surprising discovery one time when I told Momma she didn't have to leave the light on, I could easily find my way around in the dark. Not much ever changed in our small house, including the same old furniture in the same old places.

Momma quickly corrected my assumption.

"The light's not on for you, Katie Anne. It's on for me. When you're out at night, I can't rest good until I know you're back home and safe. With my bedroom door cracked open a little bit, I can see if the light is shining down the hall. If it is, you're still out. But if it's not, I can go back to sleep and rest easy."

After Daddy died, I became quite a challenge for my mother. Of course, I was clueless at the time. I was a teenager, trapped in the middle of the blissful yet horrendous stage of life when the whole world revolved around me. Every issue was pondered according to the direct effect on my life. Every conversation, every event, every trip to the store was viewed with the perspective of what it would do for me. The importance of everyone else's life was measured in direct proportion of how it flowed into my life.

Oh, to be able to delude myself that way again.

Even after all these years, I could hear Momma's voice in my head, trying to keep me on the straight and narrow. The miles I ran to Nashville weren't too far to hear the completely feminine yet steely, strong sound. The same voice singing a sweet and true alto in the front row of the choir loft every Sunday morning quickly turned harsh when trying to jerk me away from perceived wickedness. At times her words were as shocking as taking a mental slap. I wondered if I'd ever outgrow the reflex of flinching at it.

One day I came in from school thinking I'd found the perfect reply for Momma's next negative comment to me, whatever it might be. The opportunity to use my secret weapon presented itself when she called me forgetful for not putting away last night's dishes as I'd been told. I confidently thrust my sword with a dramatic flair.

"Momma, you shouldn't say things like that to me. It hurts my self-esteem."

"Listen, sugar, I grew up without any self-esteem and you can, too!"

I should have known I was no match for Momma.

Remembering the little, long-ago encounter also reminded me I needed to stay sharp this weekend.

"Hang in there, Kate," I told myself, drowning out Momma's voice repeating various warnings in my head. "You can do it. It's only for a weekend."

As soon as I made the right turn onto the road leading to the house, I saw Momma wasn't in bed after all. The place was lit up like a drunk on payday. I guided my car onto the gravel driveway and flipped the key to turn off the engine. Almost automatically, a whispered wish arose on my lips for Momma and me to get along well during this trip.

∾

As expected, I found Momma standing over the stove, stirring the contents of a large iron skillet. I easily identified the mixture for her delicious fried chocolate icing, especially since a plain yellow cake set on the counter nearby. The tantalizing smell of chocolate wafted in the air. It was a good beginning.

"How did things go for you kids?" Momma greeted me.

Although it was a stretch to describe us as kids, I didn't make an issue of the term.

"We had a fine time."

I crossed the kitchen in a few short steps. She tilted her face toward me, and I pecked the expected quick kiss on her smooth cheek.

Leaning up against the counter, I glanced around the compact kitchen, wondering how many meals Momma had fixed for me over the years. Even after Daddy died, we rarely failed to have supper together at the table each night. Our lives were no longer normal, but Momma wasn't one to give in to circumstance so easily. Even if our family was only two people. Even if Daddy was never coming back. After all those years, his chair remained untouched at the head of the wooden table. I briefly wondered where Edgar sat when he came for supper.

"Anybody else there?"

"Leah came with me, then Drew came in with Debra and Zeb. Zach got there sometime in the middle."

"That's nice, sugar. You hadn't seen them all in a long time, I guess."

Suppressing my natural inclination to launch into a full-scale recounting of the evening, I slipped back into the immature habit of providing only short answers to Momma. The more Momma questioned, the less I talked. That was the way things had worked as long as I could remember. If required to give up information, I would give up as little as possible. Name, rank and serial number only. I would have made a good soldier. Come to think, Momma would have made a good general.

Chagrined to realize how ridiculously childish I was behaving, I determined to try to come across more like the adult I had become. I purposefully gave out a few more details.

"We really did have fun, Momma. I had forgotten what a nutcase Wayne could be. Especially when Zeb and Drew joined in with him."

"He's a cut-up all right, always has been."

"They told some stories I had about forgotten and updated me on some of our old classmates. Didn't talk about anything too important, just chatted generally. Wayne's wife Amanda was supposed to come but got held up and didn't show. Do you know anything about her?"

"She's a real nice young lady, as different from Wayne as can be."

"In looks or personality?"

"Both. She don't come up to more than his shoulder, a little bit of a thing. She's turned kindly quiet, but she seems to be able to keep a good handle on him. He strikes me as a real family man."

"So old Wayne finally met his match, huh?"

"Yep. When are you finally going to meet yours?"

My own fault. I stepped right into the trap. No one to blame for the monumental blunder but myself.

"Who knows? I guess Cupid's arrows can't find me."

"Or maybe you're jumping out of his way too quick. Did you ever consider that? Are you seeing anybody special right now?"

"There's a guy named Jason I've been going out with some, but it's not serious and never will be."

"Then move on. Quit wasting your time. You can't find somebody it could get serious with while you're wasting time with him."

Time to turn the tables on Momma.

"So I'm assuming it's serious between you and Edgar?"

Even while needling her, I couldn't even look in her direction. How surreal to have a conversation in which both of us were talking about who we were dating. I thought surely this must be one of the first signs of the apocalypse, right before a plague of locusts struck.

I should have been looking at Momma. Then I could have dodged the swat from the dishtowel which came down firmly on my head.

"We're not talking about me, we're talking about you."

"Let's not."

I had gone as far down the trail as I was going to go in the information department. Remember, baby steps. I knew Momma too well to let my guard down so easily.

Momma was a fine Christian woman. And a master manipulator. In our family, instead of stating plainly what we meant, we endured an elaborate dance and then a guessing game until we finally got to the point.

Momma always held back just a little bit of what she knew in case she needed to use the information on you later, to pull the rug out from under you at just the right moment. If you were smart, you gave Momma the respect she deserved. I was determined to stay on my toes.

In her next question, I recognized the beginning steps of a dance to which only she knew the complete choreography. The casual tone of her words immediately alerted me to their importance. Momma was most serious when she acted most casually. The tactic gave the advantage to her in most situations. Except I anticipated her moves.

"What did you and your mawmaw talk about when you went to get her?"

"Nothing in particular." I remained as noncommittal as possible, although wheels turned rapidly in my brain as I tried to figure out where she was going.

"Did she say if she'd been to town yesterday?"

"No."

Lifting the heavy skillet with both hands, Momma pivoted in front of the cake on the counter. Tilting the pan over the cake's bottom layer, she sent a waterfall of thick chocolate paradise cascading to its destination. She repeated the action on two additional layers. With a good bit of icing remaining in the skillet, she nodded permission to dig in, and I didn't hesitate. My index finger circled the top and transported a swirl of delight to my awaiting tongue. Again proving the weakness of my dieting resolve, I zoned out on the magnificent taste.

Momma tapped me on the head to get my attention. Obviously, I should have worn a helmet tonight.

"Well?" she asked.

"Well, what?"

"I thought she might have been over to the co-op getting things for her garden."

Click.

All at once, the pieces of the conversation fit together. One of the few things I knew about Edgar, the man Momma was "keeping company with," was he worked at the farmers' co-op during busy seasons. Like right now.

"Was Edgar possibly working at the co-op yesterday?" I asked.

"How would I know?"

I was back in my parallel universe. One in which my mother was trying to pry information out of me about what her mother thought of her boyfriend. *Quick,* I silently begged, *someone call nine-one-one and get me out of here.* I should have left the whole conversation alone at that point, but bad habits broke free. I couldn't resist.

With Momma, the shortest distance between two points was around a mountain, through a valley, and in the opposite direction. You were forced to listen extremely carefully to each word or else misdirection was inevitable. I called her brand of conversation the "technical truth." Rarely did you catch her in an outright lie, but you usually didn't get the whole truth either. Not without a whole lot of effort, at least.

"I don't know, Momma. Do you know?"

"I didn't say I knew."

No wonder I chose the legal profession. Constructing a line of questioning to get at the truth, the whole truth, and nothing but the truth comprised a significant part of everyday conversations with Momma.

"But do you know?" I asked.

"Sometimes he's there."

It didn't matter the least bit to me where Edgar, this mystery man I had never even seen and had only heard about hours ago, spent yesterday, but I was every bit as bullheaded as Momma. I guess I'd never quit trying to change her, in the same way she'd never quit trying to change me.

"Was he there yesterday? Yes or no?"

"I wasn't there yesterday."

This wasn't getting me anywhere. If I couldn't get in through the back door, I decided to circle around and march straight in through the front door.

"If you want to know if MawMaw saw Edgar at the co-op yesterday, why don't you ask her straight out?"

Momma pursed her lips tightly before glaring at me.

"I didn't say I wanted to know. And even if I did, it's nothing I want to talk about with my mother."

"Gee, I know how you feel."

In spite of herself, Momma let out a quick laugh.

"Get on out of here." Another swipe with the dishtowel emphasized her lighthearted demand.

"Is there anything I can help you with first?"

Momma looked sideways at me before finally cutting a smile in my direction.

"Have I ever heard that question come out of your mouth before, Katie Anne?"

"I see I'm not appreciated here. Good night."

The Blue Hole

At the Blue Hole, several in our crowd of friends were already congregated around the pit's bank on the opposite side.

I looked around for Trisha. She and Jesse were entering the clearing behind me. As soon as she spotted me, she jogged over. She was holding a beer can, and I hoped she was still on her first drink of the night, the same one I had given her earlier. She didn't have much experience with alcohol.

The only other time I'd witnessed her drinking, two beers left her emptying her stomach on the bushes outside a high school dance. Afterward, I helped sneak her home without her parents getting suspicious. I sure didn't want a repeat of that night. We might not be successful again.

"Hey." She greeted the group and inched over to where I stood. I hooked an arm around her shoulder and pulled her closer.

"Don't get too far off with my girl, Katie Anne," instructed Jesse. He was already taking long strides toward the edge of the pit where Dennis was still goofing off.

Turning Trisha around to face me, I demanded, "spill."

Giggling, she casually raised her beer can in the air and shrugged.

"Spill," I repeated. "No way I'm letting you get by without details."

"Magical. All I can say. Magical."

Wayne sauntered up, waving his arms like he was herding cattle. "Let's go, everybody over to the party. Time's awasting."

I whispered a warning to Trisha as we began moving. "Maybe that's all you can say now, but believe me, you'll say plenty later."

❧ CHAPTER 16 ❧

I awoke to the heavenly smell of bacon frying. The alluring aroma wafted over me like the first sweet healing rain after a drought. A big country breakfast was certainly a welcome benefit of waking up in my mother's home. One thing she taught me that sunk in was there weren't many hurts bacon wouldn't help.

Was there a more magnificent way to wake up? If so, I hadn't discovered it. Yet, until that precise moment, lying there in my childhood bed, I didn't realize how much I had missed it. I did miss it, with a longing connected to much more than food.

As far as I knew, Momma cooked breakfast every day of her life, beginning the day she married Daddy. Bacon wasn't always on the menu; sometimes the meat was sausage. Or occasionally, ham. But always a meat, accompanied by biscuits, white gravy, fried apples, and homemade jam, most likely strawberry rhubarb or blackberry. Making gravy was a culinary art at which every Southern woman was expected to be expert. Of course, the process was pretty much routine after the first two or three hundred times.

A quick glance over at the bedside clock told me Momma probably postponed her early morning breakfast to let me sleep in as long as possible. However, today promised to be busy, with a full list of preparations for the benefit jam-packed into our schedule.

I headed next door to the bathroom for a quick shower and then dressed hurriedly. When I entered the kitchen, Momma stood in the same spot in front of the counter where I left her last night. She looked more at home to me there than anywhere else on earth.

"Something sure smells good."

"Put us a couple of plates on the table and we'll be ready to eat."

I did as she asked, then poured myself a cup of steaming hot coffee and topped off Momma's mug.

Her blessing over the food included an earnest prayer for a successful benefit.

Our breakfast conversation consisted of her telling me our assignments for the day. We were both anxious to get started. Anxious enough that Momma suggested leaving our dirty dishes in the sink for the second day in a row. Not that she hadn't washed yesterday's dishes by then. I figured they got the clean treatment as soon as she arrived home last night. We stacked the breakfast dishes into a sink as clean as if the porcelain had never before been touched.

Momma barely disappeared down the hallway and into her bedroom when a knock sounded from the back door.

"I'll get it, Momma."

At this time of year, with a hint of frost still in the air, the back door remained closed. Living in Nashville ingrained in me the habit of identifying the person outside before allowing entrance, so I peered through the door's pane glass window.

Standing on the other side was Trisha's mother, Miss Justine.

Oh, no. Please, no.

After an eternal second in which I simply could not seem to move, I opened the wooden door and proceeded to fumble with the screen door latch, willing the mechanism to obey my mental command to open. I sent up a prayer to the heavens that now was a good time for the rapture. *Take me now, Jesus. Or, at the very least, take Miss Justine.* But neither scenario occurred.

In all the times I had visited home since moving to Nashville, I had never once run into Miss Justine. I put the situation down to careful timing and a lot of luck on my part. After all, before I moved away, Miss Justine and her family were in and out of our house with Momma and me nearly as much as we were in and out of theirs.

Wrapped up in myself and my own feelings, I never even considered the possibility that while I was trying to avoid Miss Justine, she might be trying to avoid me. The instant realization hit as an unexpected shock.

Miss Justine and my mother were extremely close friends over the years. In fact, other than Aunt Lora Anne and Aunt Patty Lynn, I would have to say Miss Justine was Momma's dearest friend. They shared so much in common, their relationship was natural. Their ways of life were almost identical. If you added three sons to Momma's life before Daddy died, it looked to me like you ended up with Miss Justine's exact life. At least, to a teenager who never wasted any time looking for nuances, the situation appeared cut and dried from the surface. Who knew mothers possessed hopes and dreams and secrets to set them apart from one another?

But if Miss Justine and the rest of the Hamiltons continued to be involved in Momma's daily life, there was nothing to indicate their presence to me. Their names were never mentioned in our conversations. I thought the reason was a kindness from Momma to me.

My dread of running into Miss Justine made my mouth go as dry as a cotton swab from nothing more than hearing her name. Knowing she was actually at the house, standing in front of me, set my stomach to churning like a dryer full of wet towels. She was the last person in the world I wanted to see.

Was she thinking the same thing about me? Surely she knew I would be here. Did she have to force herself to pull her car into Momma's driveway and walk up to the door, knowing she would probably see me? If nothing else, she should have noticed my car with Davidson County tags parked outside.

"Katie Anne." She spoke my name by way of greeting, snapping me out of my thoughts and prompting an automatic response.

"Hey, Miss Justine."

"I come by to drop off this cake with your momma. I sent James over to the high school with it, but he said the doors was still locked."

Was there a hidden meaning in her statement? Was I supposed to figure out the reason James, Trisha's protective older brother, would take the cake to the high school but he drew the line on visiting the Henderson household himself?

"The front doors probably are locked, but some of the

ladies from the church are at the school now to do some last-minute chores. I guess they went straight into the cafeteria through the side door."

If talking to me bothered Miss Justine, she showed no indication. She appeared the same pleasant woman I had always known, a little older looking perhaps, with a little more gray in her hair, but her heart-shaped face was still relatively wrinkle-free. Then again, my voice sounded normal enough to my own ears, yet I realized my heart was beating as fast and as sharp as a series of lightning strikes.

"But I can take the cake as I go," I offered. We already had enough baked goods lined up on the kitchen counter to open up a small bakery. One more wouldn't be any trouble.

"Is your momma home?"

While she was still speaking, Momma appeared behind me.

"Justine, honey, come on in."

I stepped back to allow Momma to move in front of the door and take over the conversation. Apparently she was interrupted between the bathroom and bedroom, and her hands clutched the edges of her robe together in front of her.

"Well, maybe I'll step in for a minute, Rayetta." Miss Justine moved over the threshold and continued following Momma the few short steps into the kitchen. "I know you're starting a full day, what with getting ready for the benefit and all. I did want to send this on over early. I got up and baked it this morning so it'd be fresh."

Miss Justine carefully eased a tall, golden brown cake down on the table. The delicacy rested on the kind of common homemade platter created by covering a piece of sturdy cardboard with aluminum foil.

"Oh, it's your apple stack cake. It always goes so good."

133

"Why, it's not much, but maybe it'll help out."

"You know it will."

Having exhausted their supply of small talk, the two women's eyes met for a few seconds, and I sensed a silent communication passing between them which left me out entirely. I was clearly forgotten for the moment.

Then Miss Justine found her voice.

"We'll all be there tonight. My prayers surely are with you and yours, Rayetta."

Miss Justine turned and left the house, easing the back door closed behind her. Momma stood still another second, both her face and body forming a stone statue.

Then the tears came.

Watching my mother cry as if her heart were broken tore me in two. It didn't happen often. She frequently produced the kind of tears to seep from the corners of her eyes, daubed dry by a single tissue press. Those tears were usually brought on by a happy memory, a poignant moment, an emotional tribute, my graduation. But heartbroken? I could count on one hand those breakdowns in my presence. When Daddy died. When PawPaw died. When Aunt Lora Anne's illness first became touch-and-go. I supposed her tears would devastate me no matter how old I was at the time.

"Momma?" My voice sounded strange to my own ears, filled with hesitancy, soft lest I say the wrong thing and make the situation worse.

But the statue came alive, and she opened her arms to draw me in. My own arms reached to encircle her, holding her close to me, laying her weeping head to my shoulder. In the single moment, I realized with wonder how fragile she appeared, how small she felt in my embrace. Was it a new phenomenon or was I too blind to notice sooner?

Lacking any idea of the right words to say, I held my tongue and waited.

After a length of time, Momma straightened up and stepped away from me, reaching for a paper towel to blot the wetness on her cheeks. My blouse was nearly soaked through at the shoulder, and she patted the material with her already moist towel.

"Forevermore! Would you look at me? We sure don't need all this foolishness now. We've got a basket full of things to get done without me standing here wasting time."

Momma's nervous chatter filled the silence but didn't quiet my anxiety. Of course, she was stressed about the upcoming benefit. Yet obviously, something else was unsettling her emotions. Was it Miss Justine? They had lived on adjoining properties for years, since shortly after they both married and were able to afford to make the payments on their own parcels of land.

"Momma?" I asked again.

She glanced quickly at me before turning her back and pretending to concentrate on lining up the same baked goods on the counter that she had already lined up.

"Don't you worry about me. I'm being foolish."

"No, you're not, Momma. Sit down here and talk to me a minute."

I sat down at the kitchen table and drew out a chair for her. She made no motion toward me, so I repeated my request. My resolve must have finally communicated itself to her, making her realize I would not be put off. Briefly, I shared her hesitation. After all, I didn't know what tree of apples I was about to shake loose. They might all fall on our heads.

Momma's hands trembled and her eyes avoided

mine as she pulled up to the same table she had pulled up to thousands of times, but never for this purpose.

"What's going on?" I probed gently, giving her my complete attention. One of her hands grasped out to clutch my own.

"I miss her."

"Who?"

Even though my dull brain already clicked the pieces of the puzzle into place, I refused to allow the realization to fully hit me. Any tiny, minute chance of an alternative reason for Momma's distress provided something to hold on to.

"Justine."

With one word, shame flooded over me. In all my replays of all the devastation caused by my irresponsible actions, the broken relationship between Momma and Miss Justine was something I had never even considered. My leaving town was supposed to have made the situation all better for everyone.

"In all these years, Justine and I have never really talked again. We don't avoid each other anymore, we just don't talk about anything that matters. Once we get beyond the weather and our gardens, there's not much left to say."

Pain flowed through my body, but the toughest words for me to hear were still ahead. Momma delivered them with her head down, still not meeting my eyes.

"The day you lost your best friend was the same day I lost mine."

"Momma, I'm so sorry." The few words sounded so inadequate, even to me, but what else could I offer?

"I couldn't bring up Trisha, and I guess she couldn't either. And I couldn't mention your name. Not because I blame you for anything, you've got to know that, Katie Anne.

But because the slightest mention of you being here was the same as saying Trisha wasn't here. I couldn't do it to her."

As Momma spoke, she lifted her head to stare out the window and continued shredding the paper towel she still clutched into little pieces, dropping them on the table in a neat pile. I didn't think she was even aware of her actions.

"As a mother, I knew every reminder of you or any of your classmates would be a fresh stab to her heart. A reminder that if Trisha was here, she would be getting a job, seeing a new man, making her own family. To see you all as adults is for Justine to see the future Trisha lost."

I never realized.

"So Justine and I just drifted apart, and I didn't fight it. She didn't either, and I don't blame her. I thought I might have done the same thing if I'd lost you."

"I'm so sorry, Momma," I repeated.

"Don't be, sugar. It's not your fault." She reached out in her familiar way and tucked a stray strand of hair behind my ear. "I hope someday you'll realize it's not. You keep replowing the same old ground. It's time to quit plowing and finally plant something permanent in your life."

❧ CHAPTER 17 ❦

A quick trip to town was the first item on my day's agenda for the benefit preparations. Momma handed me a short list of foods to pick up from the grocery store, scrawled in pencil on a piece of lined yellow paper, and sent me on my way with at least a dozen unnecessary instructions. I felt like a child again as I was warned to check expiration dates and comparison shop.

Armed with the list of errands and Momma's strict admonition to not waste time, I headed toward town.

"Don't stop and talk, just smile and wave," she instructed. "We've got a full schedule ahead of us."

Sure, as if I wanted to stop and chat with the same people I had been avoiding since high school. Sometimes Momma killed me with her insight, and sometimes she was clueless. We were obviously in the middle of one of those clueless occasions.

Momma caught me by the arm on my way out the door and handed me the keys to her old four-door sedan. She insisted I drive it since the vehicle provided more room than my car, plus she had filled up with gas the day before. No reason to waste my gas on her errands, she said. Knowing my car had plenty of cargo space for groceries and other items with room to spare, and knowing the short trip into town required minimal gas, I reverted to childhood and rolled my eyes at her as soon as she turned her back. However, I did take the keys. Easier to comply than to complain.

I could barely squeeze into the driver's side of Momma's car, which provided only a few inches between the seat and the steering wheel. Momma was slightly shorter than I was, and she also preferred to drive sitting as close to the dashboard as possible. My hand fumbled around under the seat for the manual adjustment until I finally found the lever. I slid the seat back to a more comfortable position and pulled Momma's little "driving pillow" out from under me, flinging it on the passenger seat.

As I headed out the driveway, muted strains of gospel bluegrass music filled the vehicle's interior. The sweet strains of the music I grew up on. In my family, anything by Doyle Lawson commanded nearly as much respect as the national anthem. Four-part harmony with or without a guitar, fiddle and bass. The voices of angels ringing out of the radio on *Uncloudy Day*, *Kneel At the Cross*, *I'll Fly Away*, and *This World Is Not My Home*. MawMaw delighted in hearing her sons' voices blending together on *Just A Little Talk with Jesus* and *Meeting in the Air*. Bluegrass lovers treasured songs about heaven.

Living in Nashville provided me the bonus of enjoying the best music in the world. And not only country music. My adopted city attracted top musicians in plenty of other genres, too. Every other restaurant featured a corner with only a microphone and a stool as an invitation for volunteers to give their best shot at entertaining patrons. I routinely listened to some stars who weren't stars yet, and occasionally came across a real star or two who took time to surprise customers in a small venue.

Under the circumstances, taking music for granted would be easy, yet I seldom did. My musical tastes had broadened greatly over time. In the countless genres, only heavy metal, new age, and rap were strictly avoided. All others were most welcome. Even so, bluegrass touched me in the most basic part of my soul.

The sounds coming from the radio soaked into me, and I quickly found myself singing along to the familiar tune. The awareness of my listening neighbors on the other side of my apartment wall usually kept me from singing too loudly at home, but when I got in a vehicle there was no such description as too loud. I let the lyrics belt out of my mouth as my fingers imitated steel guitar on the steering wheel and my left foot kept time with the bass.

"Thump. Thump. Thump."

Making so much noise myself, I didn't know how much time elapsed before I realized part of the noise I was hearing wasn't generated by the radio. I turned the knob to off and, sure enough, the thumping noise continued. Even though Momma's car was the first vehicle other than my Mustang I had driven in a long time, clearly something wasn't right.

The turn onto Main Street was in sight up ahead. A tire shop used to sit on the right, across from the old high school and a playground built by volunteers for the community's children. I quickly debated whether to stop now and investigate the sound or whether to take my chances and try to make it to the tire shop. My mechanical knowledge was limited, but I was fairly sure the sound indicated a tire problem, and I didn't want to ruin one of Momma's rims by running on a flat.

So I pulled over.

Traffic was light as usual for Pikeville, even on the bypass. After flipping on my flashers, I got out and examined the two tires on the driver's side of the car. No problem there. But as soon as I rounded the other side, the reason for the thumping was obvious. The back tire was nearly flat. Not a good way to make a quick trip into town.

I squatted down by the faulty tire and reviewed my options. I could change the tire myself if Momma carried a spare in the trunk, which she probably did. I could change it, but I really didn't want to. I could drive the short distance to the tire shop and risk rim damage. Or I could walk to the tire shop, hope it was open, and have somebody there come out and fix the tire.

Of course, I also could have called Momma or Uncle Cooper or somebody else for help, but living in Nashville conditioned me to solve problems on my own. Besides, if I called Momma, she would probably come unglued. She already had too much going on today. One more thing might tip her over the edge.

While I mulled over my options, I noticed a young couple walking on the grassy side of the bypass in my direction. They were both about the same height and dressed in jeans and tee-shirts. The woman's belly pooched out to reveal an expanding pregnancy. Was everybody around me having children? Their coffee skin color led me to assume they were Mexicans, but I knew I could be wrong. In the years I had been gone from Pikeville, a growing number of people from various Central American countries had moved into the area, both legally and illegally. Locals frequently lumped them all together under the label of Mexican, even though some were from Nicaragua, Guatemala, or another nearby country.

"Hi," I greeted the couple as they neared.

Both merely nodded their heads in reply, leading me to I wonder if either of them spoke English. My high school Spanish was long behind me, and even back then I didn't make remarkable grades. I soon found out the pedestrian couple were as unskilled in English as I was in their native language.

The young man motioned to the tire and then to the trunk. Our communication wasn't verbal, but it was still communication, and I knew exactly what he meant.

I opened the trunk, and he reached for the spare.

"Si?" he questioned. I interpreted his words as asking if I wanted him to change the tire and quickly latched onto the offer.

"Yes, please," I responded. A liberated woman I was, but a fool I was not. At least not in this situation, in a hurry and with an emerging sun beginning to beat down on us.

He turned his head and spoke a few words to the woman. She moved back over into the grass at the side of the road and sat down.

Within minutes, the young man had the spare tire on and the flat tire back in the trunk. I tossed him a rag I found in the trunk, and he wiped off his hands.

Turning back to the car, I opened my purse and pulled out a ten dollar bill.

"Gracias" was my feeble attempt at thanks as I held out the money to him.

"No, no," he protested, waving his hands in front of

him until I finally grasped one and pressed the money into his palm.

I opened the car's back door and pantomimed ushering them into the back seat, then pointed toward the right turn to indicate the direction I was taking, even though I felt quite foolish making the hand gestures.

"No." The Good Samaritan turned down my offer of a ride as he pointed straight ahead on the bypass.

"Gracias," I repeated before returning to the car and starting the engine. As I pulled away, the couple continued their journey on the grassy right-of-away, again holding hands.

The language barrier bothered me. Had I been able to effectively communicate, I could have given the couple a ride to their destination. Besides, I was downright curious about them. Did they live in Pikeville or were they only passing through?

In years past, most Mexicans in the area were migrant workers, harvesting tomatoes, green beans, apples, and other crops. They appeared when harvest started and left when harvest ended. But an increasing number were making their year-round home in and around Pikeville.

But there wasn't much time to think, so I pushed the subject from my mind. I made the right turn, quickly approaching the tire shop on the right. The old one I remembered was no longer there, but a sign for a new one was nearby. Thankfully, the bay doors were open, so I pulled the vehicle to the entrance of one and got out. Hopefully, the repair wouldn't take too long and I could be on my way shortly.

Nobody was in sight as I entered the garage, all at once enjoying a welcome coolness in the darkened concrete and block building.

"Hey," I called. "Anybody here?"

Around the corner walked a slim figure from the past. And not too distant past. In fact, from last night.

Jesse Warren.

∂

Him again. Was I merely experiencing a case of bad luck or was something else at work? Some cruel joke from above? Someone with a voodoo doll, sticking pins in my most vulnerable parts?

In my mind, Jesse was all wrapped up in the tragedy with Trisha. I couldn't think of him without thinking of her. And I didn't want to think of either one of them right now. I had already spent a good portion of my life with that door closed forever. Or so I thought. Lately, something was trying awfully hard to pry the door open, but I was trying with all my might to keep it closed.

If our accidental meeting offered any consolation to me, it was that he appeared to be at least as unsettled as I was.

As soon as Jesse's eyes registered my identity, he stopped short, rocking back on his heels. Last night I wasn't sure he recognized me, but now his reaction was unmistakable. He did. The smile he wore to welcome a potential customer died at the precise instant he saw me.

For a moment, neither of us knew what to say. The silence stretched uncomfortably as we stared across the width of the garage at each other. I didn't know how long the moment lasted, but it felt like forever.

Jesse was as shocked as I was.

My deepest wish at that precise moment was to travel

back in time, only one minute, so I could keep driving past this particular shop. I would choose somewhere else, anywhere else. I would buy Momma all new rims, if necessary.

"My tire," I finally blurted out. "Actually, my mother's tire. It went flat. Or almost flat. Not all the way flat, but low. As I was driving to town. In my mother's car, not my car."

Could I possibly sound any dumber?

Apparently, I could.

"The back tire. On the other side. You know, the passenger side. But not now. The spare's on now. The flat one is in the trunk."

My own clearly unsettled nerves seemed to provide Jesse with a bit of confidence.

"Let's take a look."

In long strides, he moved around me and headed toward Momma's car.

"Pop the trunk, and I'll get the tire out."

So that was how we were going to play things out. Businesslike all the way. Two strangers who had never met before. I was any other customer and he was any other worker. Suited me fine. Just fine. This I could handle.

Jesse rolled the tire from behind the car and into the shop with one hand in easy, practiced motions which let me know he had performed the same task many times before and was good at his job. Within minutes, he discovered a small piece of steel protruding through the tread, removed it, and plugged the tire.

"This should hold fine. These tires still have a lot of wear in them. Let me get a jack, and I'll switch this one out for the spare."

I stood quietly in the cool shade of the block garage as he made the quick exchange.

"You're ready to go." Jesse reentered the garage. He didn't even break stride but continued toward the small office at the other end of the building.

"Wait." I broke my silence. "How much do I owe you?"

Looking back over his shoulder, he waved his hand as if to brush me off.

"No charge."

Perhaps I should have left things there, but I always paid my own way. I was no charity case. This was business, and I owed him money.

"Yes, I'm going to pay you for fixing the tire. How much?"

Jesse whirled around and closed the distance between us in seconds. As he advanced on me, his mouth tightened and his eyes narrowed in anger. His words, when they came, were overflowing with a barely controlled fury. I instinctively stepped back.

"You don't know when to quit, do you? I know why you're here. To rub it in my face. Well, you're wasting your time. Your plan's not gonna work."

"What?" was all my stunned brain could think of to say.

"I saw you last night at the pizza place, laughing and talking with all your big buddies. I guess you enjoyed a good laugh about me after I left."

"I don't know what you're talking about."

My honest denial seemed to make Jesse even angrier. He advanced another step toward me.

"They want no part of me now. None of them. You all think you're so above me. For your information, I own this shop. Not only tires, all kinds of repairs. I can fix anything that runs. You may not think that's much, but it's mine. I've got a wife and a family, and I'm as good as any one of you."

My mind raced to put together all he was saying, but I still came up short on a coherent response.

"Of course you're as good as anybody, Jesse. I don't know anybody who thinks you're not."

"I know everybody blames me for what happened. After all these years, you'd think they'd let it go. But every time some kid wants to go to the Blue Hole, their parents remind them. I know what I did, and I live with it every day, so you don't have to come around here reminding me. I never forget."

As he spoke, Jesse slowly advanced toward me until I could feel the heat from his anger radiating off his whole body. He was shaking, barely able to control himself. His hands curled tightly into fists, and he appeared ready to strike out at any second. While he vented, I backed up so far I was pinned between Jesse and the hood of Momma's car. I realized I was in a vulnerable position.

"Something going on here?" A mild voice interrupted the conversation.

Grateful for any diversion, I quickly spun around to see Harmon Suggs, the man I met last night while setting up for the benefit. So wrapped up in our tense confrontation, Jesse and I had both failed to notice him drive up.

Harmon's demeanor matched his tone of voice, as if he was purposefully trying to inject some needed calm into the volatile situation.

At that point, I felt relieved to see anybody. I was afraid Jesse's behavior was getting out of hand, and I couldn't predict what action he might take next.

But Harmon's voice served to snap Jesse out of his

rage. He glanced at Harmon and then back at me before abruptly turning on his heel and stomping out the back door.

I was left standing alone with Harmon.

"Want to tell me what that was all about?" he asked.

"It's a long story. But thanks for showing up when you did."

"No problem. The right place at the right time, I guess."

"I'll say."

"You know," Harmon continued speaking in a friendly tone, lifting one foot to rest on the car's bumper, "everybody has something to eat at them if they let it. Nobody but the Lord has ever lived the perfect life. Take me, for instance. Some people look at me and all they can see is an ex-con. I messed things up so bad, and all they can see is the bad. I had it all and lost it. Threw it away. For what? A bottle? Some people think there's no good in me to be found. They look at me and only see a loser."

While talking, Harmon pulled out a pocket knife, flicked open the blade, and began cleaning his fingernails. The small gesture reminded me of my daddy. I'd watched him perform the same small task with his knife so many times over the years. Now the simple act served as a focal point for Harmon's attention. I wondered whether he used the activity as a reason to keep from looking me in the eyes or if he was giving me a way to avoid looking into his as he continued speaking.

"If you think that way about yourself, you set yourself out a pretty hard row to hoe. People who think like that must not know the God of the Bible is the God of forgiveness. The God of second chances. And third. And fourth.

"It took me a long time to accept His forgiveness, a lot

longer than it took Him to forgive me. And I'm still amazed every time He gives me the opening to help someone else with what I've been through. It's like Joseph said way back in the Old Testament after his brothers sold him into slavery and then he rescued them from starving in the famine. I can't quote the exact words, but it's something like, 'You meant it for evil but God used it for good.' That's how I feel about all the mistakes I've made in my life. Even though some people chalk me up as a lost cause, God doesn't. He's forgiven this broken down man, and even used my worst sins to let me help other people here and there."

Harmon's gentle tone of voice lulled me into wondering if he was talking to himself as much as he was to me. It sounded as if he might have repeated this mini-sermon to himself on a regular basis.

"Everybody's got something they struggle with in their lives. Jesse is no exception. He fights with himself more than anybody else."

My heart finally settled down enough to be able to respond in a nearly steady voice.

"You talk like you know Jesse pretty well."

"I come over sometimes after I get off work and hang out a little. Give him a hand occasionally if he's on a big job. Me and his daddy went to school together, were buddies when we were younger. I understand where Jesse's coming from. He's a good man, just hard on himself. Tries to carry the whole world on his shoulders. Sound familiar?"

Harmon gazed up at me. I could see compassion simmering in his eyes, and I wondered how much he knew about me. He appeared to know quite a bit about Jesse. Did he know as much information about me? If so, who told him? Jesse? Momma? MawMaw?

I didn't respond.

"You're only responsible for yourself," he continued after a brief pause, "not everybody else. Other people make their own decisions. What's done is done, and some things can't be changed. We've got to seek God's forgiveness when needed and then move on.

"Speaking of moving on, I guess I'd better let you move on. I'm sure you've got more to do than hang around here listening to my rambling."

With so many thoughts swirling around in my head, I couldn't come up with an appropriate response to his farewell. I barely managed to nod my head in halfhearted agreement before moving around to get back into Momma's car.

Harmon pushed himself off the bumper and walked the few paces into the garage.

As I pulled back onto the street, I could see him move through the garage and out the same back door Jesse left through minutes before. I didn't take time to ponder the direction their conversation might take. All I could think about was getting as far away as I could as quickly as I could.

The Blue Hole

As our adventure at the Blue Hole continued, I decided my best option was to keep a close eye on Trisha and Jesse. That way I could see for myself how things were progressing. A teenage girl without a boyfriend of her own, like me, could be plenty curious about her best friend's love life. If forced to date vicariously through Trisha, I would.

Jesse caught up with us. Taking Trisha by the hand, he pulled her ahead of me, so I dropped back with Wayne. Some of the other kids were beginning to pair up, too. I could see where the night was going. Wayne was my old standby, and I was his. I matched my steps to his longer ones.

"Looks like it's just you and me, honey," he said. "I guess you won the jackpot again tonight."

"Spare me."

We both knew we were glad to have each other, but neither one of us would admit the truth out loud.

Someone had lit a small bonfire on the entrance side to the pit. We followed its yellow glow around the pit and down to the lower ground, climbing over fallen logs and through budding brambles.

"Hold up," I demanded, jerking Wayne's hand to make him stop and let me catch up.

"Ought to have your boots on, girl. You can't be wandering around out here like some fashion model."

"Not every man wants a girl dressed head to toe in camouflage," I teased.

"All the smart ones do, honey, all the smart ones do."

True enough, plenty of camo wear was evident among our classmates, both boys and girls. In fact, homecoming week used to include a special dress-up day for everyone to be outfitted in camo clothing. But teachers discontinued the day after realizing it was indistinguishable from any other day in school. In the same way a pair of jeans matched any other clothing, so did camo.

And University of Tennessee Volunteer orange. We didn't mind the old joke at all: *Why is orange the perfect color? Wear it Saturday to the game, Sunday to hunt, and Monday for community service.*

❧ CHAPTER 19 ❧

"Katie Anne, be sure you come through my lane to check out when you get through shopping. I've got something for you."

I heard the clear voice calling out to me as soon as I stepped inside the grocery store, snapping me out of my mental wanderings. Momma's list on the little piece of yellow paper was clutched in my hand. While I headed to the row of shopping carts near the front, I looked around to identify the sound's origin.

I spotted Sheila Swafford in the second checkout lane, wearing a red smock over a white shirt and jeans, a familiar sight even after all this time. I attended school with her children and she taught me in Sunday school when I was younger, but her natural habitat was in front of the cash register on checkout lane two.

"Hey, Miss Sheila. Sure thing. I'll be through in a few minutes."

"Don't forget me now."

I nodded my head in consent and wheeled the shopping cart through the produce section and down the first aisle. After my uncomfortable encounter with Jesse, I felt relieved to see the cashier's friendly face.

Strolling through the grocery store was almost like entering a time capsule, one that transported me back to my high school days when I worked as a cashier in this exact store. Part-time, two or three evenings a week. Wearing the dreaded red smock. I clocked in straight from school and stayed until the store closed at nine. A big enough payday to keep me in gas money.

"Driving's not free." I heard Momma's frequent statement replay itself over in my mind. "There's gas, insurance, and maintenance all to pay. You don't have to work…unless you want to drive."

I did want to drive. Definitely. And working wasn't so bad anyway. My job gave me a little independence.

Bringing myself back to the moment, I ran down the shopping list and realized Momma had written out the items in the order I reached them in the store. Classic Momma, forever organized.

Back in the meat department, the ground beef for the chili was ready to go. I quickly moved up and down the remaining aisles, picking the few necessary items off the shelves. I reached the bread section and counted out the correct number of hot dog buns before proceeding to the checkout lanes.

Lane two, of course.

Only one customer stood in line ahead of me, allowing me barely enough time to glance at the covers of a few gossip magazines. Nothing there to fully capture my interest, but I kept up with celebrity relationship changes as well as the next woman. You never knew when a good-looking actor or musician might cross your path unexpectedly. If one crossed mine, I wanted to know if he was available or not. I drew the line at messing with other women's men. I fully believed the saying: "God will never send you somebody else's husband."

Miss Sheila broke into my tabloid daydreams by taking firm hold of my cart and pulling it toward her. As she began scanning each item, I asked how she was. A routine question, granted, but I actually did want to know.

"Honey, they're working me harder than a borrowed mule. But I'll make it. I'm glad we're as busy as we are, what with people going out of town to shop so much. I wish they'd see we're all better off if they spend their dollars here in town instead of somewhere else."

The mere thought prompted her to shake her head in frustration before changing the subject.

"Did you get what all you need for the benefit?"

"I think so. I got everything on Momma's list anyway, so it won't be my fault if I didn't."

"Well, if you left off anything, I expect I'll see you back in a bit."

"Yep, you may see me a couple more times today."

Anyone overhearing me talk with Miss Sheila would think we had last seen each other yesterday. The conversation flowed naturally between two friends.

"You'll have a good crowd tonight, and the weather looks like it's going to cooperate. Have you got things about ready?"

"Everything seems to be right on schedule so far."

While we talked, Miss Sheila scanned and bagged all my groceries, and the total showed up on my side of the register. I swiped my credit card, and she handed me the receipt. Then she reached under the counter and pulled out her purse.

"I sure hate to say this, but I'm gonna have to work straight through till closing tonight. Two of the girls on the next shift can't make it in. That's the trouble with these teenage girls. They say they're sick, but I suspect some boy made them a better offer. Anyway, even with me staying, we'll still be shorthanded. If you don't care, would you take this money to the benefit tonight and put it in for me? Be sure to tell your aunt Lora Anne and all the family how upset I am that I can't be there."

Miss Sheila counted a few bills out of her wallet and pressed them into my hand. When our eyes met, I could see sincerity shining from her. No doubt this was a woman who cared about my family.

"I will, Miss Sheila. I'll let them know you'd be there if you could."

"Thanks, honey. And it's so good to see you, too. You need to start coming back home more regular."

～

As if on autopilot, I easily navigated the short distance from town back home, making turns and anticipating obstacles by rote. Fortunately, finding my way home actually was like riding a bicycle. No telling how many times I had traveled the exact route, over and over. Was the number in the hundreds or the thousands? I wondered.

Pushing away thoughts of my encounter with Jesse was becoming more difficult. I did fine on the drive from his garage to the grocery store, mostly because I was still in shock.

Could it be Jesse blamed himself for the events that transpired so long ago? All during the time when I thought he blamed me, could he have blamed himself? The possibility hit me like a train barreling straight down the track and into my awareness.

Wrapped up in my own grief, in my own pain, how was it that I had never seriously considered the feelings of others and the countless ways their lives were impacted by that night? Was I so selfish? Right now the answer wasn't one I wanted to confirm. I knew I wouldn't like the result.

My thoughts sped round and round inside my head as if on a racetrack. First I thought about Trisha, then Miss Justine, then Jesse, then Momma, back to Trisha, and around the track again.

Those thoughts wouldn't do, not at all. I had to get back in control of myself and focus on my tasks for the day. Focus on today. With all we needed to accomplish, I didn't have time to be distracted by painful memories.

"All right, Katie Anne." My voice sounded quite stern as I began giving myself a talk. "First things first. You need all your energy and abilities to deal with Aunt Lora Anne and what's best for her. All this other mess has waited a long time. It can wait a little longer. You can think about this all you want to next week. But put it out of your mind right now."

Actually, the voice in my head when I talked to myself sounded exactly like Momma's voice. That was probably why I called myself Katie Anne instead of Kate. So I wasn't really talking to myself, I was having Momma talk to me, forcing myself to listen. Probably because I took things more seriously coming from her. At least in most cases.

A great deal of effort was required, but I forced myself to concentrate on my driving and the beautiful scenery around me. With a minimal amount of prodding, an old habit kicked in and I began trying to identify the make and model of other vehicles on the road as soon as I spotted them. I may have driven an older model car, but I had a passion for anything with wheels and I was usually correct in my identifications.

There was more traffic on the road than when I made the trip into town earlier in the morning. More evidence of the county's growing population, made up of "foreigners" from places like Michigan and Florida, flocking to the Tennessee mountains to escape the heat/cold and high property taxes. Add to the mix the Central Americans in search of employment and a better standard of living.

Vehicles of all types were on the road, including a good percentage of pickup trucks. A man in Pikeville without a pickup was slightly suspect in the eyes of the native population. His woman drove a car or an SUV, and he drove a truck. That is, unless both of them drove trucks.

However, I left the traffic behind when I made the right turn onto "our road." When I first began driving, I remembered taking notice of the few vehicles I spotted on our road. Mostly neighbors. Those, I didn't mind. But let a stranger intrude on my territory and I wanted to know why. I once considered it a personal affront for anyone who didn't live along our stretch of road to use it. Unrecognized drivers were subjected to my flinty stare of disapproval.

My determination to clear my head and concentrate on the day before me was successfully accomplished on the short drive from town. I resolved to do my share and more to make this benefit a success. My aunt Lora Anne deserved the help.

And I did expect the benefit to be a success. In spite of my own situation, I knew the citizens of my hometown to be decent, caring, generous people at their core. They could be counted on to come together in enthusiastic, loving support of one of their own, especially one like Aunt Lora Anne, who had done so much for so many of them in the past. When she needed them most, I harbored no doubt her friends and neighbors would come through for her.

My thoughts of friends and loved ones finally triggered my memory. With a sinking feeling, I remembered my promise to call my friend Lainey last night. Her final instruction to me before I left Nashville was to call. Better late than never, I thought as I dialed her home phone number on my cell. If she was at work, I didn't want to bother her.

No luck. The answering machine clicked in after a few rings. I waited for her message to play and then recorded my own.

"Hi. Sorry I didn't get back to you last night. My mother has me on a strict schedule. She hasn't threatened grounding me off the phone yet, but it's a distinct possibility. Hope your day is going well. Catch you later."

As soon as I hung up, I realized I hadn't even identified myself in the message. No problem. How many other calls could she get from people whose mother might ground them? And yes, I might have stretched my excuse for not calling as planned a little for my own sake. Using what was available in front of me made good sense.

Lainey might be too busy to realize I hadn't called her anyway. Being a rising attorney in an established "old money" law firm meant she worked long hours, including many weekends. Getting ahead was all about the billable hours. Her time was truly not her own.

Seeing up close the pressures Lainey faced left me content with my paralegal position and mostly forty-hour work weeks. The money was certainly less than an attorney's salary but adequate, and I had time for a life. Maybe not an outrageously exciting life, but I was fairly satisfied.

"Be glad you're not from a family of attorneys," Lainey complained to me on more than one occasion. "We're always in an unspoken competition. More money. Bigger house. More prestige. It's a game that never ends."

"So why do you keep playing?"

"Good question. Apparently it's also a game you can't quit. Like one of those songs that never ends."

Thinking about my friend's problem let me feel a little bit less selfish. See, I could put others first, I thought, mentally patting myself on the back. The diversion also helped steer my thoughts into more comfortable territory. My nerves were back on an even keel and my heart rate felt normal. Mission accomplished.

Now all I needed to do was maintain the same attitude the rest of the weekend. The goal sounded doable, even for me. The realization left me feeling pretty good.

When I turned Momma's car back into her driveway, a surprise awaited me.

The Blue Hole

CHAPTER 20

At the Blue Hole, Wayne and I neared the fire and our friends gathered there.

"Wayne, buddy, come here and look at this," hollered Deacon.

Wayne moved toward him, and I gravitated toward Debra, lounging cross-legged on the rocky ground with Leanne, Molly, Jonica, and Iris. I didn't know Iris as well as the others since she had attended grammar school on Rigsby mountain and we weren't in any classes together in high school. But I did know her well enough to speak to.

I leaned back on a large rock next to Molly. I noticed Trisha and Jesse out of the corner of my right eye, but decided to give them plenty of room. I didn't want to be a third wheel. My best friend was with a boy she had a crush on, so good for her. I knew I would force every detail out of her sooner or later.

"We've already got the fire going, so let's see what we can noodle, boys."

161

Dennis never quit trying to be the center of attention. Grabbing a catfish with your bare hands was a tough sport. Reaching into a hole underwater to wrestle a catfish often left a person with bites and scratches all over their arms and chest. Catfish weren't known to give up easily, and neither were country boys.

"Jump in and let's see your stuff," challenged Zeb. "You catch it, I'll clean it, Debra'll cook it. She's already got the fire going."

"Speak for yourself, you male chauvinist. You can cook it yourself."

"If Dennis catches anything, I'll clean it and cook it both," promised Wayne. "That's how sure I am he can't outdo a catfish."

"Oh, the lack of faith in me." Dennis faked a swoon as he raised a hand to his forehead. "Luckily, I already caught a mess of catfish and transformed them into these tasty hot dogs." He waved toward a couple packs of wieners near the fire.

"He means these hot dogs we stopped at the store and bought." Leanne, who rode up the mountain with Dennis, was quick to correct him.

We all knew Dennis was just putting on an act, since the Blue Hole didn't have any fish anyway. If the boys wanted to noodle, they'd have to try it somewhere else.

Most of the group gathered around the fire, the same way we spent so many nights during our high school years at various locations. Our parents generally trusted us with each other, although most of them would have changed their minds had they known about the alcohol and tobacco usually present on our outings. We didn't consider it any big deal, but we knew they would, so we were careful not to mention it.

"Here, Katie Anne, take a swig of my beer." Dennis made the offer by holding a can toward me.

"Haha. My momma raised me better."

We all knew taking a drink from an opened can offered by one of these jokers invited trouble, and not because of any drug they might have added to harm us. Other girls might worry about secondhand smoke, but we worried about secondhand chew. Many of the boys chewed tobacco and grabbed any nearby empty can to use as a spit cup. Yuck. Spotting boys who chewed was easy since the round imprint of a chewing tobacco can quickly wore into the back pocket of their jeans. The tobacco companies even targeted girls with flavored tobaccos like vanilla and raspberry.

"Well, here's one hadn't been opened."

I popped the top on the lid of my second beer of the night while Wayne broke off nearby limbs the right size for roasting the hot dogs.

Trisha and Jesse were out of sight. I figured they wandered nearer to the water. Things must be going well. I was glad for my friend. She deserved every good thing she got for putting up with me, if for no other reason.

≈ CHAPTER 21 ≈

No wonder Lainey hadn't answered at home when I called her a few minutes ago. Parked in the space next to my car was her late model luxury sedan, what I referred to as her "successful attorney" car.

Reinforcements had arrived!

By the time I opened the trunk to unload the groceries, Lainey had moved through the screen door and toward me, arms outstretched and coordinating bracelets jangling against each other.

"You sure are a welcome sight," I greeted her, reaching out my own arms for her quick but firm embrace. "Why didn't you tell me you were coming?"

"You know my schedule. I was afraid I'd get tied up in depositions this morning and not be able to make the trip at the last minute. I would have been disappointed if it happened, but I didn't want you disappointed, too. When I saw I could get here as early as midday, I thought I'd come ahead and try to give you a hand with the preparations."

"Well, you didn't have to come. I know it's a long drive and a lot of effort for you. But I'm glad you did."

"Me, too. Let me help you with those bags."

"An offer I won't turn down."

In the house, Momma was already turning on stove eyes under two large iron skillets.

"Bring the ground beef right over here. Don't even bother to put the meat in the refrigerator. Your aunt Patty Lynn called and changed the plan on me. We agreed last night to take it on to the high school and fry it up there, but she's changed her mind this morning. She thinks it'll be less trouble for me to cook the meat here. Then we can put it right into the chili when we get to the school. Less trouble for her, she means. Oh, she said to take some by there and she'd fry part of it, but there's no need to. It won't be much more to set in and do up the whole thing."

"I can do it, Momma, while you do something else."

"That's all right. I can handle this. I've got a little something else in mind for you to do. But first you sit Lainey down there at the table and visit a few minutes. Wasn't it the sweetest thing she come all the way down here to help us out?"

As usual, Momma didn't wait for an answer but continued the monologue on her own. Next she hit on her two favorite topics, one right after the other.

"How was the weather in Nashville this morning, Lainey? Did you have much traffic on the drive? I know them big trucks make me nervous to drive alongside. I sure am glad the weather today is turning out pretty. Of course, we'd go on and have the benefit no matter what, but it's so much nicer to have the sun shining. Makes it all easier."

I looked at the clock, surprised by how much time

had passed during my trip to town. Momma caught my gaze.

"Katie Anne, you stayed gone so long, it's time for a bite of dinner already. I figured we'd eat a little early, and then we'll have a snack before the benefit starts. Does it sound all right with you, Lainey? I reckon you must be fairly hungry after your drive."

"Sounds fine with me."

"Around here, dinner is what we call lunch." I felt obligated to explain the difference to Lainey.

"Oh. Then what do you call supper?"

"Amazingly enough, we call it supper."

Momma cut in with her opinion. "I don't know why some folks are determined to say dinner when what they clearly mean to say is supper. They have some funny ways. I don't understand, and I don't want to."

She continued along the same subject as she turned down the heat on the stove and crossed over to open the refrigerator door.

"Katie Anne, you get us out some plates and napkins. And get us all a glass of tea. Is tea fine with you, Lainey?"

Iced tea, the nectar of the South. The beverage came two ways: sweet and unsweet. Actually three: some people ordered half and half.

"Sounds great to me."

Momma pulled out a package of bologna, along with cheese slices, a jar of mayonnaise, and a bowl of homemade slaw. Momma was known for her delicious slaw as long as I could remember, and she was called on to supply the delicacy for most every occasion.

She grabbed a loaf of lite bread from the top of the refrigerator and set it on the table with the rest of the food. A bite of dinner coming right up.

After Momma said the blessing, I gave her a carefully edited account of her flat tire episode, not mentioning Jesse or our confrontation. Then she and Lainey kept the conversation going while I ate in silence, with Lainey updating Momma about what was going on in her life. Nothing I didn't already know.

When Momma saw me place the last bite of sandwich in my mouth, she struck.

Once again, her oh-so-casual tone launched me from relaxed to high alert in seconds.

"Katie Anne, the next thing I need you to do is go over to the church and pick up whatever baked goods are there and take them on to the school."

When I looked up at her, she appeared to be concentrating awfully hard on dishing out a second helping of slaw onto her plate. Big faker.

No one could claim Momma didn't know how to take advantage of an opportunity. Had Lainey not been present, making a case for sending me to the church would have proved much more difficult for her. Lainey didn't know she was playing right into Momma's hands. If nothing else, my friend's presence guaranteed I would not resort to a full-blown tantrum.

Church was the last place I wanted to go. Momma and I both knew it. I'd refused to set foot in the doors since before my high school graduation. If God had let me down, my church had thrown me down. At least, that was how I felt.

In the brief period of time between losing Trisha and moving off to Nashville, I felt like an outcast. None of the people who talked so much about how we as a church were one body, were united in Christ, stood with me. I stood alone. Except for Momma. We didn't discuss it, but we didn't need to. She stood with me.

This new chore of hers was a setup. A way to ease me into the church on an errand I couldn't refuse. And who would be on hand when I arrived? Could the who in question possibly be the pastor? Clearly a setup.

Time to turn the tables on Momma.

"Sure, Momma." I saw the surprised relief in her expression before dropping a bomb of my own. "Lainey, you'll go with me, won't you?"

"No." Momma quickly cut in before my friend had a chance to decide for herself. "After her long drive, Lainey needs some rest. And I thought she could stay here and help me with a few things. You'll stay here with me, won't you, Lainey?"

Momma put on her best "pretty please" face which cried out, "If you love me, you'll do this one simple thing for me."

I put on my "if you don't want me to throttle you on the spot, you'll do this one simple thing for me" face.

My poor buddy looked back and forth between us, afraid to come down on either side. I soon took pity and made the decision for her.

"Momma, with all the food there, you know I'll need somebody to help me load it up. You'll come with me, Lainey."

Case closed.

Relieved not to be forced to choose between the two of us, Lainey nodded her head in agreement. Momma pursed her lips tightly, unhappy she had lost the skirmish but at the same time, knowing she'd won the war. She could afford to be generous. So I wasn't going by myself, but I was going. With any luck, Lainey would also get the preacher's special attention.

Within minutes, we cleared the table and Lainey and I headed off to the church.

⁊

"All right, what was that all about?"

I knew I would face Lainey's line of questioning as soon as she got me alone in the car. But her curiosity was definitely the lesser of two evils. Either I could go and face the music alone, or she could go with me and I could possibly avoid listening to the music at all.

"See how popular you are? Everyone wants you with them."

I also knew a smart aleck answer wouldn't satisfy her long-term, but diversion was all I could think of to begin with. It gave me time to form a more acceptable reply.

"So we're going to be flippant, are we? That's the Kate I know and love. Or should I call you Katie Anne?"

"Certainly. And then I shall call you Elaine. Let's do that." Her given name wasn't bad at all. Except to her.

"I don't know why you never went on to law school. With your mouth, you could argue in front of the Supreme Court."

By this time, I was able to frame my response to her first question and soften my words.

"Here's the scoop. Momma has been trying to get me back into church for a long time, one way or the other. Nothing else has worked, so she cooked up this little trip."

"It's merely picking up a few things. What's the big deal?"

"Indeed."

Our exchange struck the perfect note of nonchalance.

Lainey might have been my closest friend, but no need to get into all the messy family issues. Or explain how much I dreaded entering the church doors.

Might as well get the visit over with. I knew Momma would expect me to attend services tomorrow. Anybody in her household on Sunday morning went to church. Period. No exceptions other than with a notarized doctor's excuse.

By this time, I didn't know if I was skimming the surface of the issues because I was ashamed to admit the entire situation to Lainey, or if I didn't want to pick the scab off the wound for my own sake. At any rate, I felt confident I could keep the errand brief and my demeanor upbeat.

"Here we are."

I pulled Momma's car up as close to the side door of the church as I could get and popped open the trunk. Then I made a mistake. I took a minute to look up at the building and felt waves of memories flood over me.

❧ CHAPTER 22 ❧

Trisha and I were about fourteen years old, newly christened teenagers barely in high school, when one of my more inspired ideas hit.

Music rang out from the chimes atop the church without fail twice a day, at ten in the morning and six at night, reminding the entire community of the promise of salvation nearby. Some old-time hymn on classical steroids. The strains of *Holy, Holy, Holy* floated across the residential sections of town and out into the farmland like the aroma of freshly baked bread enticing people home.

Adults were enthralled by the melodies from the first day the workmen arrived from Chattanooga to install the chimes. Of course, one person's music was another person's noise. And the sound was all noise to some of us teenagers. Or so we said.

Then I was struck by a brilliant plan. What sounded like chimes was actually a CD playing on a timer. Wouldn't it be hilarious if we switched out the chimes disc for some better music, something in the rock category, something with a beat?

In my defense, the scheme did sound hilarious at the time.

Once the idea was birthed, Trisha and I needed only to choose the replacement song. We giggled for days, pouring over possibilities, imagining song after song traveling through the airwaves and into surrounding houses. Finally, we settled on a rock collection, and we decided to pick a random number and let fate have the final say on the song selection.

"I don't think we should really do it. What if we get caught?"

As if on cue, Trisha regularly voiced an objection before any plan was actually carried out. Her objection was as much a ritual as having me override it.

"We're not going to get caught."

Famous last words.

We snuck into the church annex on Saturday evening, after the chimes played both times for the day, and set things up for the next morning. In our own minds, we took every precaution. No one saw us enter the church. Once inside, Trisha was the lookout while I quickly made the music switch. We tiptoed out the back door and safely away.

There was one slight flaw in our plan, but we didn't realize the problem at the time. To get into town in the first place, we tagged along with Daddy. Claiming we needed some makeup, we had him drop us off in front of the drug store and promised to walk on up to the barber shop to meet him when we were finished. The combination of means, motive, and opportunity had convicted less guilty criminals and would soon lower the hammer on us.

The next morning, I was ready for church early.

"I don't know what's caused this desire to get to church without me hollering at you to get ready, but I won't look a gift horse," Momma commented.

"Just anxious to worship the Lord."

And I thought I was being so smooth.

The timing couldn't have been more perfect—or deadly. Daddy pulled his truck into the church parking lot and opened the door at the exact moment the chimes began blaring out the introduction to one of rock's greatest classics.

Momma wasted no time whirling around on me. I could see the gears turning in her mind as she clicked together my unflattering comments about the chimes, my unscheduled trip to town yesterday, and the contents of my music collection.

I might have carried it off had I not tried to look innocent in my own defense. My attempt at a blank expression served only to convict me more.

Momma reached across and quickly grabbed my arm in a vise grip. Cars had been towed with less force.

Daddy was my saving grace. By then he was grinning from ear to ear, leaning his head back in the truck window as he set his cap on the dashboard. The moment church let out and he climbed back in the truck, he would return it firmly atop his head.

"Now, Rayetta." His tone of voice was calm and measured as he addressed Momma, as if reasoning with a bull ready to charge. "You don't have no proof against her. Besides, if there's nothing wrong with hearing this music at home, there's nothing wrong with hearing the same thing at church."

"Don't you Rayetta me, Earl Henderson. I won't

have my daughter mocking the church. This is a shame and disgrace. What will the ladies in my class say?"

"They won't say nothing. They won't know nothing less you tell them."

Momma froze in place as she carefully weighed the options in her mind. Throw a loud scene everyone at church could see. Or bluff things out and take a chance the plan might work. And Momma could pretend. Had she chosen the stage, she would have been famous. A great, award-winning actress. Momma lived in her own little world. If she could pretend everything was fine, then it was.

"This is not over, young lady."

I invited myself home from church with MawMaw for the afternoon. A strategic move that worked brilliantly. Momma never mentioned the chime incident again.

I never got my CD back either.

∂

Youth camp the summer after tenth grade. The first great love of my young life jumped out of the back of a big, yellow converted school bus and onto the mountain land of Fall Creek Falls State Park.

Suddenly, fireworks exploded in my world, brightly-colored sparks shooting into the galaxy, signaling an event of epic importance. I didn't recall actually hearing angels sing, but I couldn't say they didn't either.

What I did remember was a halo appearing around the head of a tall, lanky, golden-haired dreamboat who instantly clicked into place as the man of my dreams. Skeptics might point out the halo was actually rays of the sun glowing behind him. Not me. In my heart of hearts, I knew he had a halo. Dozens of romantic movies had prepared me to recognize the magical moment.

Time stood still. I was frozen in my tracks, even though I sensed the activity of others nearby. For whatever length of time I could hold my breath, I held it.

The park's claim to fame might have been as the highest waterfalls east of the Rocky Mountains. But to me, the most interesting part of my week stood right in front of me.

On its own, church camp was a glorious adventure. A whole week with my friends, away from parental supervision, roaming around together, sharing inside jokes, staying up late and giggling. Although we were mere miles away from town, and in fact, still in our home county, the group camp at the park was a magical world away from our daily lives. Swimming, hiking, boating, golf, and horseback riding awaited us.

As the host church, we arrived on Sunday afternoon and conducted evening services there, since the park was near enough for the rest of the church to drive out to attend. On Monday morning, buses and vans began arriving, carrying teens from a few other churches to join us for the rest of the week.

My dream man stretched his arms up to the sky and opened his mouth for a huge yawn, revealing a gleaming set of silver braces. An easy grin settled on his face as he glanced around, taking in his surroundings.

An eternity must have passed before his eyes settled on me.

"Hey."

"Hey," I replied.

"I'm Chad."

"Katie Anne."

I was enraptured. He had spoken. See, he wasn't only a pretty face, he could speak, too. And he seemed to be staring at me with the same intensity I was staring at him.

Just then, an unwelcome voice burst into our private communication.

"Get out of the way, will you? We gotta unload all this stuff."

A head poked out of the back of the bus, and I thought I must be seeing things. This burst of passion had addled my brain. The head was identical to my dream man's head.

Twins?

"He's Chase. We're twins. Don't get too far away, Katie Anne. I'll catch up with you later."

To my delight, he kept his promise. We were inseparable the rest of the week. In the way of teenagers, too inexperienced to guard their hearts against certain disaster ahead, we shared our deepest secrets in stolen moments away from the prying eyes of camp counselors.

It was the summer after we lost Daddy, and my young heart remained bruised and tender. Chad was exactly what I needed to convince me my life still offered beauty and promise.

We snuck away for long walks, clutching sweaty hands in the sweltering heat. We ate together in the mess hall, sharing meals of hot dogs and spaghetti. We sat side-by-side on the long, hard benches in chapel, singing silly camp songs and halfway listening to the preaching while trading furtive glances with each other.

Back in my cabin at night, I suddenly transformed into the girl the other girls wanted to know all the details from. What did he say? What did I do? Had he tried to kiss me? What was I going to do if he did?

Teenage girls being teenage girls, a little jealousy crept in, too.

"Chad's ears stick out too much for me."

"I don't want to kiss a boy with braces anyway."

"I think his brother is cuter."

"The girls from his church say his family is dirt poor."

Ordinarily, I would have slapped somebody silly over any one of the insults. The fact that I let their petty comments sail over my head stood as a testament to the depths of my devotion.

The days quickly blended into each other, and before I realized, Friday descended upon us. Tradition dictated a bit of mischief on the final night of camp. Counselors eased up a little on the rules, and campers resolved to get away with as much as they could.

Naturally a bit of a drama queen, I was genuinely bereft at the thought of being torn away from my true love the next day. I persuaded Chad to meet me at the stroke of midnight on the path to the golf course. His unwillingness to so boldly break the rules was overcome by my heartfelt pleas.

The distance of years clearly illuminated the foolhardiness of our actions. Besides the obvious problem of having a hundred teenagers run wild in pitch dark over thousands of acres of forestland, the mountain was known for the danger of snakes slithering freely. But we knew nothing bad could happen to us. We would live forever.

We raced to the ninth hole and removed the flag to take back to camp as proof of our adventure. I was winded and already breathing heavily when it happened. Chad leaned down and angled his face toward mine. Moist lips covered my own. His arms wound around me in a tender embrace.

I would have remained in the position forever had we not been suddenly interrupted by shouted whispers.

"Hurry up! Hurry up!"

Approaching from behind me were Trisha and another girl from our cabin, Stephanie. Knowing Trisha broke a rule without my prodding clearly convinced me of the great urgency of the situation. To get caught meant getting sent home in disgrace. Trisha wouldn't take the risk without an extremely good reason.

"They're doing bed check. We told them you were in the bathhouse. Come on!"

Our romantic spell broken, we took off at top speed, splitting up at the edge of the group camp. The girls ran to our cabin, and Chad continued to the boys' area. I was buried under the covers and feigning sleep by the time counselors returned.

The next morning, we learned Chad was never even reported missed. After being spotted in his own bed, Chase snuck over to Chad's bed before his cabin check was performed. Counselors never knew the difference. Oh, if only I had a twin, too.

Chad's bus pulled out early the next morning with no chance for us to have any privacy again. He leaned out the window as he left, his sad eyes locked onto mine as tears rolled down my cheeks. My heartbreak was complete. I was certain I would never love again.

I relived our sweet kiss a million times in the coming days. Even as an adult, occasionally I passed a golf course and a tiny tug on my heart brought back a faded but treasured memory.

Chad and I exchanged a few letters, each one taking a little longer for a reply, until the romance died a natural death. In the way of life going on, the appearance in eleventh grade of Bradley Williams, another tall, lanky, sandy-haired boy, greatly eased my sorrow.

ஃ

"So, it doesn't sound as if all of your experiences with this church were bad ones, does it?" Lainey asked.

Although my mind filled in many more details, until Lainey's comment I wasn't fully aware I was recounting bits of memories out loud. Apparently too many.

"I guess not." I tried to keep a note of wonder out of my voice at the mere possibility.

Quickly trying to turn the conversation down a less sentimental path, I pointed to a small, scraggly patch of grass.

"Here's something I remember. Right here off to the side of the fellowship hall entrance is where all the smokers did their fellowshipping between Sunday school and church. If they hurried, they had time for one cigarette between the services. It tore the preacher up, seeing the smokers file in, one right after the other, right before the choir came out. He could hardly stand it, but he had no choice.

"No matter how much preaching he did against the evils of tobacco, nothing changed. Of course, some of the people in the pews had done the hard work of harvesting tobacco at some point in their lives. The cash crop put actual cash in the offering plate. Somebody finally gave in and put a big, plastic urn out here, so at least the cigarette butts wouldn't be scattered all over the parking lot.

"Whenever it rained, they were forced to smoke in the bathrooms. You could smell the smoke across the whole church. Of course, it did provide a fitting environment for a fiery sermon on hell."

What I didn't tell Lainey was how easily the teenagers could sneak a smoke under the circumstances. With a group of adults smoking, nobody could tell if our smoke was firsthand or secondhand.

"Looks like times have changed," Lainey pointed out. "There's no urn out here, and I don't see any cigarette butts either. Perhaps the old reverend finally got through."

Once inside the church, I stopped a minute to look at the names engraved on the plaque hanging on the foyer wall, names of people who founded the church over fifty years ago. I read down part of the charter member list.

Saints with a vision. Most of them passed on now. I had known all of them well. All except Mr. Ken. My memories of him were faint, but anybody who attended the church eventually heard his story from the pulpit. Mr. Ken was so faithful to attend every service that one Wednesday night when he didn't show up on time, some men of the church went looking for him. They took for granted if he wasn't at church, something was terribly wrong. It was. They found him at home, felled by a stroke. Talk about faithful. I was certain I could never live up to the ideal.

"Any more memories?" Lainey's question broke into my thoughts.

"A million. But most of them end with me getting caught in my latest escapade and facing the wrath of Momma."

"Those are the ones I want to hear. I'll have something else to hang over your head."

"Thank you so much, but I don't think you need any more than you've already got."

Passing the Sunday school classroom for teens triggered a recollection of the night we attended a sleepover at our teacher's house and toilet-papered the house across the street. I had a broken leg at the time so I was running in a cast, but I managed to keep up with the rest of the hooligans. Once again, were so clueless we thought we could deny a guilt so obvious to everyone else.

Our prank phone calls were another riot in our own minds. All routine child's play, but we thought we invented every scam ourselves.

And then there was the time we decided to climb the steeple. The only access is from the roof itself. Come to think, that was how I broke my leg.

But I had stalled long enough. Might as well get my punishment behind me.

Taking a deep breath, I opened the door leading directly into the fellowship hall. Although I was still crossing my fingers to get in, pick up the food, and get back out without encountering anyone else, I knew it was a long shot.

Even while I pulled the door open from the outside, a hand pushed it open from the inside.

Busted.

❧ CHAPTER 23 ❦

"Here you are, dear."

Old Miss Hilda Stephens appeared in the doorway, her face nearly nose to nose with mine, except she stood a couple of inches shorter than I was. And when I said nose, I meant a huge honker, looking out of place on the rest of her little apple-shaped body. The way she squinted at me, she could have used a pair of thick glasses resting atop her large nose. No offense.

Instinctively, I took a step backward, nearly toppling over Lainey who was following close behind me. I regained my balance, but Miss Hilda didn't seem to notice my misstep as she began welcoming us.

"You girls come on in here now. I've been keeping a lookout for you, Katie Anne. Brother Carl told me he hoped to have a few words with you when you stopped by."

Another one of Momma's plans neatly coming together. Even though I had expected no less, I was rendered speechless. A rare occasion to be sure.

My reaction didn't phase Miss Hilda. She had presided over the comings and goings of this congregation for years, since her former church down the valley split over which groups would be allowed to use their fellowship hall. Miss Hilda was determined under her benevolent guidance the same type of tragedy wouldn't happen here.

She also served as the church's secretary, as firmly entrenched as she was marginally competent. Years ago, there weren't many ways to get to Brother Carl without going through her, and apparently the situation hadn't changed.

"I'll help your friend here get this food loaded up while you go on up and see Brother Carl. He's in his study. Just tap on the door," Miss Hilda instructed. "And take as long as you want, we'll be fine together."

Confident she had me headed in the right direction, she dismissed me and focused all her attention on Lainey. Taking my friend by the arm, Miss Hilda led her over to a table laden with cakes, pies, and other desserts.

"The ladies have been carrying in sweets all morning, one after the other. They'll mostly be at the benefit, but it helps to know beforehand what you've got to work with. I wrote their names down on this sheet of paper so the family could have it. We always do it that way. Makes it easier when they're writing the thank you notes. Organization is so very important. I fixed the angel food cake in the blue pan. I love my sweets, but I'm having to cut way back since the doctor diagnosed me with the sugar diabetes. It runs in my family. Now, who are you?"

Lainey was in good hands with Miss Hilda. I headed up the back steps and into the lion's den.

ॐ

I confidently assumed Momma had effectively primed Brother Carl to deliver a one-on-one sermon tailored specifically to the audience of me. The proverbial three points and a poem. Points one through three would be focused on getting me back into church on a regular, three-service-per-week basis. The only question remaining was how he would tie in the poem. But Brother Carl possessed more than adequate oratory skills. I was certain he would rise to the challenge with great expertise.

Entering the cramped, wood-paneled secretary's office, I curiously took in my surroundings. The office doubled as Sunday school headquarters and a mini copy center, too. Shelves lining the walls overflowed with lesson books for each age division, as well as instructional books on producing plays, putting on puppet shows, and learning sign language. Desks and chairs fought copiers and filing cabinets for space.

A computer sat on what I assumed to be Miss Hilda's desk. The equipment was actually turned on. Had I misjudged Miss Hilda's competence? After all, jumping to conclusions was my favorite exercise.

On the wall nearest the entrance were graphs charting the year's attendance ups and downs. Mostly ups. Members of the flock were fairly consistent in their faithful attendance. Where space permitted, timeless maps of the Holy Land, the Children of Israel's route through the desert, and Paul's missionary journeys hung slightly askew, their edges curled up with age.

What I could see of the floor revealed the same square tile that lined the floors of the rest of the building in a hideous yellow-green I doubted would ever come back in style. Everywhere but the sanctuary. Green carpet had covered the floor in there as long as I could remember, and I couldn't imagine it changing.

Before I had time to make more than a cursory look around the room, I heard a chair squeak in the adjoining office. The heavy clomp of footsteps let me know my time was about up. I was strapped into the electric chair and the prison warden's hand was reaching for the switch. I inhaled a deep breath and prepared to meet my fate with dignity.

"Hey there, Katie Anne."

Brother Carl greeted me with a wide smile and out-stretched hand. I've never known a preacher who didn't want to shake hands first thing when they saw you. Apparently the practice was stressed in seminary classes.

We both showed signs of having aged in the inter-vening years. His slightly bulging midsection gave evidence of a sedentary lifestyle, while his receding hairline was a testament to his mother's genetics. Overall, time had been kind to him, failing to dim the bright blue eyes topped by long lashes his female parishioners must envy. A strong jaw line shouted, "You can trust me."

Dressed in khakis and a short-sleeve, button-up shirt, Brother Carl projected a neat, clean image from head to toe.

Vainly, I hoped my appearance held up as well under his scrutiny.

"I'm glad you could come by," he said after I returned his initial greeting. "Your mother said she would pass along my invitation to talk a few minutes if you found time during the day. I know things are busy, and I'm sure your family is glad you were able to come home and help out."

Family loyalty kept me from ratting out Momma to her preacher. I would hardly call her sneaky maneuvering to get me here an invitation. However, it did accomplish the same purpose in the end, so points to Momma in this round. Undoubtedly, I would come up with something in the not-too-distant future to even the score.

As he continued talking, Brother Carl ushered me into the back office.

"Miss Hilda volunteered to come in today and help with the food. I told your mother if no one from the family got time to come by, I would deliver what people dropped off here over at the school."

He was digging Momma's hole deeper and didn't even know it. But I did.

"How kind of you, Brother Carl, but I brought along a friend downstairs to help me. In fact, she and Miss Hilda are loading up the car now. Actually, I have only a couple of minutes to spare."

Good thinking, I congratulated myself. Plan an escape route as soon as possible. I knew how the game was played. I had been taken to the woodshed before. The goal was merely to get the encounter over with and move on. Minimize the casualties as much as possible.

"Well, take a seat anyway, Katie Anne. I'll try not to hold you too long. I'm sure Miss Hilda can keep your friend occupied while we chat."

Brother Carl grinned back at me. Maybe I wasn't as slick as I thought. It seemed he'd played the game before, too.

He motioned me to sit down in one of two blue wingback chairs facing a wide mahogany desk that dominated the room. An attached station supported a computer and printer. His office's décor was decidedly more modern and attractive than in the outer office. Painted a light eggshell blue, the walls were enhanced by white crown molding and chair rail. An attractive set of shelving behind me displayed an array of books in a wide variety of sizes, although I sat too far away to read any of the titles. A window to my left overlooked the parking lot and basketball goal.

Overall, a comfortable office set up for administrative work or pastoral counseling, whichever was called for at a specific time. In my humble opinion, whoever decorated in here needed to be given free reign over the secretary's space, too.

Brother Carl noticed me looking around appreciatively.

"All my wife's doing. I can't match black pants with black shoes, so she's in charge of all the color coordinating in the family. You know how I can tell she's got good taste, don't you?"

"She married you."

"Right answer."

My attention was drawn to a large painting on the wall behind the desk which depicted Jesus as the Good Shepherd of the flock, lovingly gathering up His lambs in His arms. The trusting animals looked so safe and peaceful.

"The subject of that picture is kind of what I want to talk to you about, Katie Anne." Brother Carl rolled his desk chair sideways so he could still see both me and the painting. "This picture means a lot to me. Every time I look at it, I'm reminded of the Good Shepherd and how He watches over His sheep. I'm reminded of the flock God has entrusted to me, for me to care for as lovingly and protectively as He does."

His statement puzzled me. I didn't know where he was going with this. Well, I still thought I knew where he wanted to end up, but I certainly didn't know how he planned to get there from here.

"Katie Anne, I want to apologize to you."

What? Back this train up. The pastor of the church wanted to apologize to me? Somewhere between Momma telling him to give me a lecture on getting back in church and him relaying the message on to me, Brother Carl had gotten off track. Way off track. Preachers did not apologize to regular people—even when they needed to. Some kind of preacher rule, written in stone along with the Ten Commandments. I had never heard of the rule being broken before, much less seen it happen in person.

"I did a great disservice to you when you left this church, Katie Anne. I let you go without a word. I was the undershepherd God placed in your life, to help protect you and guide you and keep you safe. I failed in my duty, and I have asked God to forgive me. I'm asking you to forgive me, too."

Brother Carl turned his chair around and looked me straight in the eyes as he delivered the surprising words, his expression one of genuine regret. I had no doubt of his sincerity.

After a moment of silent disbelief, my manners kicked in, and I automatically attempted to deny the meaning behind what he said.

"I don't know what you're talking about. You don't have any reason to apologize to me…"

"Yes, I certainly do. And I know I do. I put all my focus on trying to help Trisha's family, and I ignored you and what you were going through at the time." Brother Carl paused to run a hand through his thinning dark hair. "Oh, I rationalized my actions quite well. Trisha's parents and brothers were my immediate concern, so I was doing the right thing by doing all I could for them."

He continued, "It didn't help that I've always been

awkward with teenagers."

I stuttered out the beginning of another protest. How had I ever thought Brother Carl was clueless?

Instead, he put up a hand to cut me off.

"Don't try to deny it. It's one of my real weaknesses as a pastor. Fortunately, since then we've been able to bring a youth pastor on staff. He helps fill in the gap now. I know it doesn't help you or change what you've been through. With you, the truth is I was plain old chicken. You were a pretty intimidating teenager to deal with."

"I know," I moaned, feeling lower than a sinkhole. "I was rotten."

Brother Carl smiled. "I think the politically correct description is mischievous. The truth is, I was a young man when I came here. I had only been at one other church for a short time before coming to Pikeville. I was well aware some of the congregation thought I was too young and inexperienced to be their pastor. I immediately set out to prove them wrong by taking a tough stance on everything. I started out so full of myself, it's taken these years of God working with me to make me realize how big the love of God is and to start to understand the magnitude of His forgiveness. Only now do I think I have some idea of what being a good shepherd is."

"I don't know what to say."

"You don't need to say anything, but what I'd like to hear you say is you forgive me."

"I forgive you." I automatically repeated the words.

"Thank you. I know it doesn't change the past and I know you live somewhere else now, but I still care about you and want you to know I'm here for you at any time. Our God is the God of forgiveness, the God of second chances."

The words sounded extremely familiar. In fact, I'd

heard them earlier in the day.

"Have you been talking to Harmon Suggs?"

Brother Carl responded, "You know I'd never repeat a conversation with anyone else. The same as I won't repeat anything you've said to me. Everything is strictly confidential."

"I'm sorry I asked." My mind swirled in such a jumbled mess, I seemed capable of speaking only one short sentence at a time.

"Unfortunately, you're not the first person God has nudged me to apologize to when I failed a member of my flock. I have learned over the years the Bible tells us not only to speak the truth, but to speak the truth in love. Without adding the love, speaking the truth can be a dangerous thing."

"I don't think I understand, Brother Carl."

As anxious as I was to quickly flee the confines of Brother Carl's office, my curiosity overcame my better judgment.

"When I first arrived at this church, when you were growing up, I preached God as a God of fire and brimstone. That in itself isn't wrong. Judgment Day awaits us all. We'll all stand before God someday, every person who ever lived, and give an account of our lives. The Bible is plain on that particular point. So I wanted to get people into the family of God any way I could. To spur them into action, into repentance, even if only out of fear of spending eternity in the fiery pits of hell."

"You sure scared me as a kid," I agreed.

So many nights of my childhood, as I lay in bed gazing at a sliver of light shining into my room, I relived the scary words of his sermons. The person who described the man who "preached hell so hot that you could feel the heat" described Brother Carl perfectly. And when the smokers snuck cigarettes in the bathrooms, I could even smell the fire.

From behind an ordinary wooden pulpit, Brother Carl made me believe the flames were licking at my feet and demons were cackling my name. In a dramatic illustration, his voice rose from a whisper to a thunder and hit every emotion in between. Those occasions certainly kept the congregation awake.

The only remedy was to walk the aisle and repent.

Then there were his warnings about the rapture and the seven seals and all the other events of Revelation. The seven years. The hundred and forty-four thousand. For a while back there, Brother Carl attempted to unlock all the mysteries of the final book of the Bible.

All the warnings accomplished for me was to convey the fear that somehow when Jesus came back for His people, He could forget a little kid like me. An easy oversight no one would blame Him for. Any time I looked around in a store and couldn't find Momma, I suffered through blinding panic until I spotted her again.

Brother Carl wasn't finished yet.

"But looking back, I can see I focused too much on the wrath of God and not enough on His love. I preached what I knew, what I grew up hearing. Do what's right and God is happy with you. Do what's wrong, and He'll reach down and knock you over the head with a hammer. It's not true at all. God always wants the pure best for His children. It was my own understanding of God that was lacking."

Was I hearing what I thought I was hearing? Or had I entered my parallel universe once again? The one in which everyone acted the opposite of how I expected them to behave?

"It's all a question of balance," he said. "Everything

I preached was the truth. But it needed to be balanced out by the tremendous love of God. The love is the main thing. Without the love, the rest of it has no meaning."

As Brother Carl finished speaking, he shook his head, as if only then realizing a mini-sermon just tumbled out of his mouth.

"Well, I promised not to hold you too long." He rose from his chair to indicate my release. "Let's pray together before you leave."

Without waiting for agreement, he bowed his head and uttered a short but heartfelt prayer.

As soon as he spoke the word amen, I began moving toward the door, but he held up a hand to delay my departure. For the first time, I recognized uncertainty in his demeanor.

"Katie Anne, maybe I ought to leave things as they are, but I'm going to rely on God's instruction to 'speak the truth in love' right now. I realize I don't know a whole lot about your current life, but nobody can go forward in life by looking back. If there's any part of you still locked in the past, I encourage you to deal with it. You can't move on until you do. If you need to go back to the Blue Hole to do it, I'll go with you anytime."

"Thanks. I'll think about it."

I knew I was lying right there in church, and as a result, expected to be struck dead at any moment. We were only in the office, but it still counted as church. Nothing short of twelve wild stallions could drag me back to the Blue Hole.

Besides, tonight's benefit was my top priority. There would be plenty of time to figure out all the other stuff later. No sense in mixing the concrete until you were ready to set the posts.

The Blue Hole

Around the campfire at the Blue Hole, Zeb began strumming the guitar he brought with him. Wherever he was, his beat-up, red acoustic guitar was usually nearby.

A loud chord ignited action from a couple of the other boys, who jumped to their feet to accompany Zeb on air guitar. One of them, Hayden, had clearly already surpassed his limit on alcohol, whether beer or something stronger. He staggered around until he tripped and went sprawling on the hard ground. The others ignored him, confident he'd recover by the time we got ready to leave.

Wayne offered me a roasting stick with the end whittled off to a nice, sharp point. I accepted the piece of wood and stuck on a hot dog before laying it over a hot spot in the crackling fire. The flames licked inches under the meat, quickly browning the outside.

I wasn't hungry, but some food would help balance out the beer on my stomach.

Zeb settled down and picked the opening strains to

an old song we all knew. Zeb's specialty was the honky-tonk favorites of years ago. He knew every Hank Williams, Sr. tune and loved to play them. No matter how much we begged or booed, he rarely budged. Occasionally, he gave in and humored us with a current song, but not often. As a result, we all knew the old songs, too.

Some of us tried to sing well, and others tried to sing loud. The loud ones won every time.

Before we knew it, we had sung every song we could think of twice, and yawns were openly acknowledged. Midnight was shortly upon us. I needed to get home, and so did the rest of the group.

I wandered over to where Hayden still lay on the ground and gently nudged him with my foot.

"Let's go, Sleeping Beauty."

"Help me get him to the truck," Wayne said to nobody in particular. Brad ambled over and reached down for an arm. Together the two struggled to get Hayden to his feet.

Apparently I was on my own getting back to the makeshift parking lot.

I looked around for Trisha and spotted her and Jesse sitting on a huge boulder about halfway up the side of the Blue Hole. I began walking in their direction, sticking within a few yards of the pit's edge where little vegetation grew to trip me up.

"Hey, ready to go?" I asked.

Trisha gazed up at me.

❧ CHAPTER 25 ❧

Lainey and I arrived back at Momma's house to a whirlwind of activity. Elijah may have been taken up into the air with less commotion, flaming chariot and all. A veritable parade of ladies, some I recognized and some I didn't, scurried in and out of the back door hauling armloads of food, baskets, utensils, linens, and more.

The sheer quantity of vehicles in the driveway prevented me from turning in, so I pulled the car to the shoulder in front of the house and out of the way.

In spite of the activity, Momma was obviously keeping an eye out for our return. As Lainey and I neared the back door, Momma's head was visible through the kitchen windows, framed on either side by curtains bearing an intricate magnolia design. Her piercing green eyes stared straight at me, probably trying to determine my mood from my demeanor to figure out how much trouble she faced.

No doubt the little schemer was anxious to investigate the results of her latest setup job. I was sure Brother Carl didn't deliver quite the message Momma expected him to, but I still believed she was the one behind the visit. However, the whole situation required more in-depth thinking to figure everything out, and I didn't have time yet.

A couple of possibilities rolled around in my mind.

One, as I originally thought, Momma strong-armed Brother Carl into sitting me down and giving me a good lecture about church attendance and how even though occupying a pew didn't get you into heaven, it let other people know you were on your way. Then he double-crossed her by unexpectedly baring his own soul and relating to me as if he were a regular person and I was, too. I'm sure she never imagined that particular scenario while considering the possible outcomes.

Two, Momma's only involvement was supposed to be Brother Carl asking her to tell me he wanted to see me. But she decided maneuvering me into going to the church was a better strategy than telling me the truth outright. Knowing Momma, that possibility was also conceivable. After all, manipulation was her favorite hobby.

I knew she itched to learn every scrap of information about my discussion with Brother Carl she could, in any way she could. Unwilling to allow her the satisfaction, I would never comply. After all, evading her questions was my favorite hobby.

We were quite a pair.

After holding the screen door open for a woman whose arms were loaded down with paper plates and cups, I motioned Lainey to enter the house first.

Momma did the expected and hurried over to us, leaving the other ladies to wait for instructions.

"You're back. How did things at the church go?"

Her eyes searched my face for a sign of any small detail she could pick up. Anything as a clue. I didn't oblige. Instead, I purposely set my face to register blank on the Momma scale.

"You tell her all about it, Lainey. I'm going to run in and get a clip for my hair. It keeps falling down in my face."

As proof, I slung my head back at the same time I lifted a hand to brush a stray strand of hair out of my eyes.

At that precise moment, a honk sounded from the driveway, drawing Momma's attention outside and away from me.

"I'd better see what that is. You get done whatever you need to, Katie Anne. We've got about forty-five minutes before we need to leave for the school. And I'll want you to pick up your MawMaw on the way. Lainey can go with me and help me if she don't care to."

&

The first thing I noticed at MawMaw's big white farmhouse was the green mailbox with sticky white letters spelling out the name McReynolds. The box sat atop a weathered wooden fence post out where the yard met the road. The mailbox door stood open, mail spilling out onto the side of the empty road. The mixture of envelopes and colorful sale circulars immediately caught my eye and alerted my senses something wasn't right.

The mail carrier on MawMaw's route, Mr. Calvin, was as punctual as a clock, as punctual as he was old. Maybe because MawMaw and her cronies kept an eye on him six days a week, fifty-two weeks a year. Mail delivery was the means some of them use to time their daily schedules, and woe be to Mr. Calvin if he deviated more than speck from the routine, government check day or not. But especially government check day. The ladies plotted careful track of his progress by telephone. The first report came early in the day at the beginning of the mail route. By the time of the second phone call, MawMaw could predict within a narrow window what time her mail would arrive.

Rather than make an extra trip to the post office in town, MawMaw preferred to leave her outgoing mail in the box for Mr. Calvin to pick up. When she needed stamps, she left money to cover the expense and raised the little red flag as notice to him.

Each day, as soon as MawMaw spotted the mail carrier's old navy blue sedan approaching, Mr. Calvin straddling the seat to work the steering wheel and pedals with his left side and stuff the mail into the boxes with his right, she was down the front steps and into the yard.

I couldn't imagine MawMaw leaving her mail scattered on the ground without a good reason. My mind quickly threw out a number of possibilities, but I couldn't call any of them good. The scenarios spanned from reasonable explanations to ridiculous fantasies.

Maybe right when MawMaw stuck her hand in the mailbox, she heard the phone in the house ring so she abandoned the mail to answer it...

Maybe a wasp looking for a new home crawled in the mailbox and stung an unsuspecting MawMaw when she opened the little door...

Maybe Mr. Calvin finally popped the question to MawMaw and they've eloped to Las Vegas for a quickie wedding...

The possibilities scrambled wildly through my

unsettled mind while I quickly parked my car and got out, racing across the yard and then bounding up the wooden steps two at a time.

"MawMaw! MawMaw! Where are you?" I shouted.

No answer.

The massive pocket doors to both the parlor on the left and dining room on the right were open. No sign of MawMaw in either one.

I dashed down the hall to check the kitchen and bedroom. As I neared the bedroom, I heard a noise. I cracked the door open.

"I said I'm in here, honey."

Relief flooded over me. My nerves were racing faster than a prison escapee trying to outrun a bloodhound. MawMaw looked up at me from a prone position atop the double bed she occupied every night of her adult life, first with PawPaw and then without. But I had never seen her in bed during the daytime. She was fully dressed, stretched out on top of the same double wedding ring quilt that had covered her bed as long as I could remember. Seeing her resting during the day was a new and unsettling experience.

"MawMaw, are you all right?" I leaned over her, searching her face for clues.

"I'll be all right. I laid down for a few minutes. Is it time to go already? I declare, I'm getting sorrier and sorrier all the time. I don't mean to hold you up none."

"You're not holding me up, MawMaw, but I do want you to tell me what happened."

Her skin appeared a pallid white, and her breathing sounded labored. She lifted her head for a moment before gently easing back down.

Why, oh why, didn't I go into nursing when Momma

encouraged me to? I should be taking MawMaw's blood pressure or something. Please, God, I'll do whatever Momma wants me to do from now on.

"I'm an old woman, that's what happened."

"Tell me, MawMaw."

She quickly recognized the determination in my face and reached the correct conclusion. I would not let this episode slide. An explanation, if nothing else, was demanded.

"When I first got up this morning, I felt a little light-headed, but I put it out of my mind and went on about my business. After me and your uncle Cooper eat lunch, he headed on over to Terry Merriman's farm to help him pull a calf. He asked me if I needed him to come back home and carry me to the benefit, but I said no, your momma said she'd send you over. I didn't tell him nothing about how I was feeling or he would have made too much of it. After he left, I piddled around in the kitchen, watching for Mr. Calvin to come by carrying the mail. My Social Security check should be here today or Monday."

As soon as the realization hit that she lay in bed while her Social Security check went unguarded in the front yard, MawMaw sat straight up.

"Lands, my check!"

I caught her as she swung her legs over the side, preparing to stand.

"Hold up, cowgirl. If your check was fine a minute ago, it's still fine. I'll go out and look as soon as you finish telling me what happened."

MawMaw glared at me.

I glared back.

She broke first.

"When Mr. Calvin pulled up in the yard, I started out

the front door. I got to the mailbox. I saw his car pull away."

MawMaw quit talking and looked down at the floor, as if searching for a trap door to magically open and allow her to escape my questioning.

"Then what?"

"Then nothing."

"What do you mean nothing?"

"I mean it's the last I can remember real clear. I believe I opened the mailbox, but my mind's kind of fuzzy from then on."

Her right hand lay on the colorful homemade quilt, a hand weathered by hard work and unadorned by jewelry. I reached down and cradled it in my own hands before carefully examining her face, relying on the little medical information I possessed. No obvious signs of a stroke, her complexion color was improving, and she was talking as sensibly as ever.

What should I do?

My first choice was to have her seen by a physician, but this time on a Saturday afternoon meant a lengthy emergency room visit. I could call the county ambulance service for transport. Either of these suggestions would bring on an uphill battle from MawMaw.

She stared up at me, fully aware of the thoughts running through my mind.

"Katie Anne, this little episode ain't worth mentioning to nobody else. To talk about this would mean stirring things up. There's no need in it and no time for it."

"But MawMaw…"

"I mean it. Not a word to nobody. Tonight is for your aunt Lora Anne. I'm fine now. I reckon all this flurrying around got a mite too much for this old woman. But I've rested, and I'll be good as ever once I get up and stir about some. It won't take but a few minutes to get situated and ready to go. You can help me all you want to."

MawMaw's decision stood firm. My advice was both unwanted and unwelcome.

"But MawMaw…"

"I'll jerk my good clothes on right quick. You get on out there in the yard and hunt my Social Security check."

෫

Uncle Cooper arrived back at the house at the same time I was carrying in the mail. Fortunately, MawMaw's check was the first piece of mail I found. The envelope lay upside down on the sidewalk below the front steps. Evidently, the check was the last item she dropped. Even partially incapacitated, MawMaw must have clutched the precious check as long as she could.

The amount of the check wasn't great, I knew, but the relatively small bit of money each month saved MawMaw from being dependent on her children. That fact alone made the check almost priceless in her way of thinking. Uncle Cooper chipped in his fair share and more when he could sneak some extra cash in to the household budget without her noticing. He was forced to be creative, because MawMaw wasn't keen on losing any of her independence.

"You bringing in the mail, Katie Anne? How come your mawmaw didn't already get it? She generally meets Mr. Calvin at the road. Is everything all right?"

"She's inside getting ready to go." I could tell the technical truth as well as Momma. I just wasn't sure if the talent was a good quality to possess or not.

"I told her I'd carry her over with me in the truck."

"I know, but I wanted to spend the time with her anyway."

Uncle Cooper accepted my glossing over of the truth without question.

"In that case, I'm going on to the barn to feed before I get cleaned up, and I'll be over later on."

"Don't worry about MawMaw. I'll see she gets to and from the benefit tonight so you can concentrate on one of your other women."

I couldn't resist teasing my favorite uncle, but my comment didn't get a rise out of him. Like the rest of us, he had other things on his mind. He started around the corner of the house on the worn path leading out to the barn.

When I returned inside, MawMaw was leaned up against the railing of the stairway. I knew what she wanted and didn't make her wait.

"Right here's your check, MawMaw."

She quickly snatched the valuable envelope from my hand and headed back toward her bedroom.

"I'll put this up in a safe place till I can get to the bank."

"MawMaw, why don't you have your check direct deposited in the bank each month so you don't have to worry about it? That way you'll know you've got money available on the same day every month."

"Don't you start in on me too, Katie Anne. It's all I hear nowadays. I don't trust them computers to make sure my money comes on time. If I put the check in the bank myself, I know it's there."

To tell MawMaw a computer wrote the check she was holding in the first place would go nowhere fast, so I saved my breath and moved on to another hopeless topic as I followed her down the wide hall to her room.

"What do you say we give Tara a call and let her stop by here and check you out before we go on to the benefit? Let her look you over and take your blood pressure as a precaution."

Tara was the oldest of my aunt Patty Lynn's six children and sister to my cut-up cousin Drew. She was also a registered nurse at the county hospital. MawMaw held great regard for her medical skills, and Uncle Cooper often referred to her as "the best doctor I know." Tara would be here on the run if she thought she were needed.

"There's no point. I had me a little spell, and now it's over. I told you not to say another word about it, and I mean what I say."

She did. If ever anything was true about MawMaw, it was that she meant what she said And so I dropped the subject with a firm promise to myself to keep a good eye on her all evening. At the first sign of any tiny problem, MawMaw would be forced to accept medical treatment, like it or not. I would rat her out in a second if necessary for her health, but perhaps it wouldn't be necessary.

❧ CHAPTER 26 ❦

A volunteer dressed in a bright orange vest and holding a giant flashlight waved me into the parking lot at the high school. I made the left turn as directed, and another flash of color fastened my attention on a man up ahead who motioned me to pull my car into a specific spot.

Members of the county rescue squad routinely handled parking duties at local events, a pleasant change of pace from their normal chores of extracting victims at wrecks, and trudging through acres and acres in search of the occasional lost hiker, as well as water search and rescue.

Although MawMaw and I arrived nearly an hour before the benefit was scheduled to begin, several cars were already lined up near the school entrance. I waved a greeting to the volunteer and helped MawMaw out of the car and into the building where Momma waited.

"Where in the world have you been so long, Katie Anne Henderson? I told you to run get your MawMaw and get straight over here."

An agitated Momma was a bundle of flying nerves and preparing to make a hard landing right on top of my head as soon as MawMaw and I entered through the school's double doors.

"Don't light in on the girl, Rayetta. I'll take full responsibility for holding her up this time. I'm moving kindly slow today." MawMaw ably defended me while at the same time setting up an early excuse should she need to explain her own behavior throughout the evening. It was pretty smart thinking and helped reassure me that her earlier spell might not prove significant in the long run.

Momma's sharp gaze darted between the two of us, searching for any sign of weakness to pounce on, but both of us played innocent to perfection. Momma quickly decided to drop the subject, thereby saving her energy for a later round. After all, the tag team of Kate and Ettalene possessed some wildly impressive moves and required a great deal of muscle to defeat.

"Well, now that you're here you need to get busy, Katie Anne. You and Leah are to make sure everything is set up for the auction and ready to go at six o'clock, as soon as the musicians get through playing."

Confident of my complete and immediate obedience for once, she turned her full attention to MawMaw.

"I sent one of the boys out to my car to bring in a lawn chair for you, so you don't have to sit on them old hard bleachers. Me and Patty Lynn and the girls have got the food well in hand to start serving. People should be tromping in here in another thirty minutes or so. Why don't you go on in and set down so you don't get all wore out too soon?"

"I'm not fixing to get wore out, Rayetta. I'm here to work, too. Put me in front of a job needs doing and I'll get it done." Any insinuation MawMaw couldn't keep up in the work department with others years younger did not set well with her.

"Why don't you see to Katie Anne and Leah then. Make sure they've got things right. Make sure they don't forget anything. There won't be any time to stop and do what we forgot once things get going. It's likely to be a madhouse in here tonight."

Great. There I stood, an independent career woman reduced to being watched over by my grandmother like a five-year-old. But the die was already cast. The only consolation was having Leah join me in the same boat.

"Momma, what have you done with Lainey?"

"I sent her into the gym, where you're supposed to be. Now go on."

MawMaw was already on her way down the hall, her tan rubber-soled shoes squeaking on the tile floor with every quick step. I hurried to catch up.

The delay at MawMaw's house put us a few minutes behind Momma's strict schedule, but I didn't see any real cause for concern. When we left the school last night, all of the auction items were lined up and ready for bidding. Momma herself said the food preparation was underway. The parking was definitely covered. I was confident other responsibilities assumed by various family members and friends were being handled every bit as conscientiously.

Entering the school's gym, my confidence was reinforced by the activity in progress. The auction items, displayed to the best of my organizational abilities, waited for their new owners atop tables lined up in front of the bleachers on the side nearest the doors. A rotating group of auctioneers would offer the treasures from a position front and center of the crowd.

"Hey, Tara." I called out to a familiar figure across the huge room.

Aunt Patty Lynn's daughter turned her head and broke out in a welcoming smile when she spotted me. Or maybe she was smiling at MawMaw. Either way, a warm glow hit my heart dead center before chilling slightly at MawMaw's whisper to me.

"If you know what's good for you, you'll watch your tongue around Tara," she warned. "Don't say nothing about my little spell to nobody, but especially not Tara."

Sheesh! I'd already promised to keep her health glitch between the two of us. How many times did I have to tell her before she believed me?

"My crazy little brother said y'all went out for pizza last night when you got through here, Katie Anne. Knowing I missed it makes me even sorrier I wasn't able to help get things ready last night. He said y'all had a blast."

Tara's greeting accompanied her enthusiastic hugs of both me and MawMaw.

"We did. I sure enjoyed being with Drew and the others. I hadn't laughed so much in I don't know when. I laughed enough my stomach muscles are sore today. Come to think of it, since I'm sore, can I count it as exercise?"

"Absolutely! In that case, we'll all have to get together again while you're here, but next time I won't miss it. I guess you know I was on duty last night. The hospital has got me on more double shifts every time I turn around. But I guess I ought to be glad to have the work."

"How is the hospital doing these days?"

"We're getting by fine. A lot of small towns have lost their hospitals in the last several years, so we're extremely fortunate to have ours. The complicated trauma cases are transferred out, usually to Chattanooga, but we're generally able to stabilize the patients beforehand. Getting immediate care makes a difference in a lot of situations."

MawMaw had been silent long enough.

"I don't ever want to be shipped out nowhere, Tara. You mark my words. I'm telling you here and now, and I'm leaving it up to you to see my wishes are done."

Not that MawMaw's wishes were a deep, dark secret. Everyone in the family, and probably in the whole county, knew she didn't see any need in "putting all those machines on you to make you breathe when you can't do it on your own."

Tara was saved from a reply by a shout from the middle of the room where the band was getting ready.

I turned my attention to the cluster of teenagers setting up musical instruments.

"Are those your boys?"

"Yep. Seth and Derek's band is going to play a set tonight before the auction. I'd better get back over there and finish with the final instructions, otherwise they'll be playing some heavy metal stuff. I was just giving them a mini-lecture on what types of songs are appropriate for their great-aunt's benefit."

With a quick wave, Tara turned back toward her sons and their friends, continuing to issue directions to them.

MawMaw and I zeroed in on the activity closer to us. Leah and Lainey stood with their heads together at a folding table set up near the door. Lainey was obviously getting a quick lesson in keeping track of the financial side of a benefit. Easy enough. I was certainly no math wizard, but even I grasped the basic four: addition, subtraction, multiplication, and division. No fancy accounting necessary. A healthy dose of common sense would drive the bus as far as we needed to travel.

Leah looked up.

"About time you showed up. Does Aunt Rayetta know you're here?"

"Yes. I've already been duly reprimanded. Where do I need to begin?"

"How about fixing some signs to go on the chance boxes, and then we can decide how we want to divvy up the other jobs."

I moved over to the next table which held three cardboard boxes with a small slot cut in each top. We were selling chances on the four items most popular at benefits: a handmade quilt, shotgun, recliner, and television set. Correction: technically we were not selling chances, we were giving away the items and at the same time allowing people to make a donation to the worthy cause.

Selling chances was gambling in Tennessee, and gambling was illegal in Tennessee. Unless you were state government and ran your own lottery. Fortunately, the powers that be were smart enough to leave small-time charitable fundraising alone. In return, small-time fundraisers tried to be respectful of the law by remembering to call the activity "giving away for a donation."

Leah's penmanship was never prize-winning, thus prompting her to assign me the sign making duties. I quickly and neatly lettered four mini-posters with the name of the item and the "suggested donation" amount.

In spite of her earlier protests, MawMaw settled comfortably in her lawn chair perch in the entrance corner of the gym, directly in front of the first row of bleachers, ready for the show to begin.

By the time Leah and I wrapped up the last of the auction details, assisted by Lainey, several people were beginning to straggle in. Most of them carried plastic containers from the concession stand laden with pinto beans and cornbread, hot dogs and chili, or nachos and cheese. As far as I knew, all successful benefits featured those diet staples.

I noticed Tara giving her sons the sign to crank up the music, and soon the pleasant sounds of classic country floated throughout the gym and into the hallways. The oldest boy, Seth, was the spitting image of his daddy and the apparent leader of the band, playing guitar and singing lead. His brother, Derek, joined him on guitar and backup vocals. The other two musicians were unfamiliar to me.

"Hey, Katie Anne." Leah's voice rose over the music. "What do you think about Lainey taking care of the chances while you work with the auctioneer to keep the flow going steady. I'll assign bidder numbers since I'll probably know most of the people coming in."

"Fine with me. We can switch up later to give everybody a break."

So far, so good.

∼

"Wha'd a you bid? Who'll give me twenty, twenty, twenty. Now thirty, thirty, thirty…"

The rapid-fire rhythm of the auctioneer's speech stirred up the growing throng of bidders relaxing against the wooden bleachers. A close ear to his exact words was necessary to keep up with the action.

The auction segment of the benefit was well underway, and bidding ran fierce. I stayed on the run, supplying the auctioneer a widely varied selection of items, one after the other, trying to keep them random in order to keep the bidders interested. If the momentum ever shifted…well, we didn't want the momentum to shift.

Randell Lee, another former high school classmate of mine, was an entertaining auctioneer known for calling people out of the crowd and putting them on the spot. A historically effective technique when raising money for a worthy cause.

"Ronny Watson, here's what you've been waiting to bid on, a lovely teapot. Your wife told one of these boys she'd like to have one, and we all know you're cheap but not too cheap to buy a teapot for her."

In the stands, Ronny's face flushed red in embarrassment while his wife laughed, but he dipped his head in agreement to begin the bidding in the next round.

Several of my male cousins were operating as "spotters," scanning the crowd for signals from bidders. With all the movement going on, the job was harder than it sounded. When they identified someone holding up an index card with the number Leah assigned to them, they let out a loud whoop. Having registered all the bidders, Leah moved on to busily keep track of successful bids and bidders with assistance from Tara. Lainey was still selling chances. The dozen or so of us were operating like a well-oiled machine.

"Going…going….sold! To bidder number fifty-two." Randell banged the gavel, and Ronny Watson ended up with the teapot after all.

The frenzy of activity allowed me to keep my mind focused on the job I was doing and off who might be watching me do it. However, my attention was captured in a single instant by the noise of a lone person clapping. The sound quickly ran across the crowd, with people in the stands rising to their feet as if a celebrity had entered the gym. I glanced around to identify the cause of the commotion.

There in the doorway stood Uncle Herbert pushing Aunt Lora Anne's wheelchair through the doorway. Aunt Lora Anne was a tiny figure, shrunken and pale beneath a crocheted afghan covering her body nearly to her neck. Following were the couple's three sons and their families. Their two little granddaughters skipped around the wheelchair, oblivious to the thick emotions swirling in the air.

Equal parts of overwhelming love and overwhelming fear suddenly clutched my heart in a tangled mess. Love for Aunt Lora Anne and fear of losing her. The lump in my throat swelled so big I thought my neck would explode. Tears overflowed my eyes and trickled down my cheeks.

What a tribute to Aunt Lora Anne, a woman obviously deeply loved by many, many people. How blessed I was to be a part of her life and have her as a part of mine. The clapping of the crowd gradually died down, but friends and neighbors continued to stand silently in respect.

When my cousin Bryant tenderly picked his mother up out of her wheelchair and gently placed her into an awaiting recliner, I struggled unsuccessfully for composure. My trickle of tears widened into a steady stream. Surely it was the sweetest sight I would ever witness on this earth.

Aunt Lora Anne looked up from her new position and lifted a weak hand in a fluttery wave. For a second, my awareness of everyone else fell away, and I got the feeling Aunt Lora Anne was the only other person in the room with me.

Gradually I heard the sound of another round of clapping spread through the gym, breaking into my thoughts.

I looked around and became aware I wasn't the only person moved to tears by the intimate scene. MawMaw's expression was full of sorrow and her eyes were full of tears. Several women were using their food napkins to wipe the wetness from their cheeks, and grown men were sniffling.

As the noise died out and people returned to their seats, the experienced auctioneer made a neat transition to return focus to the auction and turn the sincere emotions into solid cash.

"Let Miss Lora Anne see how high you'll go on this next item. What have we got to sell, Katie Anne?"

Now seemed like the perfect time to pull out one of the big ticket items, so I handed over the certificate for a weekend for two in Nashville with tickets to the Grand Ole Opry's Saturday night show.

"Here you go, get your wallets ready. Let's start off the bidding at an even one hundred dollars and keep going from there."

"Who'll start us off? Hundred dollar bill, hundred, hundred… Now one-fifty, one-fifty…two…two…"

Still trying to pull myself together, my eyes swept the crowd in appreciation and wonder. The love and concern of this community for their neighbor was overwhelming. Who could ask for more support than was shown this night in this place by these people? An outside force threatened one of their own, and they were gathering up all resources to fight. Sure, they were the same individual people with their own problems and worries, yet they had enough to share with someone else. The realization humbled me in a way I hadn't been humbled in a long time.

I continued trying to reign in my emotions, but it was as though a whirling fan was blowing a stack of papers through the air. I couldn't catch them quickly enough.

Leah appeared at my right shoulder, slipped an arm around me, and gave me a quick squeeze.

"Hurts, doesn't it?"

"Sure does."

"Why don't you step out for a little break. Tara can keep track of the bids by herself for a few minutes, and I'll take over for you here."

Nodding in appreciation, I ducked out as inconspicuously as possible. A quick trip to the ladies' room provided time to repair my makeup, and a stop at the concession stand for a snack might do me good.

As I rounded the corner into the main hallway, I was startled by a loud commotion.

❧ CHAPTER 27 ❦

An embarrassed Harmon Suggs was trapped between the counter of the concession stand and a scrawny young woman rapidly shaking a finger inches from his face while delivering a blistering tirade against him. I stood too far away to make out all of the muffled insults her high-pitched voice was hurling at him, but clearly her message was anything but a friendly inquiry about his health.

A small crowd was already beginning to gather around the two of them, made up of people waiting in line for food and others drawn to the area by the loud voice. I maneuvered myself through the people and nearer to the escalating confrontation.

The young woman apparently had plenty more ugly words in store to shout at Harmon.

"My little niece never got a chance for any kind of a life. You took her life, you miserable drunk. Who do you think you are, coming here around decent people? You ain't nothing but a jailbird."

Spewing anger and self-righteousness, the young woman shook as the horrible words poured from her mouth in a steady stream of venom. Harmon seemed to shrink before my eyes, head cast down toward his shoes, the tips of his ears bright red as he made himself the smallest target possible.

"I'm awful sorry. I know..."

"You don't know nothing! And yes, you are awful!"

By then Momma was charging out of the concession stand door to take control of the volatile situation. I let out the breath I hadn't even realized I was holding. Circumstances were tricky, but Momma majored in tricky before this girl was born. I held complete confidence in her abilities.

"Hold on here a minute," she commanded in a loud voice soaked in authority.

The young woman whirled around to face Momma toe-to-toe.

"Do you know who he is? He killed my little niece. My sister never has been the same. Her old man left her and it's been downhill ever since. This man ain't worth spitting on."

"You hush that kind of talk right now. Harmon Suggs is a good man who made a terrible mistake, and the law says he's paid what he owes. If you can't act no better than this, you can turn around and march your tail home. We don't need you here."

The young woman briefly attempted to stare Momma down, but the steely determination in Momma's face and the firm set of her jaw quickly convinced the woman she had no chance for a win there.

She turned to leave, jerking her sagging purse strap back to her shoulder. I happened to be standing directly in her path to the door, but she could easily have stepped around me. She chose not to. Advancing as close to me as she had been to Harmon and then Momma, she stopped and fastened a hand on one hip.

"And who do you think you are? Get out of my way!" she demanded.

Before I could overcome my shock and make a decision on how to react, she did step around me on her way out of the building. She stomped off, muttering something about how some people didn't even appreciate it when you went to a benefit to try to help their kin.

"Who's next in line?" Aunt Patty Lynn quickly jumped into the uncomfortable silence from inside the concession stand. "We've got plenty of food left, and the chili is homemade."

As a few customers awkwardly shuffled up to the order window, Momma gently placed a hand on Harmon's arm and guided him over to the side of the hallway for a private discussion out of the hearing of others. He continued to stare at his feet as Momma began talking.

I took a deep breath and shook my head in amazement. Was it merely a few minutes ago I felt so good about all these people? What happened? How many complicated relationships and emotions swirled beneath the surface of goodwill in this building? Yet, on the other hand, the young woman was only one person in a crowd of a few hundred people. I probably shouldn't let her actions taint the kindness and generosity of all the others.

The anguish of the little girl's family was no doubt bone deep and agonizingly real, despite the inappropriate way the woman chose to express her pain. Their loss wasn't fair.

But why did the young woman yell at me? Was I a convenient target who randomly appeared in her path? Or did her words hide a deeper message directed specifically at me? I searched my brain for a connection between us but came up empty.

My heart hurt for Harmon and the embarrassment he suffered because of the woman's vicious verbal attack. And I was moved not only because of the attack, but because of his past and the heavy baggage he dragged around behind him. Harmon's entire life was being judged by the most horrible act he ever committed, by the most horrible decision he ever made.

In an instant, my brain clicked on the falsehood of the measuring stick. A person's entire life could not be judged on the basis of one horrible decision, no matter how devastating the outcome. If only I could apply the same truth to my own situation and make peace with the one event still haunting my life, silently influencing my every action.

"How's it going out there?"

Startled out of my musing, I gazed up to see my cousin Farrah, formerly known as Clara, waiting for an answer from me. She leaned against the concession counter, spooning pinto beans into bowls, trying to appear casual while casting sideways glances over at Harmon and Momma.

"What?" I asked.

"I sure hate it happened, but it was bound to at some point. Maybe it'll be better for Harmon to have it out in the open."

Expecting Farrah to pile on, I was surprised by her lack of judgment. Perhaps it was time I took Momma's advice and eased up on her, too.

"Well, it's over now so the less said the better."

Time for me to quickly change the subject.

"The auction's going good. Bidding is pretty high on most things."

"I sure am glad. Food's selling, too. It better, after all the beans I cooked last night and today. I'm not wanting to carry any of them home."

A noise arose from the floor at her feet, and Farrah directed her attention downward. "Little man, we're going to spill something hot right on top of your head if you keep rolling around on this floor. We're going to have to find your daddy."

A little towheaded toddler built like a tank scrambled off the floor and lifted his arms toward his mother.

"I don't have time now, Tucker."

"How about I take him with me for a little while?" I suggested. "He can help me on the auction floor. Do you want to, Tucker?"

He leaned his head back as far as it would go to peer up at me with big blue eyes. I did my part by leaning over the counter to give him a better look at me. He quickly sent me an approving nod and headed around the counter on a run. As he barreled into me, I swooped him up in my arms. The little fellow was solid all right. My arms would get a workout toting him around.

Farrah narrowed her eyes at me as if uncertain I could be trusted with her son. After all, she and I had just had the first civil conversation of our lives.

"You be sure to keep up with him. He can be a little devil if you don't keep your eyes locked on him every minute. He gets into every blessed thing."

With my back turned to my cousin and her instructions, I rolled my eyes without thinking about young Tucker's attention on me. He began to giggle, and I quickly headed away from the concession stand before any words left his mouth. I didn't want him tattling on me and my facial contortions.

"You funny. What you name?"

While answering Tucker, my own curiosity prompted me to peek in the direction of Harmon and Momma. After all, my mother was involved, and I needed to make sure the situation was under control for her sake. I wasn't being nosy, I was concerned.

Momma's lips were still moving a mile a minute, but the frown on her face was replaced by the faintest hint of a smile and her stance was relaxed. Harmon leaned on the block wall behind him, intently soaking in every word Momma uttered and throwing in an occasional nod of agreement.

Disaster averted.

As I reentered the gym, Tucker firmly settled on one hip and his little grubby fingers pulling on the fragile silver chain around my neck, I immediately confirmed the pace of the auction was still going strong and breathed a sigh of satisfaction. Only about half of the items were sold, so we couldn't afford a slowdown this early in the game. Fortunately, the situation looked as if we didn't have to worry.

Bidder signs flashed one after the other from the bleachers. I couldn't see which item they were trying to buy, but I didn't care. I only cared that they bought something. Experience taught me some of them didn't really care what they bought either. Some people came with a determined amount of money to donate and they were going to spend their dollars one way or another.

Aunt Lora Anne and Uncle Herbert would put any money donated to good use. They certainly deserve the help. Both were well-known in the community for their years of helping others in whatever way they could. Uncle Herbert was a county commissioner, while Aunt Lora Ann had served on the county fair board forever. They'd both been involved in everything from Little League to football and band booster clubs, to the chamber of commerce, to the library. They'd also been active in the volunteer fire department and helped with many other benefits for many of their neighbors here tonight.

Lainey remained seated at the table with the boxes for the giveaways, but her business had slowed and she was ready for a diversion. She eyed the little fellow in my arms with a sly grin. The noise in the gym blared so loudly, she was forced to lean in close to make a comment.

"Well, well, isn't he a little young, even for you?"

"Ha ha. This is my new friend and little cousin, Tucker. Technically, my cousin's son. Or my uncle's grandson. Or my first cousin, once removed. Or, as we say it around here, my second cousin. The last part isn't technically correct, but it's still how we count things."

"Sorry I asked."

"How are the chance sales going?" I looked down to see only part of one roll of tear-off tickets remaining on the table.

"Most everyone bought tickets when they first came in, so it's slow now. I'll have to admit, it's a new experience. Everyone wants to know who I am, as if they can't fathom the idea of someone they don't recognize behind here helping. Some of them ask me outright, but other people stand right in front of the table and discuss who I might be, like I can't hear them or something."

"Welcome to Pikeville, Tennessee, always on the lookout for possible terrorists and church prospects."

The sounds of a guitar strumming finally registered with me over the auction noise at about the same time Tucker pointed a stubby index finger at the opposite side of the gym.

"Theth."

"What did you say?"

"Theth."

Obviously, I had uncovered another flaw in my personality. I could not interpret toddler speak. When I looked to Lainey for help, she merely shrugged her shoulders in defeat. But I was game to attempt to figure him out.

While I was figuring, Tucker quickly became impatient. He began kicking his legs against me and pulling away. I had no problem recognizing what that meant, and I let him slide down my leg and to the floor. No sooner did he hit the ground than he switched into torpedo mode and raced off in a blast. Evidently, Tucker operated in two speeds: stand still and blue streak.

He bulldozed into the back of a young man strumming a guitar. The fellow's knees bent forward with the impact, but fortunately, he managed to right himself before falling completely. I recognized him as Tara's oldest son, Seth, the leader of the band playing before the auction began.

"Theth," Tucker cried out, grabbing the young man around both legs in a captive embrace.

Oh, Seth. If I'd harbored any doubt, now I was certain Tucker had known exactly where he was going.

To add to Seth's surprise at being ambushed from behind, he was blindfolded while he played tunes for the cake walks, a variation of musical chairs. In front of him were circles on the floor, about a dozen or so with a person standing on each one. A circle was taken away during each round while Seth strummed his guitar. When he stopped the song at a random point, the walkers scrambled to make it to a plate. Whoever came up short was disqualified. The rounds continued until only one person remained. The winner's prize was a cake. Besides the obvious reward of an entire cake, the game provided entertainment for youngsters too squirmy to sit still for long while the auction was underway.

Since Seth quit playing as soon as Tucker grabbed him, the cake walk participants quickly scrambled to find a plate of their own to claim. Two teenage girls ended up on the same one, and the lady who appeared to be in charge was forced to make an executive decision on who stayed and who was disqualified.

The good-natured conflict allowed me time to peel Tucker off Seth's skinny frame and scoop him back up in my arms. An obviously relieved Seth, having removed his blindfold as soon as he was hit, smiled appreciatively at me.

"Thanks for the rescue, Katester."

"Katester! Katester! Katester!" Tucker set up a blaring chant close to my ear, clapping his pudgy hands together and convincing me he wouldn't forget my new nickname anytime soon. Lainey appeared next to me.

"Seth, did you meet my friend Lainey? She's from Nashville."

A blush crept up Seth's teenage face as he gazed at my attractive, stylish friend. Chalk up another male smitten by Lainey the Heartbreaker. For a moment, he seemed unable to speak.

"Nice to meet you."

"You, too. You're an extremely talented musician."

"Uh, yeah. I mean, thanks."

Completely forgotten by Seth the moment an attractive woman appeared on the scene, I thought I would do him a favor anyway.

"Here, Lainey. Take Tucker and you two enter the next cake walk while I go back over and see about the auction. Tucker, you want to cake walk with Lainey, don't you?"

Whether he fully understood the question or not, his little head nodded up and down in rapid agreement and he reached his arms out to Lainey, my poor friend with absolutely no experience dealing with children. I was certain a grubby hand never before dared touch her fair skin. In my mind, that made it about time one did. Or two, to be exact.

Without giving Lainey an opportunity to decline my generous offer, I quickly transferred Tucker into her arms and returned to the auction area.

~

A new auctioneer had taken over the microphone, giving Randell a rest from the strain the constant calling put on an auctioneer's vocal cords. True to her word, Leah continued to keep the auctioneer supplied with a steady mixture of kitchen appliances, tools, and odd objects. Something appealing to men, then something for the women, followed by a toy for the kids. True, a few things donated for the auction should have gone directly to the garbage dump, but we had weeded out most of those last night.

To the side, Tara still kept track of the winning bids and bidders. I walked up next to her and leaned down with an offer.

"You want me to spell you for a while? You can take a

break and get something to eat or switch off with Leah either one."

Tara diverted only half her attention to me as she answered. The other half remained focused on making certain she didn't miss recording a bid.

"No, thanks. I stood up on my feet and legs all week at the hospital. It's fine with me if I stay parked in this chair all night long. Besides, I know which number belongs to which person by now so it makes the job easier."

I knew she was too busy for me to bring up another subject, but I couldn't wait.

"Later on, before you leave tonight, I want you to tell me everything you know about a man named Edgar."

She looked up in surprise.

"That's exactly the same question I was going to ask you. I mean, I know who he is, but what I'd like to know is what's going on with him and Aunt Rayetta?"

"Well, if you see him tonight, be sure to point him out to me."

Just then the auctioneer lowered the hammer to signal another successful bidder, and I lost all of Tara's attention in her effort to keep up.

When I extended the same offer to take over for Leah, she also declined a break but accepted my help.

"Since the nearest tables are starting to clear, I'm having to go farther to haul things up. It may take both of us to keep up from here on out."

I picked up a purse from a nearby pile.

"What are we going to do with this thing?"

"No problem."

Leah got the auctioneer's attention, put her hand over his microphone, and quickly made a suggestion. The auctioneer smiled and nodded before making an announcement to the crowd.

"All right, folks, Leah here is going to start passing this purse up and down the rows. When it comes to you, put some money into it, and I don't mean change, I mean the folding kind of money. Whatever you can spare. When you get through passing it, we'll auction off the whole thing, the purse and all the money in it."

Leah lifted the purse high in the air as she made her way to the bleachers and handed the pocketbook to a young man whose jaw bulged with a plug of tobacco. He tipped his cap up higher on his head and reached for his wallet.

"While you're busy, these ladies tell me it's almost time to give away the recliner. So if you want to get in on the prize, hurry down now and get your name in the drawing. You know the old saying, you can't win if you don't enter."

In response, a few people rose from their seats, and I headed over to the table Lainey had occupied earlier to handle the additional ticket sales.

This auction business operated on a precise and proven method for getting the most money out of a crowd, and the auctioneers were tops at their job, even when performing on a voluntary basis like tonight. Giving away the recliner first guaranteed heightened interest in all of the prizes. The person was never born who didn't want to win something.

Next up came the handmade quilt, always popular with the ladies, followed by the television, popular with everyone. Giving away the shotgun last guaranteed the men stayed until the end of the auction. Bledsoe County's men owned plenty of guns, yet they were forever eager to add another one to their collection.

While I helped fill out remaining tickets for the giveaways, the auctioneer propped up a small painting in front of himself and proceeded with another unique sales pitch.

"Isn't this the prettiest thing you've ever seen? This beautiful landscape looks like it was painted by Grandma Moses. Now I'm not saying it was, but it looks like it could have been. Once you buy the thing, you can find out for sure." After the description, he quickly launched into the rhythmic patter of the auctioneering world. "Now who'll give me twenty, twenty, twenty…"

By the time the painting sold and the winner of the recliner announced, the purse returned to the front after circulating throughout the crowd. To my delight, wadded bills threatened to overflow the bag's confines. Good idea, Leah.

Bidding was fierce for the purse, since bidders were promised ownership of both the purse and all its contents. I was astonished when the gavel finally banged at three hundred and twenty-seven dollars. But I was completely stunned when the winner of the bid, a truck driver and longtime family friend, donated all the money inside back to the benefit. When counted, the purse contained six hundred and three dollars. The night promised to be exceptionally profitable.

The Blue Hole

CHAPTER 28

"I said, are you ready to go?"

At the Blue Hole, I repeated my question to Trisha.

She hadn't heard me approach. When I spoke, she whipped her head around, and then her whole body swayed from the action. If the night hadn't been so dark, I was certain I would have seen a sickly green color on her face.

She gazed up at me with unfocused eyes.

"What do you want?"

"How much has she had to drink?" I demanded of Jesse.

"Who made you her momma?" he shot back. "I don't see it's any of your business either way."

A half-empty jar of moonshine set next to his left hand. It didn't take a genius to figure out they had been sharing the alcohol.

"Yeah, who made you my momma?" Trisha slurred her words. From the glazed look in her eyes, I wasn't sure she even recognized me.

Okay, time to take charge, I thought.

I reached for Trisha's arm to tug her off the rock and get her started on the way toward the vehicles.

"Back off!" Jesse shouted. He sprang off the rock to lurch unsteadily between me and Trisha, and pointed a shaking finger in my face.

I backed up, shocked. As far as I knew, Jesse was gentle as could be. I had never before heard him as much as raise his voice.

"Yeah, back off!"

If all Trisha could do was echo whatever Jesse said, she was pretty far gone. I felt responsible for her, but my hot temper was beginning to flame.

"Let's go, Trisha."

"She's with me, so you better turn around and march out of here before you get hurt."

"You're gonna hurt me? Trisha, are you gonna let him talk to me like that?"

No answer.

"I said, are you?"

Still no answer.

Trisha remained silent, looking down at her shoes while this guy threatened me! My temper rose hotter and hotter until the wrath spilled out my mouth in an unconcealed rage.

"Fine. If you wanna choose this piece of trash over your best friend, go ahead. If that's all I am to you, don't ever speak to me again!"

I turned on my heel and stomped back to the fire site where some of the guys were making sure every spark was extinguished. I knew they were probably too far away to have heard the exact words exchanged between the three of us, but they heard enough to give me a wide berth. None of them would look me in the eye.

∾ CHAPTER 29 ⊰

As soon as an extremely happy older man took possession of his new shotgun, the gym began quickly emptying of people. Leah, Tara, and I triple-teamed the bid checkout station, collecting stacks of money for the auction items purchased by the bidders. Ordered chaos ensued for the next twenty minutes or so until the bulk of the funds was collected.

Uncle Herbert and family had quietly slipped out and taken Aunt Lora Anne on home a short time earlier, both because she quickly tired from the big evening and to gently shield her from the well-meaning throngs of people whose personal concern would tire her even more.

The benefit might be officially over, but plenty of work remained.

Tucker returned to "help Katester" after only a brief time apart. Cake walking proved too structured an activity to hold his attention for long. He spent the remainder of the auction alternately racing up and down the length of the gym, rolling under the tables, and running into me full speed ahead and then laughing like a pint-sized maniac. Somehow he also managed to wriggle his place into my heart.

When Farrah entered the gym with the other ladies who worked the concession stand, Tucker paid no attention to his mother. She didn't acknowledge his presence either, instead addressing no one in particular with her words.

"How did things go in here? Y'all make any money?"

That was, after all, the big question. Not the sixty-four thousand dollar question, but up in the thousands anyway. How far up, we would know shortly. Everyone enjoyed the night's entertainment; however, we were there for the cash.

"I think we'll be pleased when we get it all added up," Leah responded.

Momma held up a large cooking pot called into double duty as a cash depository for the concession stand profits. Change jangled in the bottom with each step she took toward the bidding table.

"We done our part, let's see what you others did."

She set the heavy pot down on the table in front of Leah and moved over to sit on the bleachers with her fellow concession stand workers to observe the money counting process.

Obviously, Leah, Tara, and I were expected to handle the accounting. Lainey stuck around to help, too.

Any good counting began by separating the money by both bill and coin denomination, so we got to work on the four piles of money: auction, food, chances, and cake walk. With nearly everything donated, expenses were at a minimum. Only the television and a few food items were purchased, leaving nearly one hundred percent profit on the benefit overall.

"Here, Katie Anne, you total up the food money and

I'll take the auction. Tara, will you get the chances? And Lainey, will you get the cake walk?"

The women in my family weren't shy about taking charge, and Leah proved no exception. She quickly identified what needed to be done and let us know how we were going to do it, keeping the biggest task for herself. Fortunately, no one was shy about work either, so we accepted her plan without comment and proceeded to get busy.

With pencil in hand, I set about tallying up the checks first. Might as well get the most difficult counting out of the way before all the numbers began jumbling together in my brain. Tara and Lainey didn't have any checks or any change in their piles of money from the chances and cake walks, making their counts a little easier. In fact, most of their money came in the form of one dollar bills.

The plan sounded simple enough, but the execution was slowed by the fact that none of us routinely counted big sums of money. After all, our group contained a social worker, lawyer, paralegal, and nurse. Not an accountant in the bunch. Not even a bank teller. And, as the paralegal with limited math skills, I'd have to admit I rarely even balanced my own checkbook. In this same school, my math teacher predicted I might someday wish I'd paid more attention in class. As usual, she was right.

When Tara began counting the bills from the chances out loud right next to me, I lost place in my own count and was forced to start over. Deciding a little space was in order, I picked up my pot of food money and moved to a nearby table to give my concentration a fighting chance.

While we worked, the men helping with the auction spotting folded up the tables and moved them back into the cafeteria to be ready for school to resume on Monday.

Without a doubt, we would leave the school in at least as good a shape as we found it, and probably better.

Out of the corner of my eye, I noticed Wayne and Donnie Ray tearing down the sound system with help from Drew. My mind wandered, questioning whether Wayne's wife was still at the benefit. During the auction I picked him out of the crowd, sitting high in the bleachers with a woman on either side. From the distance, I couldn't tell much about either one, much less make a good guess about which was his wife. I was still extremely curious about the woman who stole my buddy's heart.

Reminding myself to focus on the money count, I bent my head and continued totaling the checks.

"I'm done!"

When I turned, Tara was holding a stack of bills in the air and waving them around like she won the lottery.

"Me, too."

Lainey beamed next to her, obviously proud of herself. At least her hands were down next to her sides.

The show-offs. I felt obligated to defend myself.

"Y'all had the easy ones to count."

"Yeah." Leah sided with me from her counting position. "We've got the big categories. Hold on a few minutes and we'll be done."

The two women did even better. Tara approached Leah, and Lainey moved to my table to help me.

"What's things looking like?" When Momma asked the question, all of the ladies still relaxing on the bleachers suddenly perked up. They looked worn out from a night of hard work, but were obviously anxious to hear the result.

"I think it's looking good, Aunt Rayetta," Leah answered. "Be patient with us just a few more minutes. We want to be sure to get it right."

Overcoming the odds against us due to our non-existent accounting skills, the newly opened firm of Leah and Associates did get it right. After we counted all the money once, we switched places and did a recount. Leah, Tara, Lainey, and I huddled at the cash register with our individual notepads holding the tallies from the night. When the final numbers from the two counts came up exactly the same, we felt confident enough for an announcement.

"All right, everybody." Leah's voice rang out over the straggling group of people remaining in the gymnasium. Everyone immediately quieted, eager to hear the announcement. "Here are the final numbers. We raised…"

With a dramatic hand roll, Leah let her words hang over the crowd, drawing out the anticipation.

"Hurry up," an impatient person called from the bleachers.

"If you interrupt me, I'll have to start all over," Leah warned. She began again, "We raised…twenty-three thousand, four hundred, ninety-six dollars and ninety-eight cents!"

The small group let out shouts of joy to nearly rival the noise the larger crowd generated earlier in the night. I looked at Momma and saw her body bent nearly in two, her head down in her lap as if she couldn't hold herself upright on her own strength. I felt a little dizzy myself.

Lainey grabbed me for a hug, and then Leah and Tara descended from both sides. We spun around on the gym floor, and our group hug quickly turned into a little celebration dance.

Leah's husband, Zach, halted us by grabbing his wife's shoulders from behind before we got even sillier. In his hand, he offered a small amount of money. Leah's puzzlement was evident in her expression.

"Three dollars and two cents," he explained. "I'm adding this much more to make the total an even twenty-three thousand, five hundred. It'll simplify things all around."

"Oh, you sweet, sweet man." Leah flung her arms around his neck and proceeded to pepper him with kisses. Her display of gratitude struck me as a little excessive for the small amount of additional money he offered, but maybe I was just jealous she had a man. I turned back to Lainey.

My friend was no doubt the person most amazed by the benefit's outcome.

"I had no idea! When you said in the thousands, I thought two thousand, even three at the most. But more than twenty-three thousand dollars!"

"To be honest, it's the most I've ever heard of. But you can close your mouth now."

"Either way, it's incredible!"

❧

So caught up in the success of the moment, I didn't notice Wayne standing beside Lainey until he spoke my name.

"Katie Anne, here's somebody wants to meet you, although for the life of me I can't figure why."

A tiny woman, several inches shorter than me, jabbed an elbow in his ribs at the same moment she sent a soft smile in my direction.

"Don't pay any attention to my crazy old husband. But I guess you know that already, don't you? I'm Amanda."

In spite of her small frame, Amanda's demeanor

exuded confidence and strength. She wore her dark chocolate brown hair in a bob to her shoulders, and her green eyes were steady as they met mine. In the way of women, I knew she was sizing me up to see what kind of person I was and what my interest in her husband was. I could quickly put her at ease on the last point. We were friends and that's all we ever were. Close, close friends, but only friends.

"It's so nice to finally meet Wayne's wife, Amanda. I know you took on a big job when you took him on. But looks like you're making progress."

"I'm trying my best."

"Hey, now," Wayne jumped in. "You two are forgetting what a prime example of manhood you're talking about."

His words earned him another quick jab from his wife. I decided a change of subject was in order.

"I want you both to meet a dear friend of mine from Nashville. Lainey, this is one of my old school buddies, Wayne, and his wife, Amanda."

"Nice to meet you both."

A little small talk followed, mostly about their two sons, our jobs, the benefit. All too soon, Amanda suggested to Wayne it was time to leave.

"All right. Let me go say goodnight to Miss Rayetta."

He headed toward Momma, and Amanda turned back to face me. Her eyes locked onto mine, and although her pleasant look remained, her next words surprised me.

"Katie Anne, my husband brings up your name so often I could almost be jealous of you."

"Me? There's no reason to be jealous of me. We enjoyed a lot of good times together, and suffered through some bad times too, years ago. That's all."

"That's a lot."

"We were good buddies all during school. Wayne was always like a brother to me."

Amanda continued staring at me while completely ignoring Lainey. After a few moments, she appeared to relax slightly.

"Well, I guess it's nice to have somebody like a brother."

Wayne reemerged and gathered me up for a hug.

"Katie Anne, you take care of yourself and come back to see me soon."

"You too, Wayne. You too."

Amanda smiled back at me as she placed her arm in her husband's, and they walked through the double doors of the gym and out of sight.

"Whew, I feel like I just took some kind of test there."

"You did, my friend. And the good news is you passed the test with flying colors." Lainey's words confirmed what I already knew in my mind.

"If I'm the only thing she's worried about, she's in good shape."

"I don't think she was really worried, she was just using the opportunity to make certain there was no reason to worry."

"Well, there's not. Wives everywhere can rest easy. Kate Henderson is no threat to any marriage. In fact, the sad news is, I'm not even a threat to a single man's marital status."

"You could change it anytime you wanted to. What about one of these guys?" Lainey motioned to the side of the gym. A dozen or so men were busy with the last of the cleanup work, breaking down the bleachers and pushing them against the wall.

"Sure, which one?"

"How about the delicious looking logger type with the work boots and tee shirt?"

Lainey's description fit most of the men present.

"You'll have to be more specific."

"With the forest green shirt that says, 'I Love Wildlife, It Tastes Great' on the back."

"Thanks, that's my cousin Lisa's husband, Travis. She's Leah's sister. You're trying to start a family feud. But you always did like the brawny type."

I felt a tug at my knees and looked down. Tucker had again reattached himself to me.

"Hey, little buddy."

"Go home wif' you." Those little eyes gazed up at me with hopeful adoration.

"We're not quite ready to go home yet. Come on and let's see when MawMaw wants to go home."

MawMaw continued to hold court from her lawn chair next to the gym's doors. As each person left the gym, they stopped to speak a few words to MawMaw, and she lifted her bony arms up to bring them down for a thank you hug before uttering words of blessing. To be sure, the help given this night would never be forgotten as long as MawMaw lived.

I knelt down in front of her, resting one hand in her lap and the other on top of Tucker's head. From our positions, me kneeling and MawMaw seated, the two of us were nearly the same height.

"How you holding up, MawMaw?"

"I'm holding up mighty fine. How you holding up, Katie Anne?"

"You know what I mean. Any more problems?"

"No, and you can quit worrying about me right now.

240

I seen you looking over this way a million times during the auction when you ort to have been paying attention to other things."

Despite her harsh tone, I didn't take offense. MawMaw was upset with her own body, not with me. As if in proof, she took hold of my hand in her lap, alternately stroking and patting in a ritual only she knew how to perform. Instant comfort and unconditional love conveyed in a touch.

Bored by the lack of action, Tucker crawled under MawMaw's lawn chair and darted out the door. I gathered my strength and pushed up from the floor.

"I'd better see to him."

≈

With Tucker's head start, he'd already abandoned the entrance hall. As I debated which direction to pursue, his giggle gave him away. I caught up with him in the cafeteria, and after a few minutes of fun prolonging the chase, I grabbed him by a cowboy boot and tugged him from under a table. His giggles increased into outright belly laughs. After delivering a mock stern glare, I picked him up by the ankles and carried him upside down back into the hallway, his chubby fingers clawing at my pant legs.

Tucker and I were enjoying great fun until I spotted his mother marching toward us, arms crossed tightly against her ample chest.

"Tucker, what have you been up to now? Katie Anne, don't hold him that way. He's liable to start coughing and choke to death. Tucker, get down right now. I warned you not to be a nuisance tonight."

"He hasn't been a nuisance at all. We've been having

lots of fun together tonight, haven't we, Tucker?"

Farrah continued her scolding as if she hadn't heard a word I said.

"Young man, I don't know why you can't be still. You're all the time getting into something. Come on, we're going home and straight to bed."

Tucker continued as if he hadn't heard a word his mother said. He was a smart little boy if he was already using her own weapons against her. She walked over to where he rolled on the ground in front of me, grabbed his arm and pulled. He closed his eyes and let his whole body go limp.

"I dead."

A short laugh escaped my mouth before I could stop it, earning me a fierce scowl from Farrah before she turned back to her son.

"Tucker, I am not playing this game. You get up from there and in the car or I'm calling the police. We'll see if a night in jail teaches you what happens to little boys who don't mind their mommas."

Whether the insane threat worked or Tucker tired of playing the game, he jumped up and raced out a door that was propped open while someone carried supplies back to their vehicle. The last I saw of Farrah, she was struggling to catch up with him. Perhaps next Christmas someone would buy her a series of parenting lessons. As the new childrearing expert, I was one to talk.

"You're good with the boy."

I glanced around to identify the speaker. Harmon Suggs leaned against the block wall to my left, one boot propped up against the wall behind him, his arms dangling at his sides. He used the boot to push himself forward and toward me as I replied.

"He makes it easy. He's a fun little fella."

Silence grew up between us. I was thinking about the incident earlier in the evening at the concession stand, and I assumed he was, too. Frankly, I was surprised he was still at the benefit. Had I been in his place, I would have left after the woman's hateful attack, turned tail and run, not made myself a convenient target by hanging around. In fact, that's exactly what I did years ago, turned tail and run.

Harmon was first to break the quiet.

"You're momma is a fine woman."

"Yes, she is."

"Just because God forgives you doesn't mean everybody else will, but it makes you appreciate those who do a whole lot more."

"Can I ask you something, Harmon?" His nod encouraged me to continue speaking. "Why do you stay around Pikeville? Wouldn't it be easier to start over somewhere else? Somewhere they don't know your past?"

He let out a dry chuckle.

"To tell the truth, I'm not allowed to travel out of the county because of my probation. So for that reason alone, I've got to stay here." His expression sobered. "But fact is, I'd stay here anyway. This is where my life is, where I belong. You can't outrun who you are by moving to a new town."

I was saved from having to reply by the noise of several people approaching us. Leah's husband, Zach, hauled the big pot of money in front of him, surrounded by Leah, Momma, MawMaw, and Lainey, and followed by Drew.

"I've got my deputies surrounding me to make sure nothing happens to the money," Zach joked. "Nobody I know would take on these women even for this much money."

MawMaw usually appreciated a good joke as much as

anyone, but clearly joking time was over.

"You're to go right to the bank and put that money in that place they've got to put money at night," MawMaw instructed.

"I will. You don't have to worry about it at all. Leah and I are headed straight to the bank. Drew's going to follow us to make sure nobody tries any funny business along the way. We'll put all the checks and bills in the night depository and take only the change home. The rest can go to the bank on Monday morning."

The plan satisfied MawMaw, but she still wanted the last word.

"You boys be as careful as you can."

"I'll guard this money with my life, Miss Ettalene."

"See that you do."

The Blue Hole

My temper cooled off as quickly as it heated up. I was already regretting my harsh words to Trisha when Wayne came up, grabbed my hand, and led me back toward the field where the trucks were parked. Trisha was in no condition to hear my apology tonight, so I would have to wait to offer my conciliatory words until in the morning. Whatever else I said tonight would only make the situation worse.

A few engines were already revving up for the trip back to town, but I asked Wayne if he minded waiting a few minutes to make sure Jesse and Trisha got back to the parking site safely.

"Sure, honey," he said. "Don't worry, though. Zeb said he'd drive Jesse's truck back to town, and then I'm gonna pick him up."

We climbed in Wayne's truck, and he flipped on the radio. We listened to the nearest country station through crackling static while looking for signs of the couple. After what felt like an eternity, we spotted them through the darkness.

A fog began settling on the area, reminding me of a horror movie with the villain approaching in the mist.

"There they are." Relief was evident in my voice. "They made it."

But as soon as I finished speaking, Jesse changed direction and started moving to the right. With a tug, he pulled a wobbly Trisha behind him. They were headed for the rock ledge forming this side of the Blue Hole. The rock ledge that dropped down without warning. The rock ledge that formed the top of a sheer cliff straight to the deep water below.

"What is the idiot doing?" The calm, unruffled Wayne suddenly sounded afraid. "They don't need to be out there."

"Get back here!" I could hear Zeb shouting at the couple as I lunged for the truck door.

Wayne moved faster and had already caught up with Zeb by the time I fumbled to operate the door handle.

My heart was beating so fast I couldn't breathe well. I raced toward Trisha, frantic to pull her away from the danger.

As if he hadn't heard the warnings, Jesse continued walking, barely skirting the edge of the pit. He let go of Trisha's hand, but she continued following him.

I was still running when she yelled, "See me, Katie Anne? I don't need you to tell me what to do."

In an instant, I saw the rock she was standing on collapse, taking her over the side.

Just that quick, Trisha was gone.

❧ CHAPTER 31 ❧

Euphoria over the benefit's results lingered like a cloud of pleasant perfume as Lainey and I followed the glowing red taillights of Momma's car back to the house. Once inside, we collapsed around the kitchen table, eager to relive every detail of our success. I was as excited to bring Momma up-to-date on what she missed inside the gym as she was to relate a story about every hungry person who purchased food from the concession stand. And considering Momma's storytelling abilities, that was saying something.

"I'll make us some coffee and we can finish off these few Little Debbie cakes that didn't sell. You girls set right there while I bring it to the table," Momma instructed, warming up to her mile-a-minute speech rate as she moved throughout the kitchen. "I hope y'all don't mind these packaged snacks to eat, but we run plumb out of baked goods there at the end. We figured the food pretty close though, I'll have to say. Patty Lynn dipped out the last drop of pinto beans to Joel Simmons. I was afraid Virginia was going to want some too, but she ordered a hot dog and a few of those were left. So everything worked out. We could have used a little more cornbread. That was the only thing. And if Patty Lynn hadn't started out cutting it in such big pieces, we could have made what we had go further. But I reckon nobody headed home hungry."

"I'm sure they didn't, Momma. And I don't think they headed home with much money in their pockets, either."

A sweet smile widened on Momma's weary face as she eased onto a seat at the foot of the table between Lainey and me.

"No, I don't think they did, sugar."

Her hands reached out on either side, grasping one of mine and one of Lainey's. She squeezed briefly and then stilled her hands on top of ours. Her eyes teared up as she began speaking.

"Girls, I want to tell you both how much what you've done this weekend means to me. There was plenty of other places you could have been and other things you could have been doing, but to be here for our family and for Aunt Lora Anne means the world to me. You couldn't have got me no other present in the world I would rather had."

Momma's eyes bored in on mine.

"Katie Anne, I'm glad to see you know to put first things first, and your family come first this weekend. It shows you know what's worth the most in life."

Next came Lainey's turn.

"Lainey, you stuck with us in the hard times. There's only one other friend that sticketh closer than a brother, and that's the Lord.

"I pray He richly blesses both of you for what you done here."

The lump in my throat prevented me from speaking right away. Lainey jumped into the gap.

"I'm so glad I was able to come this weekend, Miss Rayetta. The pleasure was all mine. You have a wonderful family, and I am honored to have been able to help in some small way."

"I'm thankful, too, for my daughter to have such a wonderful friend as you."

Lainey glanced at the old clock shaped like a man's pocket watch on the wall.

"But now I'd better say goodnight and get on the road."

"Oh, no. I won't hear of it," Momma protested. "You'll stay right here tonight. There's a little bed in my sewing room you can lay on tonight, and then get you an early start in the morning if you're a mind to. It's a long ways home. A woman don't need to be out on the roads alone at midnight. No telling what might happen."

"What a kind offer for you to make. But I didn't come prepared to spend the night. You have enough going on this weekend without me staying over. I'll be fine on the way home. I often travel late at night on work assignments, so I'm used to getting in late."

I could have told Lainey she was no match for Momma, even though she was a lawyer, but seeing someone else sparring verbally with Momma provided a pleasant break for me. I sat back to enjoy the show.

"No, I said you'll stay right here. Besides, I wouldn't sleep a wink worrying about you out there in the pitch dark so late. You do want me to get some rest tonight, don't you?"

The unanswerable question was Momma's specialty and her ultimate weapon. End of conversation. Lainey recognized her defeat and surrendered gracefully with merely the hint of a wry smile directed at me.

The sleeping arrangements settled, we began to replay the highlight reel of the benefit. Momma recited the names of everyone she could remember who moved through her food line and what they ordered. I broke in here and there as I thought of specific auction items, who bid on them, and how much money they brought. Lainey added a few stories about her door prize duty.

The only topic we didn't touch was Harmon Suggs. I wasn't sure Lainey knew anything about the ugly incident earlier in the evening, and if she didn't, I didn't want to explain. Besides, we were so upbeat about the benefit's result that we wanted to remember only the good parts.

Well, we didn't talk about Edgar either. Tara hadn't pointed him out to me, so I assumed he had a good reason for not attending. I'd have to pursue my investigation later.

We sat at the table more than an hour, swapping stories and laughing. I lost track of how many snack cakes I ate, but Lainey had no room to be the self-righteous dieter because she was chowing down on them, too.

Sitting at the kitchen table with Momma brought back an avalanche of sweet memories from through the years. Our family owned a perfectly good sofa and love seat in a perfectly good living room, but we always seemed to wind up at the kitchen table, somehow more comfortable on the hard wooden chairs than on the sofa's soft cushions.

Finally, the euphoria began to wear off, and we all looked weary at once. I stretched and yawned, setting off a chain reaction in Lainey and Momma.

"I don't know about you two, but I'm headed to bed. Momma, I'll show Lainey where to sleep."

"That's fine. Katie Anne, be sure to lay out an extra quilt for Lainey. There's some on the top shelf of the hall closet. You girls go on now and get you some good rest. I'll have a big breakfast waiting for you two in the morning."

With a soft embrace, Momma bid us both good night.

≈

"If you need anything during the night, knock on the wall. I'll be the one snoring on the other side."

I stood next to the twin bed in Momma's small sewing room. My friend looked up at me from her perch on the mattress, lightly bouncing up and down to test it.

"This feels like summer camp. Too bad we don't know Morse Code. If we did, we could stay up half the night sending messages back and forth to each other," Lainey suggested.

"Then thank heavens we don't. I'm feeling way too old for camp tonight. This is one night I'll be perfectly content to close my eyes and not roll over until morning."

"What, no pillow fight? If I'm going to stay over, at least make it worth my while."

Since she hadn't planned on spending the night in Pikeville, Lainey didn't bring an overnight bag with her, and she wasn't exactly low-maintenance either. So we raided my entire stock of cosmetics, plus the contents of Momma's bathroom vanity. I'm certain our combined resources fell pitifully short of Lainey's usual supply, but she was taking her temporary withdrawal from beauty products with a good attitude and a sense of adventure.

Her face washed free of makeup and duly moisturized, Lainey wore an extra tee-shirt and sweatpants of mine as makeshift pajamas. Her clothes hung over the back of

Momma's sewing chair, and her jewelry sparkled from atop the sewing machine cabinet.

"What else do you need?" I asked.

"The only thing left is to be tucked in and read a bedtime story."

"I think I'll let you handle that on your own."

"Sit down here on the bed with me a minute at least." Her voice softened with concern. "Tell me how you're doing. How does it feel to be back here at home?"

"Oh, no." I protested even as I sat on the edge of the narrow mattress and leaned back against the footboard. "Not another one of your 'feeling' questions. Don't go all touchy-feely on me right here in Pikeville. I think it's against the law here or something."

"I will hit you over the head with this pillow if you don't answer my question. Some people pay big money to tell someone else their problems. I'm saving you a ton of money here by listening for free, so start talking."

In spite of my resistance, I knew Lainey asked because she genuinely cared about me. And I also knew I would have to begin facing up to my past at some point and sorting out my world. Who better to dive into the mess with than my closest friend? I took a deep breath, swallowed my hesitation, and plunged in.

"I feel…good." I was so proud of myself for sharing, I repeated the words. "I feel good. That's how I feel."

"All right, keep going."

Opening the forbidden door to my relationship with my hometown didn't seem nearly as frightening as the prospect loomed before this weekend. There I was, a large chunk of the weekend over with, and still in one piece. Perhaps not universally loved by every single citizen in the whole county, but received rather warmly by most I came in contact with.

"When I moved to Nashville, I deliberately pushed everything about Pikeville out of my mind. Or at least all I could. It was like the first eighteen years of my life didn't even exist anymore. I didn't think about it. And then I get here this weekend and begin seeing all these people I dreaded seeing, and they're so kind, not at all judgmental like I thought they'd be. And all at once I begin remembering so many good times we shared, so many memories together, and now I'm kind of homesick. Which is really strange since I am home."

"I thought this wasn't your home anymore."

Lainey's quick retort astonished me. I had informed her countless times in the past that Pikeville wasn't my home, so why did I suddenly have to suppress the urge to contradict her?

"It's not. You're right."

Lainey stretched out on the bed above me, pulled the extra quilt around her legs, and folded her arms above her head.

"Am I?"

"You always think you're right."

"Good point," my friend agreed.

"Anyway, I'm wondering, maybe instead of pushing everything away, maybe I should have kept the good stuff. Maybe I pushed the good out with the bad."

"Ah, the baby with the bathwater scenario."

"Exactly."

I sighed in frustration before continuing.

"Anyway, it's all jumbled in my brain. I'm thinking it's best to pull a Scarlett O'Hara and not think about anything until tomorrow. Or day after tomorrow. Or day after that."

"You've put it off long enough, my friend. I think we're beginning to see real progress. You realize the big difference between then and now is back then you were a high school girl, looking at situations in the way a high school girl would. Now that you're a grown woman, you're looking at situations like a woman. Big difference in perspective."

"I believe you're trying to say I'm mature now."

"Oh no, you won't get me to commit to that, even if I'm not under oath."

I stared at the opposite wall of the room, where a cross stitched adage encouraged me to "Draw Nigh Unto God." During the brief lull in the conversation, I could almost hear the gears turning in Lainey's mind as she strategized how best to continue cross-examining me.

"What is the one thing on your mind you're trying not to tell me?"

"That's pretty nosy, Lainey, even for you." I waited for a response and didn't get one, so I gave in and answered her question.

"But here goes. When I had the flat tire today, I unknowingly went to Jesse Warren's tire shop. Trisha had a huge crush on him, and they were together that night at the Blue Hole. Some things he said made me think he blames himself for what happened and thinks everyone else blames him, too. But I gave her the first drink that night. I made her so mad at me she was reckless just to show me she could be. So why would Jesse think it all was his fault? I mean, I guess I've always blamed him a little, too, but not nearly as much as I blamed myself."

"Guilt doesn't always make sense, does it?"

"A lot of things don't make sense anymore."

Lainey remained silent but pulled one arm out from

under her head long enough to roll her hand in a motion commanding me to continue speaking.

"Brother Carl threw me for a loop today, I'll admit."

"Now we're getting somewhere. What did the good pastor have to say?"

"He actually apologized to me. Can you believe it? To paraphrase, he said he knew he let me down and as my pastor he should have tried to help me. He talked about God's love and forgiveness and second chances."

"How do you feel about what he said, Kate?"

"At first I was stunned. It was the very last thing in the world I thought he wanted to talk to me about. I was sure Momma put him up to lecturing me about dropping out of church. Then he blindsided me by saying how much God loves me. I didn't see that one coming."

Once started, I couldn't seem to stop confiding in my sweet friend. Not until I heard the words coming out of my mouth did I begin to rearrange all the broken pieces together in a new way to challenge my earlier perceptions. The process was almost like talking to myself out loud, but even better since Lainey proved to be a powerful sounding board.

"It sounds as if more than one person feels some responsibility for what happened," she pointed out.

Was my longtime guilt only a small piece of the whole picture? Were my memories so distorted? Were others also harboring guilt? Jesse already told me he was, and Brother Carl said he felt bad about his actions. What about Trisha's family? And other people on the scene that night? Once I began looking at the tragedy from a wider viewpoint, all sorts of possibilities were opening up.

"I thought if I removed myself from the area, everything would be right, or at least as right as I could make it. I was the problem, so I needed to be gone. How could I have been so selfish to not even think about what Momma would want? Or Miss Justine and her family? When I thought about them at all, I thought I was helping by leaving."

Lainey broke in. "Remember, you were a teenager. From what you've told me and what I've seen here for myself, I'd say a whole lot of people were simply doing the best they could at the time. And you probably aren't the only one who is carrying a good deal more than your fair share of responsibility."

Before answering, I looked down at the quilt without really seeing the material. The log cabin pattern ran together in my mind.

"Surprisingly enough, there is evidence you might be right."

"By the way people treated you tonight at the benefit, I got the impression a lot of them were seriously happy to see you."

My mouth turned up in a half-smile as I remembered the many friendships and family relationships renewed during the course of the evening.

"One last question, Kate, and then I'll call this therapy session closed for now. You won't even have to read me a bedtime story. Are you glad you came?"

"Yes." I startled myself again when the word slipped out so easily. "Yes, I am."

"Well, good for you."

My closest friend reached down to the foot of the bed and grasped my hand in a quick squeeze as she gave her final advice.

"Now go to sleep tonight with that thought on your mind and dream sweet dreams."

Nodding my head in agreement, I slipped off the bed and sent a brief wave in Lainey's direction before turning off the overhead light and heading to my bedroom.

☙

My daddy sat on top of his old red Alys-Chalmers tractor, balancing a toothpick in the middle of a wide grin as he gazed down at me on the dirt ground. Although the skies blazed bright with sunshine, his image appeared slightly blurred. I kept blinking my eyes to bring him into focus, but my efforts didn't work.

"Katie Anne, I knew you'd be back. You can't stay away from who you are."

The toothpick bobbed up and down in time with each word he spoke.

Daddy reached down and lifted me up to stand behind the driver's seat on the tractor. I wrapped my arms around his white tee-shirt, absorbing the warmth from his broad back.

We plowed random fields in Pikeville for hours on end, not speaking a word, but enjoying the quiet pleasures of being together. The sun beat down hot upon us...

With a start, I woke up to find bright light shining in my eyes from the only window in my room. Although disappointed for the dream to end, my heart was filled with peace. I knew our time together was only a dream, but if a dream was the only way to bring my daddy back to me, I would gladly take his presence for however long the wonderful moments lasted. I struggled to remember the few words he spoke. However, they eluded me.

For once in my life, I had taken good advice and done

what Lainey told me to: go to sleep thinking I was glad to be here.

∼

True to her word, Momma had a bountiful breakfast awaiting our hearty appetites by the time Lainey and I showed up in the kitchen. We looked at each other at the same time and burst out laughing.

"I'll put a hold on our diet until tomorrow if you will, Kate."

"A great solution if I ever heard one, Lainey."

And so the matter was decided.

After Momma said the blessing, we dug in to sausage, bacon, biscuits, gravy, scrambled eggs, fried potatoes, and apples, accompanied by plenty of real butter and homemade preserves.

"Did you sleep all right, Lainey?" Momma asked.

"Yes. Wonderfully. I don't know when I've slept so well."

"I got to worrying the little bed in my sewing room might not be comfortable enough for you. The mattress can be a little hard. I should have put Katie Anne in there and let you sleep in her bed. We can do it that way tonight if you want to. I'd surely be pleased to have you go to church with us this morning and then stay over another night."

"It sounds lovely, Miss Rayetta. But I really must get back to Nashville today. I have a ton of prep work to do before a court case tomorrow."

It was time I put my two cents in.

"Momma, don't forget, I'm going home today, too. I told you when I got here. Lainey and I both need to be back at work in the morning. Anyway, why would I have to sleep on the hard bed if Lainey stayed? I'm your daughter."

"Oh, hush, Katie Anne. Lainey, don't mind her a bit. I raised her right, so she can't blame me for her rudeness."

Lainey was enjoying the conversation, no doubt ready to jump in on Momma's side and pile on. A quick diversion was in order.

"Please pass the gravy."

After all, eating another helping of gravy seemed a small price to pay to save my own skin. Tomorrow morning I went back to dry toast and coffee without cream.

The conversation moved on, and we lingered over breakfast. Lainey was the first to push back her chair and stand.

"As much as I appreciate your hospitality, Miss Rayetta, I'd better get on the road toward Nashville."

"You come back anytime you get a chance, honey. My door is always open."

They traded hugs, followed by a hug between Lainey and me.

Since she was traveling light, Lainey had only her purse to gather up on her way to the door. Previous experience taught me she wouldn't get out of here so easily. Ten, nine, eight, seven…I had time to count backward only to seven before Momma turned around and began hurrying down the hall. Her voice trailed out behind her.

"Let me get my camera…"

Leaving any type of get-together was a process in my family. First, announce you were going to leave and get up. Then talk some more from a standing position. Hug everyone. Get your purse, coat, dishes, or whatever you were taking with you. Move toward the door. Stop to have at least one photograph taken and probably more than one. Hug everyone again. Only then were you free to leave.

Unfamiliar with the process, Lainey looked over at me quizzically. I merely shrugged. She'd figure things out soon enough, especially since she was quickly becoming my mother's favorite daughter.

"You girls stand together while I take this picture. Now, Katie Anne, you move over to the side while I get one of just Lainey. There. Katie Anne, you come here and take one of me and Lainey."

All possible variations of poses finally covered, we gathered for another hug session. As soon as Momma gave Lainey last-minute instructions detailing which route to take, where to fill up with gas, what speed to drive, and various other incidentals, she pressed a small brown sack into Lainey's hands.

"Here's you a couple of sausage biscuits for the road in case you get hungry, honey."

In the food-equals-love competition, Lainey was clearly pulling ahead of me for Momma's affection. At least I'd be the thinner one, I consoled myself.

Once Momma got Lainey started in the right direction, she turned back to me.

"Katie Anne, you jump in the shower while I clean off this table. We don't want to be late for Sunday school this morning."

Sunday school? I was hoping to get away with attending only church.

❧ CHAPTER 32 ❦

One more step and I would officially be standing inside the Fidelis Sunday school classroom. Momma already stood a couple of feet over the threshold, happily soaking in the ladies' pleased reactions to last night's over-the-top benefit success.

"Why, when Margaret called me last night to give me the final count, I could scarcely believe it."

I recognized the speaker as Miss Vera, a widow lady with a mind for numbers like a computer. If asked, I didn't doubt she could still recite the date I was born and possibly even the time. She was also a deeply loving woman, and I wasn't worried about her reception of me.

"I tried to tell her the benefit would be a record breaker." Miss Marie gave Momma a congratulatory hug. "We left before you announced the total, but Patty Lynn called me as soon as she got home."

Looking down at my watch, I noted the time at ten minutes until ten o'clock. Ten minutes until class got underway. Plenty of time for conversations I was reluctant to participate in.

Thinking I might take advantage of the ladies' excitement about the benefit, I tried to sneak inside the room and sit down without anyone noticing me. With any luck, the others would stand to talk until the bell rang to signal the beginning of class. By the time the ladies realized I was in their midst, class would already be underway.

That was my plan.

Miss Frances, the longtime class teacher with an eagle eye for visitors and possible new class members, greeted me immediately from her position behind a small table covered in white veneer. On top, her lesson book was spread out next to her Bible. In both books, several passages were highlighted or underscored for their importance. Bulletins for the day were stacked nearby.

"There you are, Katie Anne. I was hoping you would be in my class this morning."

Unfortunately for me, her comments were uttered during a rare lull in conversation by the other ladies. During the silence, all heads turned toward me, eyes gazing curiously at me. At least, that's how it felt.

Somehow the focused attention didn't bother me nearly as much as I expected. Of course, I knew even an ax murderer would be treated kindly by this group, so the whole church couldn't be gauged by their reaction.

As soon as the women noted my presence in the room, I was surrounded by gracious ladies eager to greet me with a hug and welcoming words.

"Katie Anne, you're getting prettier all the time."

Whether true or not, Miss Helen's words prompted me to release a big breath of air I hadn't realized I was holding.

As things turned out, I didn't have to say much at all. Merely smile and nod. Conversation failed me, but not the ladies. By the time the starting bell rang, I felt as warm inside as a towel fresh from the dryer.

MawMaw arrived in time to take a seat on my left in the semicircle of padded folding chairs before class officially began. She entered grumbling about being late. Although Momma usually picked her up for church, timing the trip so the two regularly arrived at least fifteen minutes before every service, this morning Uncle Cooper volunteered to bring her since Momma "had her hands full" with overnight company.

The rushed entrance forced MawMaw to change her leisurely routine of settling in and greeting her other classmates. Preoccupied, she was still fiddling with her purse and arranging her lesson book on top of her Bible when Miss Frances asked for prayer requests.

Would MawMaw speak up to add the names Ashley and Ricardo to the prayer list? I grinned in anticipation, glancing over to find Momma's lips pursed in a thin line, as if biting her own lips could keep MawMaw's mouth closed, too. But MawMaw remained oblivious, and Miss Ruby led in prayer. I didn't know if MawMaw was too flustered to give the prayer request or simply decided not to. Regardless, the round went to Momma.

"Let's read the scripture for today, ladies."

Miss Frances began introducing the lesson, entitled "God's Mercy Is Still Real," to the sound of pages rustling as each woman searched her Bible for the correct passage, Ephesians 2:1-10.

I breathed a sigh of relief when I heard the reference. Even though the Bible Momma thrust at me to carry to church this morning was the first Bible in my hands in quite a while,

I believed I could still find the book of Ephesians. Yep. The thin, fragile paper tried to stick together, but I managed to open to the correct passage in respectable time. Those Bible drills of my childhood weren't completely forgotten after all.

"Katie Anne, since you're our guest this morning, how about reading the verses for us?" Miss Frances's encouraging smile somehow made me feel I would be doing her a great favor to comply.

As I began reading the verses, I concentrated solely on pronouncing the words correctly. After the first few went smoothly, I hit verse four:

"But God, who is rich in mercy, for His great love wherewith He loved us..."

Even cynical me couldn't help being moved by the power behind the words.

I read on.

Verse eight struck me as so familiar, I had an instant crazy idea to close my eyes and quote the words from memory. Quickly dismissing the thought as too risky for prompting unwanted attention, I recited while looking at the words:

"For by grace are ye saved through faith; and that not of yourselves: it is the gift of God."

Some of the other Sunday school classes might be reading from another version, but not the Fidelis ladies, I thought. The beautiful language of the King James Version was for them.

When I finished the verses, Miss Frances thanked me for the reading. From my left, MawMaw reached over to pat my knee. From my right, Momma smiled as if I'd rushed into a burning building to rescue a cat and her kittens. I sat book-ended by their approval. Apparently they were proud I could read. Great, another new low.

As Miss Frances continued the lesson, drawing class members into the discussion with questions and humor, I confess my mind wandered. The classroom seemed so familiar in many ways and yet so foreign to my life as an adult. Looking around, I saw the white block walls appeared the same even though the carpet appeared to be new. The old green chalkboard of the past was gone, replaced by an updated dry erase board behind the teacher's small desk.

I surreptitiously shifted attention to the class members. A few I didn't recognize, but most I did. Like Momma, some of them seemed younger now than they did during my childhood. Strange how that worked.

Fidelis struck me as the perfect name for this class. The word was Latin for "faithful." Many people recognized the word as part of the Marine motto "semper fidelis," translated "always faithful."

The faces of the ladies somehow reflected the lives they'd led. Lives of righteousness and mistakes, triumphs and failures. Collectively, they'd undergone about any trial a person could name: troubled marriages, devastating financial setbacks, divorces, children addicted to drugs. Some extremely real and painful health problems settled on some of them even now, but here they were in church, praising God.

Faithful.

You didn't stick with something all your life, through all those troubles, like these ladies stuck with their faith, unless it worked. I knew I was blessed to have them grace my life.

᷎

"Katie Anne, good to see you this morning." An usher whose name I thought was Eddie Ray stuck out his right hand in greeting while handing me the morning's bulletin with his left. "It sure was a good benefit last night."

After his pleasant welcome, I moved forward and the man turned his attention to the next person entering the sanctuary for the worship service.

The strains of a popular praise song floated out from speakers as I followed MawMaw to find a seat. Momma left us in the hallway to hurry to the choir room for a final music practice before the service began. I truly didn't need to follow anyone to find out where we were going to sit. I knew our destination without a doubt: fifth row back from the front, on the left, aisle side.

Right on cue, MawMaw stepped five rows back and paused.

"You go on in first, Katie Anne, and be sure to save plenty of room for your momma to sit. I like to sit on the end."

No surprise there either. I followed her instructions while greeting Aunt Patty Lynn and Uncle Charles already seated in the row behind me, along with Tara and her husband Josh. Down the same pew were Uncle Garner and Aunt Glenna. Of Aunt Lora Anne's family, I saw only son Bryant and his wife Kayla.

Not all of MawMaw's children and their families attended this church. Uncle Leonard had preached for years at a church up the valley where his family were members. A few of MawMaw's brood joined elsewhere over the years, and a few others didn't go to church on a regular basis at all, despite her prodding. However, MawMaw's family customarily filled up the same few rows in this church every Sunday morning.

In fact, MawMaw left a little pillow she claimed was to make her seat more comfortable, but I believed she left it to mark her territory.

"Good morning!"

We settled in only moments before Brother Carl mounted the few steps to the platform and opened the service.

"Are you all ready to worship the Lord today? Then let's stand and welcome one another into His house and Him into our presence."

For a few moments, the din of voices filled the church as parishioners complied. I took the opportunity to discreetly look around, but all the movement and commotion didn't allow me to make many observations about the people present.

Instead, my attention focused on the wide screen mounted on the far wall above the choir loft where announcements flashed. First praise songs and now videos? This was not the same church of my childhood, and I was impressed by the updates.

As the service progressed, praise choruses mixed with hymnal selections in an odd blend of old and new, yet somehow the mix worked. The variety allowed each worshipper to focus on what touched their individual soul.

The order of service remained much the same as in my childhood: singing, offering, special music, preaching. Before I realized, the choir was excused and Momma sat beside me, once again sandwiching me between her and MawMaw. Brother Carl returned to the podium.

I listened for the scripture passage, John 15, found the chapter in my Bible, and prepared to tune out his words while continuing to appear alert. Instead, the title of his sermon stopped me as the words flashed on the screen and he announced it simultaneously.

"This morning I'll be sharing with you on the subject, 'How to be Uniquely You.' The verse I want to concentrate on is verse five. Let's read together from God's word."

With Brother Carl's voice leading, congregation members joined in reading the verse:

"I am the vine, ye are the branches: He that abideth in Me, and I in him, the same bringeth forth much fruit: for without Me ye can do nothing."

I didn't read aloud in unison with the congregation, earning myself a sharp glare from Momma.

"We'll be looking at three points this morning. Number one: We are firmly connected to God and to each other. Point two: God as the vine supplies us, the branches, with everything we need. Point three: As individual branches we are all different and all unique."

Christians unique? What about the little box people had been trying to cram me in all my life?

While I rolled the thought around in my head, my gaze landed on a teenager trying to discreetly send a text from his cell phone. The teen was part of a sizable group of youth filling the first several rows on the opposite side of the auditorium, along with a man I assumed to be the youth pastor. During my youth, the balcony was our territory, much to Brother Carl's consternation, I'm sure. I routinely slipped a paperback book inside my Bible to read during his sermons and passed notes with my buddies. Our note passing created a much greater distraction than the kid with the cell phone.

As I sat in silence, absorbing some but not all of Brother Carl's remarks, other bits and pieces of the weekend began replaying themselves in my mind.

Brother Carl's next words prompted me to refocus all my attention on him.

"God created you to be who you are, and He never wants to make you less than who you are. He merely refines you to be the best person you can be. And He never holds you back, He sets you free."

The truth of those words suddenly struck me in the coldest winter of my soul. All of my doubts, my pain, my disappointments yearned to be free.

Brother Carl uttered one more statement to pierce me through and through.

"You don't have to be worthy of God's love. He loves you because of who He is, not because of who you are. And not because of what you do."

I closed my eyes and for the first time in years, I breathed a simple yet sincere prayer: "Oh, God, I'm so sorry. Please help me." Even before I finished, an unfamiliar warmth spread throughout my body, melting the icy heaviness I had been carrying so long.

No thunderclaps sounded from heaven. In fact, when I opened my eyes, Momma was still looking straight ahead, hands folded on her Bible, unaware of the silent transformation taking place next to her.

Slowly, very slowly, the television set from which I viewed life began to change its picture from black and white into brilliant, living color. This was only the first step back to where I needed to be, but it was a big one.

I sat back, basking in the transformation.

&

"Good morning, Brother Carl." I greeted the pastor as

we shook hands at the back door after the service ended.

"Good morning, Katie Anne. We're glad to have you here this morning. Come on back anytime you get a chance."

I stepped out onto the church's wide front porch to wait for Momma and MawMaw, both in line right behind me. The bright, sunny day was a match for my recently reignited heart. All was right with the world.

Momma was the first to join me. From my view back into the church, I could see Brother Carl and MawMaw with their heads together on some topic. Whatever they were talking about, they were holding up the line of people anxious to get home from church and start in on a big Sunday dinner.

"Katie Anne, you take my car and go on ahead to the house. I told your mawmaw I'd ride on with her and Cooper to the homeplace so I can give her a hand putting dinner on the table in a hurry. Take the meatloaf out of the oven, and get the green beans off the stove, and the slaw is on the top shelf of the Frigidaire, and hurry on over. And don't forget to turn off the oven."

Momma made my instructions clear, and I didn't even reply with a sarcastic comment. Further proof the Lord was working in me. My heart was full of joy and peace, two unfamiliar companions.

I proceeded down the steps and around the left side of the building where Momma had parked her car. The parking lot was already half empty. A few people chatted here and there, but I circled widely around them as I approached the vehicle. For once, I wasn't trying to avoid anyone, I merely wanted to be alone with my thoughts as I celebrated my newly reclaimed faith.

When I reached the car door, I paused to dig out Momma's keys from the bottom of my purse. I was intent on my actions when I became aware of someone approaching behind me.

"You're not welcome here."

I whirled around, somehow instantly recognizing in the voice of a man the faint hints of the boy I used to know so well, feeling the threat in his tone.

Standing there at the side of the car was Trisha's brother, James, my childhood friend, dressed in a button-up white shirt, dark jeans, and cowboy boots. In the years since I'd seen him, James had shed his baby fat and his once blonde hair had turned a deeper shade. He'd also gained an arrogant, demanding air.

Caught completely off guard, I was too stunned to respond, but it didn't stop James.

"You think you can show up here one day and start coming around my family and we're all supposed to be glad to see you?"

"James, what are you talking about?"

"Don't play stupid. First you upset my mother yesterday, and now you come to my church."

Somehow I managed to reply calmly.

"Miss Justine came to our house yesterday, and I said nothing to upset her. And today I came with my mother to her church."

James didn't accept my simple explanation.

"This is my church and my home. And I don't want you here."

All I knew to do in response was open my heart in honesty.

"James, I'm sorry about Trisha. I can never say how sorry I am. If there was anything I could do to bring her back, I would do it, no matter what it was."

Instead of calming down, James seemed to become angrier, his eyes narrowing as he leaned toward me.

"Trisha always did whatever you did. You got her drunk, you made her mad, and it's your fault she's dead. Get in your car and go back wherever you came from and leave us alone."

"James, I'm so sorry."

"You can be sorry all you want, but I'll never forgive you."

Trisha's beloved brother turned on his heel and stalked off around the back of the building. I stood still for a few moments, breathing deeply and trying to pull myself together. When I felt I could move without breaking into pieces, I climbed into the car and headed home.

During the trip, I reflected on James's hurtful words and their effect on me. If he'd met me at the entrance to town last Friday night with those same words, I probably would have turned around and ran back to Nashville as fast as possible. But the events of the weekend convinced me the time had come to deal with my past so I could face my future.

God had forgiven me for all my sins. I hoped others would eventually do the same.

James's words were definitely hurtful, but were they true? Maybe the time had come to find out. Maybe, as Brother Carl suggested, it was time for a return trip to the Blue Hole. Thoughts of that night consumed me all the way to Momma's house and then on to MawMaw's.

❧ CHAPTER 33 ◈

The screen door at the front of MawMaw's house banged shut behind me as I carried in the meatloaf, green beans and slaw Momma had prepared sometime this morning. A good part of the weekend had been spent hauling things from one place to another.

"Katester! Katester!" Tucker, the little buddy I made last night, plowed into me with as much momentum as he could get from a running start in the other room. My knees began to buckle from his surprise assault.

"Hold up there, cowboy. Let me set this down before you knock me down."

"He sure did take up with you right off last night," Farrah greeted me. Her voice was neutral, and I couldn't tell if she thought her son's affection for me was a good thing or not.

I paused in the wide hallway, doing my best to balance a pan in each hand while she watched me.

"Farrah, do you think you could help me out and take

one of these into the dining room?"

Her expression never changed, but she did step forward and take the pot of beans. When she turned on her heel and entered the dining room, Tucker and I followed.

A plastic table runner covered the length of Maw-Maw's long wooden table. She was a firm believer in plastic for ease of cleanup, whether the material came in the form of tablecloths, fly swats, or lawn ornaments. Worries about the environment had not yet sunk in with her and probably never would.

The table, made years ago by PawPaw for his growing family, was hand-planed oak, worn silky smooth from years of use, and accompanied by two long benches on either side for his children. He and MawMaw each had a straight-backed chair on the ends. Since PawPaw had been gone, Uncle Cooper filled his spot at family dinners, but the switch still didn't look natural to me. I wonder if it did to anyone else.

Three sets of salt and pepper shakers were evenly distributed on the table top, and folded dishtowels were haphazardly scattered to protect the plastic from a load of hot foods prepared by either MawMaw or carried in by one of her daughters, daughters-in-law, or granddaughters.

Mashed potatoes filled a chipped green crock MawMaw started using when she and PawPaw first began housekeeping. She saw no need for new things when the old ones were still capable of doing the job.

The women were all gathered in the kitchen as usual, in a flurry of activity. Momma spotted me right away, at the same time Tucker abandoned me for the outdoors. Kitchen duty was not for him. Me either, but I was stuck.

"There you are, Katie Anne. Did you bring all the

food? Did you remember to turn off the oven?"

"Yes, Momma. They're already on the table. And I turned off the oven too."

Farrah began plopping ice cubes into tall plastic cups while her sister, Rhonda, poured a steady stream of sweet tea into them from a seemingly endless supply. Come to think, I didn't remember ever running out of sweet tea, regardless of how many refills were requested.

I was quickly put in charge of not letting the biscuits burn, although MawMaw wasn't too subtle about keeping one eye on me while the other oversaw Tara as she stirred the gravy. My cousin was the mother of three teenagers who were somewhere on the property, but MawMaw apparently didn't have any more confidence in her than she did in me. A few other women returned to the dining room to arrange enough food for two big tables onto the one table in front of them.

"All right, somebody call them to the table," MawMaw finally directed when she decided the preparations were nearing completion. "I druther do all the cooking myself than try to round up a bunch and get them in to the table."

Having already loaded a mountain of perfectly golden brown biscuits onto a platter, I grabbed the opportunity to escape the hot kitchen for a minute. Stepping out onto the front porch, I deliberately interrupted a conversation about the prospects of cattle prices, a favorite topic for the men of my family no matter what their age. I knew if I waited for its conclusion, we would all starve to death. They could get back to the discussion later.

"Dinner's ready. Where are the others?" I asked.

"Cooper got ahold of your uncle Eugene and took him out to the barn to see his new colt." Drew nodded his head toward the back of the house. "A bunch of the kids went on out after them."

"I hope them kids of mine don't try to get over into the stall," Melody's husband Jacob added. "You know they're bad for it if you turn your back."

"Cooper'll see to them if they do, don't you worry," came Drew's reply.

"Well, the rest of you come on in and get washed up," I instructed. "MawMaw says we're ready to eat."

Ignoring the steps, I made the short jump from the edge of the porch and headed out the path to the barn to spread the word that dinner was ready. Tucker sneaked up behind me and slipped his little warm hand into mine before I realized he was there. He set to giggling when I picked him up with my arms under his stomach and swung him back and forth. By the time his little cowboy boots were back on the ground, we were both grinning for all we were worth. It felt so good.

Tucker raced a few steps in front of me when we got to the barn and ducked into its shaded interior. Uncle Cooper leaned back against a post, while Uncle Eugene stood with one knee propped up between the rails of the stall. Inside was the sweetest little colt ever born, trying to stand on wobbly legs, nuzzling up against its mother.

"Me touch," Tucker demanded.

Uncle Eugene plucked his little body up and held him far enough across the short rails so he could rub one of his small hands across the colt's soft brown mane. When the colt touched his wet nose against the boy's fingers and snorted, Tucker gasped in surprise and quickly jerked back his hand. I grinned at my uncle as he returned the little boy to the ground.

"Pretty cow," Tucker proclaimed.

Uncle Eugene guffawed, shaking his head from side to side. "There's an opinion of your prize animal, Cooper. Out of the mouths of babes, out of the mouths of babes."

Before the line of conversation could get out of hand, I remembered my mission. "Where are the other kids? I thought they were out here with you."

At that exact moment, hay began raining from above. I jumped back, shaded my eyes, and peered up into the hayloft. I found what I was looking for. There crouched a small pack of bandits in the front row, each one clutching handfuls of hay, with three of their older teenage cousins hunkered down behind them.

"All right, you squirts. No dessert for any of you."

None of them appeared a bit impressed by my threat.

Uncle Cooper came to my rescue. "Game's over. You kids get on in the house and quit wasting my hay. That's all I got left from last winter."

"Yeah," added Uncle Eugene. "He needs all his hay for his 'pretty cow.'"

༄

By the time everyone assembled in the front room, ice was melting in the cups, diluting the sweet tea, and MawMaw was standing guard with a faded green fly swat, ready to administer the death penalty to any insect bold enough to enter her domain.

We squeezed up against each other, with a couple of the boys getting an elbow in the ribs to remind them to take off their caps for the blessing. Momma reached over and plucked a stray piece of hay from my hair while frowning at me.

Including myself, I counted twenty-eight people. When all of the family gathered at MawMaw's house, we sure enough were close quarters. Try finding a seat on Christmas Eve. If you didn't arrive early, you were destined to stand. Even with card tables and folding chairs set up, we frequently came up short.

But one thing we always had plenty of when we were together was food.

As the oldest male in the family, Uncle Eugene nearly always led prayer to return thanks for the food, in an unspoken responsibility. If he didn't, he was the one who asked somebody else to pray. Always a man. I didn't imagine he ever even thought of asking a woman to pray. In fact, I'm sure the possibility never crossed his mind. I didn't think I'd ever heard a woman called on to pray anywhere if a man was present.

Uncle Eugene did pray a beautiful, short prayer. It suited MawMaw.

"Sunday dinnertime ain't no time to start praying for all the missionaries," she was known to say, shaking her head in remembered disgust of long-winded blessings. "You can take them up with the Lord in private later. Just be thankful for what's set before you. I didn't fix all this food to let it get cold."

PawPaw's often repeated mealtime refrain was a warning: "Dig in, boys, but be careful you don't get an arm broke." He amused himself with the saying during nearly every meal, and then he'd cackle while us grandkids rolled our eyes at the corny remark. What I'd give to hear him say those words one more time.

His workmanship was proven by the wide array of

food his sturdy table supported. We were pretty predictable in our tastes. I could close my eyes and recite the menu from the hundreds of times I'd consumed the delicious offerings: chicken, meatloaf and ham, creamed potatoes, green beans, pinto beans, fried corn, slaw, pickles, cornbread, and biscuits. Unless the vegetables were fresh from the current year's garden, they were canned from the previous year's garden. Depending on MawMaw's mood, the chicken came fried or with dumplings.

Occasionally some hominy, sauerkraut, or a wild card casserole was thrown in for variety. And greens, squash, okra, sliced tomatoes, or whatever other garden-grown vegetables were in season. Sometimes Aunt Rachael sneaked in some spaghetti or lasagna, but those were strictly optional. This family may not have owned all the material possessions in the world, but we enjoyed great home cooking and plenty of it.

Oh, and fried apples were on the menu at MawMaw's house twice a day, breakfast and supper. She grew them in the orchard across from the house, picked them, canned them, and fried them all. Sometimes we helped her pick them, but mostly we just ate them.

The men all sat down around the large table, a throw-back to the days when the males came in from the fields for dinner and ate first so they could get back to work as soon as they finished. Now the action was another tradition that persisted unquestioned.

The women got busy filling plates for the children and settling them in at the card tables in the hallway or out on the porch. As the platters and bowls of food made the rounds of the table, the air filled with the sounds of clattering utensils and conversations on a wide variety of topics. Eventually, the men would cover hunting, farming, and sports, with a little politics thrown in occasionally for good measure.

Knowing that, the women loaded their own plates and willingly retreated to the kitchen, where the table was smaller but the talk was definitely more appealing. When I was younger and watched the men and women separate at gatherings, I didn't understand the reason. Once I got old enough to realize how much more fun the women were, the segregation made sense, and I gladly sided with them.

Aunt Rachael caught my eye, motioning to an empty chair between her and Bryant's wife, Kayla. I made my way through the maze of bodies to sit down. While I was still scooting in to the table, Aunt Glenna, built short and squat like her daughter Farrah, was already justifying her heavily laden plate of food.

"When I get to heaven, I'm going to appreciate my new body. Not like you skinny girls. Y'all won't even know the difference." She started digging in with intense concentration.

Thankfully, folks on my mother's side of the family tended to be fairly tall, and although not necessarily thin, no more than average weight.

"Don't you even think about such while you're eating," MawMaw instructed. "You're a good size, Glenna, and I hate to see a body pick at their food. Enjoy it."

"Well, I do. Like I'm always telling Garner, I'm twice the woman he married!"

"I'm the one who keeps getting bigger and bigger," complained the pregnant Leah. "I look like an elephant. I hardly have anything to wear, and I hate to buy much for no more time than I've got left."

"You can wear them again the next time you're pregnant," suggested Kayla.

"Don't even say it." Leah accompanied her lighthearted demand with a sharp stab in the air with her fork.

"I tell you who needs some clothes," cut in Aunt Glenna. "It's that Betty Hardin. This morning at church, there she was again, wearing britches, them tight as could be, and her right in the choir loft where everybody can see. We ort to be having a benefit for her, to buy her a skirt since she apparently don't own one herself. I give her a long, hard look so she'd know I don't approve."

Aunt Glenna, a member of a strict fundamental church on the mountain, set off on one of her favorite topics: women wearing pants to church on Sunday morning. Pants on Sunday night didn't bother her. She was even known to wear a pair herself on a Wednesday night when the weather was cold, but for some reason she couldn't abide pants on a Sunday morning. Maybe someday she'd join the real world in this century. Then again, probably not.

But before she could start too far into a tirade on the pants topic, Aunt Lillian, ever the preacher's wife and peacemaker, steered the subject to safer ground.

"It was so good how the ladies of your church did so much to help with the benefit last night. Was anything said about it during the service this morning?" she asked.

"Yes," said MawMaw. "The preacher said the nicest things about the benefit and told everybody thank you from the family. I got to him between Sunday school and church, right before the choir went up, and asked him to say something special. You've got to catch him at the last minute before he goes up to the pulpit. He's so bad to forget otherwise."

"I wish Lora Anne was feeling up to coming to service this morning, or at least over here to lunch, but she don't need to overdo," Momma added. "Kayla, once we get through eating, we'll fix up some plates for you and Bryant to take over there."

Her comment put us back on the subject of the benefit, and in our lingering excitement about the whole event, we began dissecting every minute of the action. Eventually, we got around to the music.

"Your boys and their band did so good last night, Tara. They played their hearts out for their aunt Lora Anne, and they sounded even better than they did the last time I heard them." Aunt Lillian tried to keep our conversations on the straight and narrow, but as she found out time and time again, the job was too big for one person to get right every time.

"Did y'all see who come in right after they started playing?" asked Farrah. "That Michelle. She really chaps my lips."

Leave it to Farrah to bring up the topic in front of the group. She and her mother could stir up trouble in a convent. Aunt Patty Lynn's former daughter-in-law was still a sore subject and probably always would be. My aunt didn't take well to anybody with the nerve to reject her baby boy, Drew.

Michelle, who married Drew in spite of both families' misgivings, surely didn't "take care of him" the way Aunt Patty Lynn thought she should.

"He gets up and goes off to work every morning without a hot bite of breakfast," she often complained during the couple's brief months of wedded unbliss. "And where is that girl? She's still in the bed. Here he is, breaking his back to support her, and she can't even see to his breakfast."

Breaking his back was stretching reality a little to those of us acquainted with Drew's work habits, but far be it from us to try to persuade Aunt Patty Lynn otherwise. Not that she would have listened anyway. She raised the perfect son and didn't appreciate anyone offering a differing opinion. Those of us who knew the biggest reason for their split was Drew's wandering eye also knew not to waste effort trying to persuade Aunt Patty Lynn that he might not have been the perfect husband.

But it took two to make a marriage—and to end one —and Michelle wasn't a prize either. She had a sharp tongue, and some speculated she was stepping out on Drew at the same time he was stepping out on her.

Leah apparently decided if she couldn't fight it, she'd join it. She rose to her feet and began an impressive imitation of Michelle. Although Leah's hair was short, when she slung her head from side to side, we had no trouble imagining Michelle's long, flowing mane being tossed about. Accompanying her body language, Leah's gift for mimicry had her enunciating in a high, nasal voice remarkably similar to the unfortunate ex-wife in question.

As we snorted with laughter, the attention of the men in the dining room refocused on us.

"Stop poking fun at people, Leah," commanded Uncle Leonard, still demanding respect even though his daughter was a full grown woman. With Aunt Lillian too timid to squash a bug, he served as the disciplinarian in their family unit.

"Daddy, I'm not poking fun, I'm doing a reenactment."

The explanation somehow made sense to Uncle Leonard, a fan of true crime shows and their frequent re-enactments.

"Oh, well, I guess that's all right then."

He turned back to his plate, and Leah returned to her seat.

"Who's ready for dessert?" Once again, Aunt Lillian expertly deflected us from digging deeper into an uncomfortable subject. Without waiting for an answer, she jumped up from the table and headed to the refrigerator. MawMaw's ancient model looked like an antique and hummed loud enough to join the church choir. But the relic still kept food cold, so she wouldn't hear of replacing it with a new one.

From the refrigerator, Aunt Lillian retrieved a covered cake pan and carried it to a card table set up in the dining room for desserts. I was fairly certain the cake was coconut. If there were two sure bets on dessert at MawMaw's, my money was on coconut cake and banana pudding. The old-fashioned kind of banana pudding with pudding made from scratch by MawMaw as soon as she got in from church, laid down her Bible, and tied on an apron.

Sure enough, while Aunt Lillian was cutting the coconut cake, Aunt Patty Lynn pulled a huge pan of warm banana pudding from its resting place inside the oven, topped by stiff peaks of luscious meringue tinged a golden brown.

Tara brought out her dessert offering, a yellow cake with chocolate frosting, another sure-fire family favorite.

"No wonder my clothes don't fit," Kayla complained as she rose from her seat to choose her dessert.

"Stretch pants, they're a marvelous thing," added Tara. "The woman who invented them deserves the Nobel Prize."

Since the weekend was already a diet disaster, I justified adding a tiny piece of coconut cake to my good-sized portion of banana pudding. The first bite of pudding transported my mouth to a happy place I never wanted to leave. During the decadent indulgence, I zoned out of the conversations swirling around me and merely enjoyed the fabulous flavors.

Tara finally broke into my concentration.

"If we ever see that enraptured expression on your face because of a man, we'll know you're a goner."

The ladies laughed at me, but I didn't care.

"If I ever find a man who can make banana pudding like this, I will be a goner. I'll have him in front of a preacher so fast you won't have time to throw the rice."

As the conversation continued, I casually got up from the table, licked my spoon clean, and set the utensil in the sink. The trash container next to the cabinets overflowed with plastic plates and cups, so I lifted out the bag and replaced it with a new one. After tying the top of the full bag securely, I headed to the door carrying it. I had a plan in mind, and MawMaw played right into my hands with her next words.

"Put the garbage outside by the back gate, Katie Anne. Cooper'll haul it off later."

Grabbing my chance to escape, I nodded my head in agreement. I quickly followed MawMaw's instructions and then darted around the other side of the house to avoid being seen. The younger children playing in the pasture next to the barn were caught up in their games and paid no attention to me.

With any luck, I wouldn't be missed for a while. Even if I was, Momma would probably put my absence down to sneaking away from clean-up duty.

As unobtrusively as possible, I made my way out to my car. Thankfully, the Mustang wasn't blocked in, and I easily maneuvered the car onto the road and headed up the mountain.

There was some place I needed to go.

The Blue Hole

≈ CHAPTER 34 ≪

Nothing had changed at the Blue Hole since the last time I was there. The road in was still rough, so I left my car at the gate and hiked the short distance to the abandoned mining pit.

The water gleamed the same brilliant, inviting blue, revealing no hint of the danger lurking in its depths. Lost in thought, I inched my way closer and closer to the ledge, replaying in my memory the long-ago events.

In a panic, Zeb kept racing toward the spot he last saw Trisha. Wayne's shout pulled him up short.

"Get back from there! More rocks are prob'ly loose." Wayne's voice trailed behind him as he quickly headed to the opposite side. "We've got the best chance going in the low way."

Zeb instantly changed directions to follow Wayne's instructions.

"Katie Anne, call the rescue squad."

In the seconds since Trisha fell, I had not moved.

I hadn't been able to. I felt as if an arctic wind had blown through and frozen me in place.

"Katie Anne, now!"

Wayne's second shout got me moving. I stumbled back to the truck. My jumbled thoughts couldn't think what to do next.

"Calm down, calm down," I demanded of myself.

All at once, truck lights appeared over my shoulder. It was Dennis. He had taken a couple of the guys home and then circled back, not ready to go home himself yet.

"Dennis," I called, waving my arms wildly and running toward him. "Go get some help, please, get some help." He was confused for a couple of minutes, unable to understand what I was trying to tell him. But as soon as he realized the situation, he quickly pulled his cell phone from his jeans pocket. Seeing it had no service, he took off toward the main road at top speed.

By then, Wayne and Zeb were out of view on the low side of the Blue Hole. The sight of a lone figure huddled on the rocks near the spot Trisha slipped over finally registered with me. For a split second, I saw Trisha in the silhouette and a burst of relief flowed through me. She hadn't fallen all the way after all. She must have grabbed onto a branch and pulled herself back up.

Then the figure moved slightly, and I realized the outline of the person I saw was Jesse, not Trisha. Another wave of anguish rolled over me, but I fought the despair. I had to think of what I should be doing to help Trisha.

Lights. We needed lights.

Now I had a purpose. I climbed in Wayne's truck, thankful for his habit of leaving the keys in the ignition. The gas pedal was too far away for my foot to reach, but I scooted forward instead of taking time to adjust the seat. I turned the key, and the truck started immediately. As soon as I hit the gas, the truck jumped off on a bumpy route forward. I inched up as close as I dared, angling the truck so the lights would shine over the pit but not be in Wayne's and Zeb's eyes when they looked up.

Scrambling out of Wayne's truck, I headed for the only other vehicle remaining in the field. Jesse's truck was an older model Chevy he spent hours refurbishing and didn't allow anyone else to drive. But I wasn't asking for permission. The passenger door was closest to me, so I jerked the handle. The door opened, and I quickly slid across the bench seat. The keys weren't in the ignition, but I when I slid my hands around in the floorboard I hit paydirt.

The old truck was a straight shift, not something I drove everyday. But my pawpaw had taught me to drive the old farm truck years ago to help in the hay fields. His truck wasn't an automatic either. I figured the skill would come back to me. The gears screeched as I popped the truck straight into second and let off on the clutch. The accompanying lurch sent me flying into the steering wheel.

I ignored the pain to my chest and kept going. The ground was plenty rough between here and the low side of the pit. In a normal situation, anyone would bet a truck couldn't make the trip. But this was not a normal situation, and I was determined to get some lights to help Wayne and Zeb in their search for Trisha.

Trisha. I couldn't think about her right now. Not about her standing in front of me one second and falling out of sight the next. It didn't matter what she said, I knew she didn't mean it. Nothing could keep us mad at each other forever.

I pressed down harder on the gas, revving the engine. I'd need some speed to climb over the rough terrain between here and there. The truck started jumping side to side, jolting me around inside the cab as we ate up the distance. I could hear big branches scraping the sides of the truck, but I kept going.

I pressed my eyes from shoulder to shoulder to wipe the tears from my cheeks so I could see to steer.

The truck was within yards of our previous fire site when the tires settled down into ruts and refused to move further. Thankfully, it was close enough for the lights to shine in a wide arc, illuminating a large part of the water.

Wayne's and Zeb's boots were abandoned on the ground at the edge of the water where they kicked them off before diving in. My sandals had already been lost somewhere, so I made a running dive and swam underwater as far as I could before surfacing. The icy cold water temperature knocked the breath from me. I looked around and spotted Zeb, but I didn't see Wayne.

"Did you find her?" I yelled to Zeb.

"Not yet."

"Where's Wayne?"

"He's looking over to the right. He's okay. I saw him a minute ago. I'm going left. Be careful." As soon as he finished speaking, Zeb arced his body into the air and then plunged back down into the water.

I did the same. I was a fairly strong swimmer, but even if I wasn't, I don't think anything could have stopped me from searching for Trisha. I had to do something.

My panic intensified with each second ticking past. Every possible crazy thought ran through my mind.

Trisha is playing a joke on me...

This hasn't happened at all, this is some kind of intricate illusion...

Law enforcement is conducting a drill and forgot to tell us...

The first person to arrive at the site to help was Billy Frank Hamilton, a farmer whose house would have been the first Dennis reached. Billy Frank came prepared. He carried a thick rope in a coil over his shoulder, and Dennis carried another one. He quickly sized up the situation and sent Dennis about halfway back up the bank to throw his rope over the side as a possible lifeline if needed.

"Get back in here, you kids," he ordered. "We don't need to be hunting more than one of you."

We ignored him until we heard the sirens that signaled the arrival of emergency help. Within minutes, spotlights shined down on us and the rescue squad's boat was launched. The squad's trained but volunteer members were doing all they could.

Totally exhausted, I swam back to shore, shivering. Wayne met me on the bank, and I could see Zeb being checked out by a member of the ambulance crew. Somebody wrapped a towel around my shoulders. I didn't know who it was. I sank to my knees, rocking back and forth, staring at the water.

≈

Momma had arrived by the time the sheriff stepped over to talk with me. I still don't know how she heard the news. She asked nothing, merely sank to the ground beside me and gathered me up in her protective, loving arms.

A constant wail of agony filled the air around me. I covered my ears, willing the noise to stop. Then I realized the sounds were coming from deep inside myself. I rocked in Momma's arms, shivering from heartbreak as well as from the cold.

I remember the sheriff asking me endless questions about who was there, what we were doing, how much alcohol we had consumed, and a thousand other things. I forced out the answers as best I could, in a halting, anguished voice, more than willing to reveal the depths of my failure if it helped find Trisha.

All of a sudden, Miss Justine flung herself to her knees in front of me.

"Katie Anne, where's Trisha? Tell me, where's Trisha?"

She grabbed me hard by the shoulders, desperate for answers.

I had none to give her.

Two agonizing days passed before rescue workers finally found the body, snagged on a submerged limb under an outcropping of rock. By then they weren't saying "Trisha" anymore, the term was "the body." Those words cut me more than anything. In fact, they were about the only words able to pierce my fog-like state of mind.

I never left the Blue Hole until the search was over. Neither did Momma. She stayed with me like a shadow, never letting me out of her sight, hovering over me, running interference between me and anyone else who dared approach me, trying to coax me into eating a few bites of a sandwich someone provided.

An examination of the body revealed Trisha struck

her head on jutting rock on the way down the ledge. She was probably dead before she hit the water.

The facts were no consolation. Trisha was still gone.

Graduation and parties and gifts and college and all the things we looked forward to together were gone along with Trisha. Life in Pikeville was too painful to bear. The only solution was to flee.

∽

Lost in my memories, at first I didn't even feel the wetness as tears streamed down my cheeks. My first grief was the loss of Trisha, my dearest friend, my childhood companion, keeper of my secrets. For the little girl she was, for the young woman she was becoming, for the woman she would never be. So many lost dreams.

I cried for Miss Justine, whose daughter was snatched from her in an instant. If I couldn't fill the hole Trisha left in my life, how could her mother? How could her father? Her brothers, grandparents, aunts, uncles, cousins?

Yet, for the first time, my tears didn't carry the tremendous burden of grief and guilt as in the past. Even through the hurt, I could still feel the peace and forgiveness that settled over me this morning like a heated quilt on the cold winter of my heart the moment I called on the Lord.

An unexpected hand on my shoulder startled me. I looked up to see my old faithful friend Wayne looming over me.

"Hey, Katie Anne."

"Hey yourself, Wayne."

"Want some company?"

Without waiting for a reply, Wayne settled himself

beside me and continued speaking. His words gave me time to discreetly wipe my eyes. Wayne played along by not mentioning my tears.

"What brings you out here, Katie Anne?"

"I could ask you the same thing."

"That's easy." Wayne threw me a grin. "Amanda made me come. She's been staring out the window all day long, looking for your car to pass the house. She was sure you'd make the drive out here. You know we bought the old Hankins place up the road a few years ago. As soon as she spotted you, she told me to come on over here and talk to you. Something about guilt and closure and blah, blah, blah. You know how women are."

I let out a short laugh.

"Good old Wayne, always so sensitive."

"Yep. But don't let it get around."

We sat in companionable silence for several minutes. With Wayne next to me, I found memories of happier times struggling to the surface.

Wayne stared straight ahead as he began speaking in a gentle tone.

"You're not the only one who wishes they could replay that night, Katie Anne. There's many a time I've thought about what I could have done—what I should have done—and things would have turned out a whole lot different."

Astounded, I shifted positions to look at him, but he wouldn't meet my gaze.

"You, Wayne? What did you do?"

"It was my idea to come up here in the first place. I was the one who brought the alcohol. We both know you couldn't have given Trisha the first beer if I hadn't brought it. What I'm saying is this, it's time to make your peace with it and move on."

Without another word, Wayne got up and walked away. I turned to see him moving across the field and toward the gate until he was out of sight.

After a few moments, I pushed myself up and onto my feet. I gave the Blue Hole one last glance before heading to the gate myself.

❧ CHAPTER 35 ❧

The men of my family were still gathered around MawMaw's dining room table as I slipped back into the house as casually as possible. From the bits of conversation I picked up, I quickly figured out my uncles and cousins were discussing the pros and cons of the crops they planned to grow this year. In Pikeville, even men with other jobs tended to be part-time farmers, raising crops or cattle for the sole reason that they loved the land.

The children and teenagers weren't in sight, but that wasn't unusual. The homeplace was an outdoor paradise with buildings to explore, animals to befriend, and mischief to make.

After a quick trip to MawMaw's bathroom to repair my makeup, I reentered the kitchen to find the women talking and laughing together.

"There are you, Katie Anne. I told everybody you'd come back in the house as soon as the dishes were done," Leah teased.

Momma quickly came to my rescue.

"Now, we had plenty of help here to warsh the dishes, Katie Anne. I guess you were out in the yard with the children, weren't you?"

Momma was giving me an easy way out, handing me a plausible explanation for my recent absence. Yet I could tell by her kind eyes I hadn't fooled her. She knew something was up. As a matter of fact, as I looked around the room, I got the feeling Farrah might by the only person who didn't suspect where I had gone and why. Sympathetic looks were offered all around.

I gave a non-committal shrug to Momma's question and sat down at the table, where Aunt Patty Lynn was browsing through a stack of photographs.

"Here, Katie Anne. These are from Tara and Josh's anniversary. He pulled a surprise on her this year. He told her he was taking her to Chattanooga to get her anniversary present, but he took her to the airport instead and they went to the Bahamas for a long weekend. He arranged for her to be off work at the hospital and packed her a suitcase and everything. All he left for her to do was get on the airplane."

"He packed for me all right," Tara broke in. "When we got to the hotel, I realized he'd put in two pairs of scrubs and no shoes. I had to go out and buy a bathing suit."

From the dining room, Josh hollered out, "But you sure looked good in it, sugar."

"Thank you, hon."

I sat still and let the sweetness of the ordinary moment settle over me. How many times like this had I missed with my family because of my own self-centeredness? My own failure to deal with my actions?

Aunt Patty Lynn handed me the photos, and I

flipped through them. My cousin and her husband shared something special together, no doubt. The proof wasn't in the quality of the slightly out of focus, off-center pictures, but in the couple's glances at each other, revealing smiles, and easy affection.

I felt an unfamiliar pang of longing for a permanent relationship with a man of my own. The thought brought me up short. Where in heaven's name had that come from? I suddenly craved another emergency therapy session with Lainey. My friend would have her hands full helping me process this latest turnaround. And yet she would be thrilled to learn of the peace that so recently had become my new traveling companion.

After passing on the photographs to Kayla, I moved from the kitchen table to the large doorway between the dining room and kitchen. From my vantage point, I could see both rooms and my loved ones gathered within. I loved them all—even a couple I didn't always like. I soaked in the sight. How ironic. In the past, I had spent so much energy fighting spending time with them, yet now I found myself longing for more.

The men's discussion had moved on to fishing, and Drew described the used bass boat he was considering buying.

"I figure I can get the other one at a good price, sell my old boat, and come out ahead."

"A boy I work with might be interested in the one you got now," Bryant told him. "How much you want for it?"

Drew named his price, which ignited a new debate on whether the figure was too high or too low. I could foresee the conversation continuing for quite a while.

MawMaw broke into my thoughts.

"Katie Anne, why don't you carry me over to your aunt Lora Anne's house? We fixed these plates of food on the table for them to have for supper. Might as well take them."

"Sure, MawMaw. Let me pull my car up to the door and I'll load them up."

From the looks of the containers on the table, more than one trip to the car would be required to carry all the food. Six disposable trays were laden with large portions of every type of food from our earlier dinner and then wrapped in plastic. Six trays of food for two people, one of them unable to eat more than a dozen or so bites at a time.

"Why, I'll take the food as I go," protested Aunt Patty Lynn. "It's not a bit out of the way. You don't have to bother Katie Anne for it."

"Or me and Bryant'll be glad to take it to them. He'll probably be wanting to stop over and see his momma and daddy this evening anyway," Kayla chimed in.

MawMaw resisted any change to her plan.

"No, me and Katie Anne will go. I'm sure she wants to see her aunt Lora Anne and uncle Herbert before she has to head back to Nashville this evening anyhow. This'll be killing two birds with one stone."

Three birds, if I was forced to guess. MawMaw seemed to be setting up an opportunity to talk to me alone. I knew she wouldn't let me get away without some private words between us, and I welcomed the additional time together.

I headed out to the car as MawMaw disappeared into her bedroom to retrieve a sweater. The moderate temperature of the afternoon didn't require an extra layer of clothing, but MawMaw seldom set foot anywhere in spring or fall without a sweater. She was a firm believer in being prepared for any occasion.

By the time I pulled the car nearer to the house, Tara, Leah, and Kayla were on the porch carrying two trays each, and MawMaw was standing with her sweater draped over one arm and her pocketbook dangling from the other. MawMaw oversaw us load the food carefully in the floorboards to avoid spills.

"We won't be gone long," she told my cousins. "Y'all stay here and enjoy the afternoon till we get back."

❧

The drive to Aunt Lora Anne and Uncle Herbert's house took under ten minutes. The couple lived in a modest brick rancher on East Valley Road. Uncle Herbert and his brothers built the house on their family farm when the couple first became engaged, and they'd never lived anywhere else. The home had seen them through their honeymoon, raising three sons, his retirement, and now through her illness.

Since the trip was short, I knew if MawMaw had much to say to me, she wouldn't waste time leading up to the subject, she would jump right in.

I was right.

"Katie Anne, you being here this weekend has meant a lot to me. I hope you know."

"The weekend has meant a lot to me, too, MawMaw."

"I know times are different now for you girls. When me and my sisters was growing up, we thought about getting married from the time we played with little old corncob dolls. It's what girls did, they got married as soon as they was old enough and raised a bunch of young'uns. The men farmed the land, and the women kept the house. Now you girls can get an education and work at any kind of job you take a mind to do."

Listening intently, I was certain I knew where MawMaw was going with her remarks. Fortunately, her method of communication was more direct than Momma's, and she got to the point quickly.

"That don't mean you go off and forget your family."

I took my eyes off the road long enough to look directly at MawMaw, willing her to see the truth of my words.

"I've never forgotten my family. I'm ashamed to admit I've ignored them sometimes, but I've never forgotten them."

As we rode across the two-lane bridge over the Sequatchie River, I decided MawMaw and I needed a longer conversation than our short errand provided. I eased the car into the church parking lot on the other side of the bridge. The small, white structure on the National Historic Register barely escaped flooding every time the river overflowed, yet the area provided a peaceful spot for our talk.

Before I turned off the ignition, I pushed the button to roll down the driver's side window for some ventilation. Folding my right leg under me, I turned in my seat to give MawMaw my full attention.

"MawMaw…"

"Katie Anne…"

MawMaw held up her hand to stop me before I could continue.

"Katie Anne, when you left here after high school, you broke our hearts. Not only because you were gone, but how you left. I never would have believed you would have stayed away this long."

I opened my mouth to remind her of all the day trips I had made through the years, but she cut me off short.

"Flying in and out of here for a few hours at a time

don't count. The real Katie Anne was gone from us for a long time. We want her back."

In halting words, I tried to describe my recent transformation.

"MawMaw, being home this weekend has opened my eyes to some truths I've needed to see for a long time, things you've been trying to tell me, things Momma's been trying to tell me." I hesitated before adding, "Things God's been trying to tell me."

A faint smile crept onto MawMaw's face, but she remained silent.

"I thought God failed me, but all of a sudden I see how miserably I've failed Him. I thought He abandoned me, when the fact is I abandoned Him. When Trisha died, I never even turned to Him. Instead, I shut Him out completely, along with everyone else who loved me. To think He's still there, ready with open arms for me to come back to Him, is amazing.

"I thought I didn't deserve His love. And now I see it doesn't matter if I deserve it or not, He loves me anyway. When Brother Carl said this morning about God loves us because of who He is, not because of who we are, everything suddenly came together for me."

Tears flowed down MawMaw's face, and I admit my cheeks were wet, too. For a woman who didn't cry easily, I was shedding plenty of tears this weekend. Yet I knew they weren't hurting tears but healing tears, and all of a sudden I wanted them to run all over me, bathing every square inch of my body, washing me clean.

"Looks like you don't need my little talk after all."

"Oh, MawMaw, I can never get enough of your wisdom."

"Then remember this one little piece of advice: Your past is not your potential."

In spite of myself, I couldn't hold back a little snort of laughter.

"Why, MawMaw, you've been watching those daytime talk shows again, haven't you?"

"Don't be flip with me, girl. There's nothing wrong with some of it. A body can skip over the bad parts and keep the good parts. Some of it's not fit to watch, but some of it is. I may be an old lady, but I can still hear the truth when it's told. That's what I'm telling you to do, Katie Anne. Keep the good and let the rest go."

She continued, "While I'm at it, I'll give you another good one: Let your mess be your message."

"Like Harmon Suggs?"

"Exactly like Harmon. He made a bad mistake and hurt a lot of people. But now he's helping a lot of people, too. He's still living with some of the earthly consequences of his sin, but the Lord has forgiven him."

I looked down at my hands while softly uttering my next words.

"MawMaw, do you forgive me?"

"Oh, sweet girl, there's nothing for me to forgive. The only thing I want is the Lord's best for you."

"I still don't understand everything, MawMaw, but I know I've got the important parts straightened out."

~

Aunt Lora Anne was in bed asleep when we arrived with the food. Uncle Herbert encouraged me to wake her up to say goodbye, but I didn't want to interrupt her rest.

Instead, I wrote her a short note telling her how much I loved her and promising to call the next evening.

After a short chat with Uncle Herbert, MawMaw and I returned to the homeplace to find most of the men in the side yard enjoying a fierce game of horseshoes. The winning team would play all challengers until the champions of the day were determined.

As we strolled up the sidewalk, I hid a grin as I noticed Uncle Cooper pocketing a small stack of bills off the edge of the porch. If MawMaw caught them wagering on anything, including horseshoes, she was likely to line them up and whip every one of them. Gambling was gambling to her, and she wouldn't tolerate the sin in any form.

"Katie Anne, I'm needing a partner. Can you hit the post?"

I looked around to see Tara's oldest son, Seth, waiting for my answer.

Drew hooted.

"Can she hit the post? Why, she can't hardly even hit the ground when she falls down."

The question was settled. I was playing.

"How much money to get in the game? Maybe I can borrow some from MawMaw."

Drew laughed at the dig, but Uncle Leonard, the preacher, ignored me. He never put money in the pot, but he never tried to stop the wagering either.

The game in progress ended quickly, and Seth and I stepped up to face off against the winners, Josh and Uncle Charles, Seth's dad and grandpa. With friendly insults flying back and forth, the game was shaping up to be a grudge match. I hoped I wouldn't let Seth down.

Since I hadn't played horseshoes in years, they let me

take a few practice throws. The first horseshoe fell woefully short, earning me some catcalls, but the second clanked a wonderful sound, settling firmly around the post.

In spite of our best efforts, Josh and Uncle Charles made short work of our team. It turned out Seth was even worse than I was, while Uncle Charles was just short of turning pro.

Seth shrugged off the loss.

"Thanks for playing, Katie Anne. We'll get them next time."

I agreed and headed up the porch steps and into the house. Time to say goodbye and get back on the road toward home.

The kitchen was uncharacteristically empty, so I called out Momma's name.

"We're up here, Katie Anne."

I followed the sound of her voice to one of the upstairs bedrooms. Momma and my aunts hovered over a quilt MawMaw draped over the spare bed. The beautiful double wedding ring pattern in coordinating blue fabrics showed off her exquisite needlework.

Aunt Glenna picked up one corner of the quilt. "This is gorgeous. You could get a lot of money if you sold this."

"I won't be selling this one. I'm saving this quilt to give to my next grandchild who gets married."

In a classic cart-before-the-horse action, MawMaw looked up at me, her only unmarried grandchild in the room.

"I don't think so, MawMaw, but it certainly would be an incentive."

Momma came toward me, and I slipped an arm around her, quietly guiding her into the hallway and into an empty room across the hall. There was something I needed to say, something long overdue, and I didn't want an audience.

I turned to face her, looked straight into her eyes, and opened my heart to give her a rare glimpse inside.

"I finally got some things figured out this weekend, Momma. Thank you for all you've ever done for me, and I'm sorry for ever hurting you."

Her eyes welled up with tears, and as she drew me closer to her, she choked back a sob.

"I love you so much, Katie Anne."

"I love you, too, Momma."

The short exchange filled in the gaping hole between us. The few words weren't much, but for right now, they were enough.

Finished inspecting the quilt, the women followed us downstairs. As we moved toward the front door, little Tucker jumped from his hiding place, surprising the group and spraying us all with water from a squirt gun.

I took out the door after him, grabbing him up before he could scramble down off the porch.

"Now you're going to have to give me a kiss before I go home, Tucker."

His little body flopped like a fish on a hook, trying to get away from the dreaded kiss. When I lowered him to the ground, he flew from the threat and around the house.

One goodbye down, twenty-something to go. Might as well get started.

"Hey, everybody. I'm heading out."

After my general announcement, I began making the rounds of the horseshoe players, both getting and giving the one-armed, sideways hugs common between men and women of our family. Two of my uncles offered me gas money, and nearly all of my male relatives shared a piece of advice, most of their words involving my safety or my love life. Drew began a general discussion on the latter topic with his instruction.

"Don't waste your time on them city boys, Katie Anne. Get you a man who'll keep your garden hoed and your freezer filled with venison for the winter."

"Drew, why don't you all get together and come up with some kind of checklist for me to hand out before I go out on a date with a man."

"It's a right good idea. We'll get to work on fixing one up for you."

Tara poked her brother's arm as she defended me.

"Katie Anne's got a good head on her shoulders. She can find a man on her own if she wants one. Besides, I don't think you're anybody to be giving dating advice. When exactly is your divorce final?"

Drew clutched his chest as if wounded and staggered back toward the horseshoe game. Tara chuckled and pulled me into a hug.

"Don't be such a stranger."

The same sentiment was echoed as I made the rounds of hugs from my aunts. I promised each one to be back in Pikeville soon. My aunt Patty Lynn thrust a plate of leftovers into my hands in case starvation set in during the two-hour drive.

My last two goodbyes were saved for MawMaw and Momma.

Finally, I was ready to get in my car and begin the trip back to Nashville. I opened the car door.

"Katie Anne, wait right there till I get my camera."

Instead of becoming aggravated as usual, I quietly closed the car door and enjoyed the pleasant conversations around me until Momma returned.

I posed as many different ways, with as many different people as Momma wanted. When she ran out of ideas, I took the camera from her and handed it to my cousin.

"Here, Tara, take one of just Momma and me, up close."

I leaned over near Momma and laid my cheek against hers. After Tara snapped the picture, I gave Momma one last hug and waved a general goodbye to all before getting in the old Mustang. I backed out of the driveway, shifted gears, and drove away.

In my rearview mirror, I could see the horseshoe play resume, but Momma and MawMaw continued standing at the edge of the yard, waving loving hands at me until I was completely out of sight.

As soon as I turned onto the bypass, I set cruise control and settled in for the ride, already thinking about when I'd be back.

∂

If you enjoyed this book, please consider leaving a positive review on Amazon.com. Thank you!

I'm happy to hear from readers at:
ruthsappburton@gmail.com

You're welcome to visit Pikeville, Tennessee, in the heart of the beautiful Sequatchie Valley, home to some of the best people in the world, as well as some of the most gorgeous scenery on earth.